THE FUNERAL
OF
TITANIC THOMPSON

The Funeral Of Titanic Thompson

ISBN # 1-887617-12-4

Cover Artwork by Anna McBrayer
Cover Design by Anna McBrayer
Typography and layout by Anna McBrayer

A Sincere Disclaimer

THE FUNERAL
OF
TITANIC THOMPSON

Lowell Douglas

A Fiction Novel Based on Hearsay Facts about A Fairytale Funeral of Golf's Greatest Right-Handed and Left-Handed Player and One of America's Greatest Gamblers and Hustlers Accompanied by Real-life Characters Playing Fairytale Parts in a Fairytale Setting. If It Didn't Happen This Way, It Could Have, and It Should Have!

Dedicated To All Of My "Titanic" Wannabes:

Andy, Al, Adam, Alex, Ben, Bob, Bill, Barry, Bud, Brian, Bryan, Bruce, Brad, Boyd, Carroll, Chuck, Charles, Chris, C.R., Craig, Dickie, Donald, Danny, Dan, Dave, David, Don, Doug, Dale, Dwayne, Dennis, Daniel, Dean, Ed, Eddie, Ellis, Frank, Fred, Floyd, Gerald, George, Gene, Gary, Greg, Glen, Glenn, Harry, Henry, Harvey, Hilton, Hal, Harold, Jack, James, Jimmy, Jeff, Jerry, J.R., John, Johnny, Joe, Jay, Joey, Josh, Kevin, Kenny, Kelly, Lewis, Ken, Keith, Leonard, Larry, Lou, Lawrence, Lanny, Mike, Marvin, Michael, Martin, Mac, Mack, Marc, Mark, Matt, Milton, Melvin, Monty, Mel, Norton, Nick, Neil, Nevelle, Pat, Peter, Phil, Paul, Pigeon, Richard, Randy, Ron, Ray, Roger, Rod, Rusty, Russ, Robert, Rick, Steve, Sam, Scott, Tony, Terry, Tim, Tom, Tommy, Thomas, Todd, Wes, William, Wort, Walter, Walker, Willard, Vern, Vic, Zeke, and to all of the members of Coronado Country Club that so thoroughly entertains all of us every year with their wonderful Canyon Capers.

The Legend of the World's Greatest Gambler
Titanic Thompson
1892-1974

The greatest gambler and hustler in American history was born of humble and hardworking parents, Sarah and Lee Thomas in Rogers, Arkansas on November 30, 1892; the gambling legend was named Alvin Clarence Thomas.

Through the next 82 years, Alvin Clarence Thomas was destined to touch the lives and pocketbooks of almost every high-stakes golfer, card player, dice thrower, checker player, pool hustler, horseshoe pitcher, bowler, pistol marksman, skeet shooter, and general gambler that ever tried the shortcut to the American dream of quick dollars and high life-styles.

His legend is full of gambling fixes and outright skill. Often, the recipient of his tactics never knew whether he was hustled or just plain out-skilled. Titanic, as he was to be known shortly after his twentieth birthday, was a brilliant strategist with unbelievable skill in setting up a wager or a game to his mathematical advantage. He loved the limelight; he loved the status of being a river-boat-gambler, and he loved the money that his profession provided. No gamble was too high, and no thrill of winning was too small. He never set out to be a millionaire, he just always wanted to live like one.

Many notable authors and news writers such as Walter Winchell and Damon Runyon envisioned the day when they would be the selected one who was to tell Titanic's life-long story. But it was not to be. Only Carlton Stowers in his 1982 book – "The Unsinkable Titanic Thompson" – was to give the present world a biographical taste of the fortunes of this unique individual. And because of Carlton Stowers' book, many of the long lost stories of

11

Titanic Thompson can be included in this compilation of memories. I am grateful for his past research and his perfect memory, and I give him worlds of credit for many of the events that are included herein.

As is the part of every true legend's biography, many of the integral parts tend to become fictionalized. The fact is; too many people have passed the stories forward for they're not to be natural exaggerations, and Titanic's case is no exception. In a large percentage of "Titanic Stories," only savory and questionable characters witnessed Ti's experiences, so, there were natural embellishments to save face amongst peers. But in other instances, prominent and other creditable individuals also serve as verification to his unbelievable talents, planning, and scheming. The viewing of Ti's exploits were not reserved to a chosen few.

To put things in perspective between then and now, one has to realize that when Titanic Thompson was performing – and he was a true "Academy Award" performer – the dollars in question were really worth more than a hundred times what they are today. Sam Snead, Ben Hogan, and Byron Nelson were wonders if they made $10,000 in a single year on the professional golf tour – in that day, yet, Titanic played matches for more than $10,000 a hole! That's a million dollars in today's money! Because of the instant nature of cash to Titanic – in one pocket and out the other – it is difficult to calculate his overall lifetime winnings, but it had to exceed a hundred million – e.g., he and his partner won over a million dollars at one poker sitting! True, he died a poor man in a Central Texas nursing home, but he spent well over twenty percent of his winnings indulging in his high-priced lifestyle. He had homes in Beverly Hills, California, in Arizona, in Texas, in Oklahoma, and many other affluent places. He owned ten Pierce Arrow road cars at one time. He gave one of his wives an oil royalty income of $15,000 per month for the rest of her life when they divorced. Money was like water to the man, and he quenched his thirst often and well with it.

Titanic was tough, yet philanthropic. He appreciated his position that enabled him to help the people that no one else ever thought about. He never underpaid anyone. He was always the most generous tipper to his caddies – win or loose. However, when he went to work – planning and scheming his next victim, he was ruthless. When he won, he always collected – maybe not the moment after the victory, but sooner or later he got his due. He had five wives, and there is no record about him saying anything negative about any of them. He killed five people, and even the authorities agreed with his actions. On the straight and narrow, Alvin Clarence Thomas could have well been President of the United States or President of General Motors – not only did he have exceptional physical skills, but he did his mental homework; whatever his task, he carefully designed a plan, and then he carried it out.

So much for Titanic's background and his lifelong mindset, try to sit back and enjoy some of his more salient experiences – the forthcoming tales are not to be doubted, and they are not to be believed – they are to be recreated and lived.

Chapter 1

"Come on, Carlo, I've been training you a long time for this. Only rich folks have a Shakespeare rod and reel. Today, I'm gonna be one of those folks. Come on; you gotta keep up; we gotta be there waiting. Gotta be there sittin' and fishing. Gotta look as if we just belong there. Come on, big guy!"

Carlo was a big, black-and-brown mixed breed of a dog – a Heinz 57 variety at best. This day, Carlos was to meet one of the richest men in the Arkansas' river bottom area.

Alvin Clarence Thomas cleared a nice spot under an overhanging oak tree to sit and watch his bobbin tan-colored cork ride the ripples of the slow-flowing river. This was a special place that young Alvin had staked out early in the spring as his favorite fishing spot. Only two days ago, someone else had noticed the same spot, and he was sure to return. That day – two days ago – this middle-aged local banker had walked off with certainly the best string of fish he had ever caught.

Alvin had done his homework; he had inquired around the fishing camps as to who this well-dressed man was and when he was likely to return. Turns out he was a local banker - Richard C. Sims, III - down from Philadelphia - an up-eastern carpetbagger in the eyes of Alvin's parents. The young boy was told that the only thing that mattered to the banker guy other than work was fishing. He had the best equipment money could buy, and he had a tackle box second to none in these parts.

Carlo and Alvin were almost asleep on the side of the bank under that sprawling oak when they were awakened by the slam of a door.

"Get ready, Carlo get ready! Here he comes! Try not to act too surprised. Just watch the cork."

The banker was hardly dressed for fishin'. He still had on his vested suit and tie and shined banker shoes. He almost slipped all the way down the bank before grabbing a sibling of a tree to break his sure-to-be tumble.

As Richard righted himself, Carlo stepped from behind the tree and half-startled him. Then Mr. Sims noticed the long legs of a young boy sticking out beyond the massive tree trunk.

"Hope I'm not disturbing," Richard said with an inquisitive pitch.

"No sir, just fishing."

"Well, are they biting?"

"Depends on what you're using for bait, I guess, unless you got a dog like Carlo here. You know, Carlo can call the fish. I never leave here without a dozen or so."

"Sure, boy. I might not look like I know anything about fishing because I'm so dressed up, but I'll guarantee you, I'm the best fisherman in these parts, and I sure don't need a dog to call the fish for me."

They both had a good laugh. Then Carlo insisted on being in on the conversation so he barked. Just at that time, the cork went under. Alvin grabbed the pole and gave a mighty yank. Sure enough, there was a fish on. Alvin fought it for a few minutes and then pulled in a nice yellow catfish.

"See, I told you my dog could call the fish!" You don't think it was an accident, do you, that the fish bit just as Carlo let out a bark? Do you?"

"Well, I'm not saying it couldn't happen, but if you say he can do it, I'll just sit down right here and dip my line in with yours and see if your dog can call those fish as well for me as he does for you. By the way, what's your name?"

"I'm Alvin Thomas, and I live up the road that way a piece. Go to school at Rogers. You won't tell anybody I'm not sick today, will you?"

"Well, are you sick? Or are you just sick of school, and you want to do a little fishing?"

"I guess it don't matter. I ain't in school, and I am here fishin'. That's what I like to do. Been fishin' in this spot for over a year – me and Carlo. I don't mind if you wet your line with me. There's enough fish to go around."

"Thanks, Alvin. My name is Richard Sims, and I work for the bank up the road. What'll you say we do a little fishing?"

The two sat about two yards apart and closely watched each other's technique. Alvin was a straight-line cork fisherman with no apparent talent except in finding the right fishing hole. Mr. Sims knew how to handle a rod and reel with obvious talent, and he had probably stumbled on the best fishing hole.

After each had caught five or six fish, Alvin was ready to spring his trap. He had somewhat made friends with Mr. Sims, and he felt the time was right.

"Mr. Sims. I was just kiddin' about Carlo here callin' in fish, but I'll bet you almost anything he is the smartest dog within a 100 miles of here."

As always, Richard started every sentence with "well." "Well, Alvin, what makes you think your dog is so smart? Can he do tricks, or is he a good quail dog or anything like that?"

"He ain't much good at sniffin' out birds, but he sure can bring `em back to me when I shoot `em. But I guess the best thing he can do is chase rocks."

"Chase rocks. I never heard of any dog chasing rocks. What good is that? And, what do you mean?"

"Well, I can throw a rock and he can find it and bring it back to me – just like a bird. In fact, I can throw this here rock, or any rock like it, into the river there, and he will go under-water and fetch it."

"Well, son, I come from pretty far away, and I've seen lots of dogs in my time, but I got to give it to you if you've trained that mutt to bring something back from under the water – particularly in a river like this that's all muddy and has a current to it. Why don't you show me?"

"Well, sir, it took a long time to train Carlo – lots of patience and discipline. He is one fine dog. I'll tell you what I'll do. I'll bet my dog, Carlo, against that rod and reel you got there that I can mark one of these rocks, throw it in the shallows there, and get Carlo to go and fetch it."

"I really got no use for another dog, my son, but I gotta admit I'm fascinated by the bet. Can I mark the rock?"

"Sure, but you gotta put an "X" on it. Both sides, `cause it may turn over when it gets into the water."

"Okay, you got yourself a bet. Hand me that rock."

The banker pulled a fountain pen from his coat that was lying neatly folded right next to him. Richard was either going to teach this young kid a lesson about betting, or he was going to have some story to tell his banking cohorts.

"Hold it, Mr. Banker. You can't mark it with something that's going to wash off as soon as it hits the water. Use that pencil that's in your other pocket instead."

"Fine, Alvin, I wasn't trying to pull something on you. I didn't even think about the mark washing off."

Richard Sims, III marked the rock, stood up and threw the rock underhanded out into the river ten feet from the bank, carefully picking a place that he knew would be at least six feet deep. At the splash of the rock, Carlo hit the water. Carlo was no dummy, he had seen the banker mark the rock, and he knew he was going to be counted on to perform. Carlo went out of sight. Richard moved as close to the bank as he dared to see what miracle just might be happening. In ten seconds, Carlo was snout up, mouth full of rock, and heading for a down-river bank slope to get on dry land. In 20 more seconds, Carlo deposited the rock at the feet of Alvin.

"I'll be damned. That dog jumped in the river and brought me back my rock. Young man, you have done a masterful job of training that dog. That is unbelievable. I wish you could come to my bank and train my employees that way."

Mr. Sims was dying laughing as he tried to brush off the flung water drops from Carlo's shaking to get dry. Then he sat back down and started to fish again.

Alvin then turned to the banker and said, "Mighty good rod and reel you're fishin' with there, Mr. Banker. If you're nice to me and Carlo, we might let you borrow it again sometime."

"Awe shucks, kid, don't spoil such a good show by pretending you won my rod and reel. You know I wasn't going to take your dog from you if he didn't come back with that rock."

"Don't matter whether you intended to collect or not, Mr. Sims. I'm telling you honestly, I set you up. I planned this bet for near three weeks – ever since you started coming to my fishin' hole. Now you don't want me to go runnin' to your bank customers telling them that you wouldn't pay off a bet to a school kid, would ya? Specially since you were with me when I was supposed to be in school."

Richard Sims, III was startled. After a moment of breath catching and river staring, the banker turned to Alvin, smiled, and handed him his rod and reel. Then he bent over, grabbed his coat and tackle box, and began to move toward the path up to the road.

"Good luck, Alvin. I wish I knew who to bet that you'd be one successful gentleman!"

Alvin Clarence Thomas' destined life was born. It was personified not by rules of chance, but rules of planning, prediction, and calculation.

Chapter 2

On the way to Titanic Thompson's funeral in Ft. Worth, Texas, many of Titanic's past friends and acquaintances simply couldn't, and didn't try to, get rid of the memories of times they had shared with the now-deceased. It was a time of reflection that was fostered in sadness, yet it was a time of enjoyment that they were privileged to be able to suddenly relive experiences with this man who was so multitalented. For most, there were many stories to remember, but for some, there was a single incident that life latched onto. In a preamble to the upcoming funeral none of these remembering souls had any idea they would be accompanied by so many other mourners. They were in for a treat beyond their wildest imagination.

Reduced to the written word, the following are probable thoughts from many of Ti's closest funeral attendees as they journeyed from their homes to a funeral beyond their imagination:

****

From one of the grandsons of one of the reported underworld figures who was a frequent protégé of Titanic Thompson who was elected and sent by family members to represent the family organization at the funeral:

Except for a few rumored games in another part of Chicago, this game may have been the biggest poker game in the history of the mid west. It included seven of the biggest high-rollers ever to sit shoulder to shoulder around a felt-covered table. And there was an alternate – invited to sit in only when one member of the cerebral seven had to take a personal break of some sort. The game had gone on for over 30 hours when the few winners finally got the losers to agree to slip down the road for some food. Stiff drinkers had no chance in a prolonged game like this; only coffee drinkers and pill junkies could possibly keep their attention through the zillions of hands being dealt, and all of these were bound to get sick to their stomachs if food was not regular on the agenda.

The alternate was assigned the task of watching over the table and cards just as they lay while the game was temporarily adjourned. The last hand was completed, the cards were pushed to the middle of the table, and each participant made a mental note of the chips that lay in front of him. The alternate never had an idea of messing with anybody's money, chips, or the five decks of cards that decorated the table. There were no plastic cards in those days, and every one of these players was adept at picking out any type of markings. The alternate guarded the integrity of the tools of this game with his life.

The first member of the smoky seven entered the local restaurant and asked that a banquet table be set for the group in one of the back banquet rooms. The owner of the establishment was quick to summon the necessary help to get the gentlemen properly set up to their wishes – he knew he was in for a big guest check, and he knew it would all be in cash. During this abeyance of gambling while waiting to be seated, Titanic was deep in thought.

"One doesn't assemble this many men notorious for gambling without setting them up for a little fun, even if it would be for stakes much less than their poker wagerings," Titanic thought.

"Don't any one of you order any potatoes; steak is the order of choice. Besides, potatoes from this part of the country are soft and lacking in substance. White potatoes around here are more like sweet potatoes where I come from."

Ti knew that he was going to get a backlash from one of his homegrown hosts. "Well, I don't have any of your potatoes, but I'll damn well bet your sweet-potato ass that our spuds here are as good as wherever yours are grown."

"Well," Titanic said. "There's got to be a way of testing

whether your potato is as good as what I grew up on. Tell you what I'm prepared to do. A good potato, right out of the soil, is so hard you can hardly push a dime into it. I'm willing to bet you that I can stand ten feet away from one of your homegrown spuds here and throw a United States quarter into it – make it stick. Now, to make things fair, I'll do it within ten tries!"

"You got a bet. How much?"

"First, we gotta get a few potatoes to choose from. Mr. Waiter, can you get us a few uncooked potatoes? The bigger the better, straight out of the sack, but they gotta be fresh out of the ground."

"Yes, sir; we got a bunch of `em in the kitchen."

In two minutes, the waiter returned with five huge potatoes, all wiped off, but evident that they were fresh out of the ground within a couple of days. Titanic stuck out both hands for the waiter to relinquish his possession to him.

"They seem to be a pretty good sample to me. Carl, you want to choose one for me to pluck a quarter into?"

"What's the bet, Titanic? Ain't no sense messin' up a good potato unless we got a bet on it."

"All right, we've been playing an average hand in that back room down yonder for at least 500 a hand. I believe I got four aces here. Are you going to let me bluff you? Or are you going to call my 500?"

"Ti, this ain't no trick, is it? You got ten throws from ten feet. I'll put this napkin on the floor ten feet away from the wall. You can't step over the napkin till the coin hits the potato. Put your potato over there against that wall – lay it down, stand it up, or set it in a chair – I don't care. I just want to see you pull this off."

Titanic did just as his poker-playing partner asked. Then he stepped back and toed the end of a napkin.

Titanic's first throw was high and way right. His second would have hit the potato right in the middle, but it was wide left – an obvious over-correction.

"Hey, Ti! I'll take another 500 giving you two to one odds on your next five throws."

"Call," Ti said. "Any other gamblers?"

Titanic gave the crowd an evil smile waiting for another taker

23

or two. No luck.

Titanic hit the potato with the next two throws, but the quarters glanced off the sides of the spud. Then Ti took careful aim; he carefully placed the toes of his shoes two inches behind the napkin, and leaned over so far in a falling motion that he was almost parallel to the floor when he let go of the throw. At six foot three, and an arm length of over 40, Ti's release was just over a foot away from the target. Like a click on a good golf shot, the quarter clicked right into the middle of that spud, and all of the remaining five non-bettors began to clap and yell. Ti never took his eye off his target, even as he fell flat on his stomach. The whole restaurant was disrupted. Everyone began to ask about the commotion.

The waiter made all the rounds – to each table – carefully describing the bet and its execution. Then he and his helper delivered the ordered meal and awaited his record tip-to-be. Everything happened just like Ti had thought, except he got an extra thousand on the two-to-one bet. The sum total of his restaurant experience was no where near the betting amount at the poker table, but it was a quick 1,500 while he was waiting for dinner.

****

From one of Titanic Thompson's most dearly beloved friends, Nick "The Greek" Dandolos:

Nick "The Greek" Dandolos and Titanic were friends from way back. They gambled against each other on a regular basis, but sometimes they were the best ever at being partners. From pool tables to poker, and from checkers to golf, no one survived when these two made a team of themselves. On this occasion, Titanic had designed a set-up golfing wager that he knew could not be turned down. Titanic never stayed too long in one town, and he had a sixth sense that warned him when it was time to move on. It was never because he lost his welcome, it was because word spread so fast about his talents and setups that everyone who had any gamble in him soon heard that there was little chance in beating Titanic at almost anything. So it was ordained in this city that time was up, and it was time for Titanic to move on. He knew just how far to push the curve in order to someday return. He knew time cured hard feelings, so he was careful to utilize this old fable to his advantage only when he was ready to depart a certain spot. He'd come back, but not until time had again made him welcome. But first, he had one more trick in his bag.

The "Greek" had set up a golf game 100 miles north of Chicago in early March with two of the town's notorious golf hustlers per Titanic's scrutinized plan. The match was publicized through all of the gambling and social channels in the area by the "Greek" and all of his acquaintances. It was to be the "Greek" and Titanic versus the two local hustling pros – heads up – no strokes. The two hustlers had previously played with the "Greek," and they knew he was a good golfer, but absolutely no match for either of them on this course - even if they had a bad day. They had heard stories of Titanic, but the golf gods have always said that no one good golfer could beat two nearly-as-good golfers ….odds, odds, odds. Practically everybody who was anybody came to the course that day to witness Titanic and the "Greek" take on the locals. The match was close throughout – even the "Greek" won one hole on his own ball, but as time wound down, Titanic took over and birdied the last two holes for a modest win. Thank goodness, "The Greek" had a few thousand in side bets to make the affair worthwhile.

However, Titanic was looking for bigger fish to fry. Purposely, all day long, Titanic never got out his driver. He drove on every par four and par five with a three wood. When the round was over, "The Greek" intimated to the gathered gallery of losers that Ti did that on purpose just to make the match interesting. Titanic then joined in with the crowd and began to highly exaggerate his talents with a driver.

"Why, one day when I was down in Dallas, I got so out of sorts with one guy claiming to be the world's longest driver, I spotted him 50 yards, and I still out-drove him. To tell the truth, I bet I hit that drive 500 yards."

The murmurs in the crowd soon rose to several boisterous challenges. "I'll bet you nobody can hit a drive 500 yards – not even you, Titanic."

"Who said that?" Ti turned to look over his shoulder to find the challenger. "I just might take you up on that bet right here and right now. But I'm not going to work myself up in a frenzy for just a little dough. You gotta put some serious money where your mouth is."

Well, the biggest, orneriest-looking guy in the whole crowd stepped forward, stuck out his chest, and turned back to the 60 or 70 throng behind him. "You all know that I can pretty much hit a golf ball further than any man in this town, and there's no way I can hit a golf ball 400 yards, much less 500 yards. And certainly not on this golf course, and certainly not in this cold weather. You're good, Titanic, but you can't hit a golf ball 500 yards today on this golf course. I bet we can get at least 20 bets of $1,000 each that says you can't. Is that too much money for you?"

Titanic looked first up at the heavens, and then glanced over to "The Greek." "Guys, this ain't no bluff. If you want to put down the rules of the wager in writing, I've got the money to accept your challenge. Just let me see your rules."

The big gentleman asked if anyone had a piece of paper and a pencil. A man at the back with his wife called out that he could furnish both, and he strode to the front.

"All right, you have to hit the ball from one of our regular tees, and it has to come to rest in the fairway of the hole the tee is on. We'll give you three chances."

Titanic kind of stubbed his toe in the ground and looked up at the big chap. "I like your rules, only a few changes. No golf course is designed for a golf ball to be hit 500 yards, so there is no way you can limit me to a fairway. Secondly, I might need five instead of three tries at it. And third, I'll put my money up here with the "Greek." Ya'll got to do the same. Then we got a bet."

Twenty-two bettors lined up to sign their names and to plop down either their personal checks or their cash. Then the big fellow took off his hat and placed all of everybody's money and the list of names into it.

"Where's your loot, Mr. Titanic?"

Ti went over to his golf bag and withdrew a wad of $100 bills that would choke a hippo. Slowly and methodically, Titanic count-ed out 220 of them. Titanic then reached into the hat and retrieved the piece of paper that had the rules of the wager written on it. He carefully read it, folded it in quarters, and shoved it into his pock-et. Then he put his money into the hat.

"Here, Greek, you do the honor of holding the purse."

Titanic then went back to his golf bag and got out his driver and five ragged but playable golf balls. On noticing the age of the balls Titanic had picked, one of the bettors challenged the structure of the golf balls.

"You don't have some high-powered golf ball there that can explode like a cannon, do you?"

"Nope. In fact, I'll use your golf balls if you wanna give 'em to me."

Titanic gestured back toward the 17th green. "Seventeen is a par five, right?"

All sorts of positive responses came from the crowd.

"That's the tee I'll be using."

It took almost 15 minutes for everyone present at the betting site to line up on either side of the 17th tee. When everyone was settled in, Titanic carefully placed his tee and ball into the almost-frozen tee surface. On his first swing, he hit the furthermost golf ball that anyone in the crowd had ever seen. Then Titanic rested his driver head on the ground and leaned against the grip.

"I reckon that ball went about 290 yards. Anybody doubt that?"

"No" was the consensus in replies.

Then Titanic drove another tee into the ground and placed another ball on it. Then, to the amazement of the crowd, Titanic turned completely around – 180 degrees from his original tee shot. He slowly took his backswing, and then he uncoiled a drive that will go down in the annals of history. The ball carried far and high – just short of the middle of the frozen lake. He stood there for a full 30 seconds until he turned to the side of the tee where the largest of the crowd had gathered.

"I guess that ball went dang near a mile – maybe over a mile. If anyone here wants to go measure it, I'll sure accompany 'em."

Not one soul said a thing. They had all been "had," and they knew it. It was in writing. Titanic went over to "The Greek" and as he reached for the hat, he said as loud as he could without shouting, "Greek, you should have bet on me."

Surely he had just saved "The Greek" from a country-club lynching.

****

From another reported underworld grandson of a different family than his other traveling companion:

Al Capone and his entourage of bodyguards were walking down one of the main streets in Chicago with Titanic and a few other notable gangland gamblers late one night after a lengthy poker game.

"Titanic, you're about the best gambler I've ever seen. I know you were cheatin'. But I can't prove it. I'm the best at what I do, and I'll give you the benefit of the doubt that you're the best at what you do. Given that - I got no business gambling with you, except I enjoy your company. And I don't mind paying for clever entertainment. Besides, I enjoy watching those poor fools that think they got a chance with you, and they don't. There is absolutely no gamble to it – the longer the game lasts, the deader they become. They got no chance!"

Just as Al Capone was finishing his last sentence, the group came upon a rolling sidewalk fruit stand.

Al summoned the fruit dealer. "Are you the boss of this grand fruit stand?"

"Yes sir, Mr. Capone. What can I do for you?"

"The guys are getting a little cranky – I think they need some fruit. How about some oranges for everybody?" Then big Al handed the vendor a crisp $50 bill.

"Gee thanks, Mr. Capone. You know we don't get to see you around here as much as we used to. Please come back real soon."

"Thanks, pal, I'll do that."

The posse had gotten less than 20 yards down the sidewalk

when Titanic stopped and addressed big Al. "I've been thinking about what you said back there, Al. I don't think I could sleep tonight if I didn't give you a chance to get your money back. How about me bettin' you that I can roll this orange from right here into that gutter across the street in one try?"

"Ti, you never stop the hustle, do you? I'm not going to bet you with your game, not now or in the future. Now, I've heard stories about how good an arm you've got. Heard that you could have been a major leaguer at one time. Is that so?"

"Well Al, I got no idea whether I would have made it to the majors or not, but I did have a pretty good arm a while ago – still do as a matter of fact."

"Okay Ti, what do you want to bet that you can throw that there orange on top of that six- story building across the street – from here?"

After a lengthy pause, Titanic responded. "Al, I'll take that bet under one condition – I've already pulled half the cover off this good ole orange, let me run back to that fruit stand and get me another – then you can name your poison."

"Okay, hurry up!"

"Titanic was swift afoot, and he was face-to-face with the fruit-stand operator in five seconds.

"Mister, I really don't like oranges very much. I wonder if you'd let me exchange my orange for that big lemon over there?"

"You're a friend of big Al's, aren't you? Any friend of Al Capone is a friend of mine. Have your pick."

The street lights were dim, and neither Mr. Capone nor anyone else in the party noticed that Titanic had switched his soft orange for a hardened lemon.

"Al, I figured I won close to 5,000 from you tonight; any part of that you want, I'll call your bet."

"Titanic, I'm the one that suggested this wager, and right now I can tell I'm already gonna lose. You are something special! I've already kissed my five G's goodbye. I'm only goin' to bet you 500.

It'll be worth it seeing somebody throw an orange on top of that building from here."

Titanic took no chance of anyone noticing his switch, so he

hurriedly turned and fired. He threw that lemon, disguised as an orange, clean over that six-story building. No one heard it make a sound wherever it hit, but everyone saw it fly over the front of that building.

Al finished watching that fruit thing fly way over the roof of the designated building, and he turned to Titanic with both palms up and said, "I told you that you were something special. You can come to work for me anytime. How about tomorrow?"

"Thanks Al, but I can't afford the pay-cut."

Without another word, Al reached into his pocket and rolled off five new crisp ones – brand new $100 dollar bills.

****

From a frequent poker player with Titanic Thompson heralding from one of Titanic's favorite gambling cities:

In Joplin, Missouri, there was a dark back room where eight guys were trying to beat each other's brains out in a no-limit poker game. None of the participants were good losers, and the game soon became rowdy. The host tried to calm everyone down by announcing an immediate cessation of the game until everyone simmered down a bit and came to his senses.

Titanic pushed back from the table. "I think our host has a special intuition. I think he is right to let us all catch our breath and get our friendly faces back on before we restart. Now, to kill a little time, how about a little non-poker wager – one-on-one – that I can throw 50 out of 52 of these here cards into ole Jake's hat over there. That's about six feet or so from here."

Two of the participants immediately challenged the bet for $100 apiece. As Titanic cleared his throwing path, two more chums chimed in at $100 apiece.

"Do I get any extra if I make all 52?"

"Hell no, Ti, just chunk the cards."

The first card hit the rim of the hat and almost bounced out, but that was as close as Titanic came to missing a throw – 52 in a row!

As Titanic was collecting this separate wager, he smiled and gave the losers another offer. "I feel bad about that, boys. You really didn't have a chance. I practice that every night before I go to bed. Now I'm working on another trick that's pretty much impossible. That's pitching all 52 cards under that there door; bouncing them off the floor and into the hat on the other side. Anybody want to get their money back?"

"Damn right," came the first answer. All the others were too chicken not to follow suit.

Titanic then opened the door to a 90 degree angle from the wall. He lay the same hat down on the linoleum floor about a foot from the middle of the open door. He carefully placed the hat where the chimney of the hat was at a low angle so the cards could bounce into it after they bounced under the open door. Then Titanic moved his chair perpendicular to the open door on the opposite side of where he had positioned the hat.

"Ya'll see that I can't see that bloomin' hat, don't ya?"

"Yeah, we see. Now give us a chance to get our money back. You going to make 50 out of 52, just like the first bet?"

"Naw boys, that's probably impossible, not bein' able to see that hat or nothin'. But here's what I'll do. I'll bet you double or nothin' that I will make 32 out of the 52, and if I get lucky and make more, you owe me ten dollars a card for every one I make over 32. That's my only bet – take it or leave it."

All of these guys had been taken before by Titanic's shenanigans, but this trick just couldn't be done – they all agreed.

"We're all in."

Titanic got up from his chair and began to pitch the cards from a slightly higher angle than before – so they would bounce off the floor and clear the hat rim on the other side. When 32 cards had found their bouncing way into the hat, Titanic still had 19 left in his hand.

"Boys, I'll let you each one of you buy yourself out of the rest of the bet for another $50 dollars apiece."

They had had enough; all accepted the buyout. But just for

kicks, Titanic had to show them that he had been generous. Out of the final 19 cards that Ti pitched, all but one found the inside of that hat's chimney – 50 out of 52 – under a door – bouncing off a linoleum floor – and into a hat!

****

From another poker buddy of Titanic's, but this time from Titanic's frequently visited oil patch town in East Texas:

Titanic had just awakened from a well-deserved four-hour afternoon nap after playing 31 hours straight of high-stakes poker. The game had been held in the basement of this town's classiest hotel, and Titanic had walked away with $6,000 dollars.

Ti arose slowly. He slipped on his heavily wrinkled pants from the day before, and grabbed a T-shirt from his suitcase. As he looked into that suitcase, he noticed his sloppy but mega-comfortable house slippers. He had just won a ton of money, and he was in no mood to care about the fashion clauses of this hotel. He slipped on his slippers and headed down to the dining room for a bite to eat.

As luck would have it, several of Ti's poker buddies had the same train of thought. There was a large waiting area bench at the front of the dinning room entrance, and three of these buddies took up almost all of the seating area on this single bench. As Ti strode up to the breakfast café, his partners in crime from the previous night gave Titanic more than a casual glance, and Titanic took a little grief because of his dress.

"Hey, Ti, did you sleep in that garb? You like Rip Van Winkle – like you just woke up from a long winter's nap – still wearing your house slippers."

"Boys, I hope you had as good a rest as I had. I know I took some of your money last night, but that don't give you any right to make fun of my slippers. Not only are these slippers the most comfortable I've ever had, but they're extremely talented in their own right."

"What in the hell do you mean by that, Ti?"

"Well, these here slippers must know what's up and what's down. I can kick this right slipper here ten feet in the air, and without touching it with my hand, it'll come right back down and land on the same foot I kicked it off with."

"Okay, I'll play your silly game. How much are we goin' to bet that you can't make that happen in a single try?"

"I might need two tries, but I figure I can do it. How about a $100 apiece?"

The three all looked at each other in a mini-huddle and then gave Titanic a unified nod that the bet was on.

Titanic then rose, loosened his right slipper, and kicked it ceiling-bound. The ceilings in hotels of that age were 15 to 20 feet high, and there was no worry about the slipper reaching that height; besides, Ti was much too talented for that. The slipper didn't twirl, but it somersaulted toe over heel at least three or four times. At just the right time, Titanic stuck his foot out, pointed his toes, and the slipper landed right on his foot.

With a big smile, Titanic slowly put his foot to the floor and said, "Boys, I really wasn't sure I could still do that, but you jogged my memory of some ten years ago when I perfected that little trick. It's good to know I can still do it. Consider yourselves very lucky. I've won a lot more money on that stunt than you're having to pay me. Now let's go have an afternoon breakfast; the meal's on me."

****

From Poker-Player-Roger, an avid card shark and a sometimes golf hustler remembering in one day how he lost at both of his unusual professions:

At a similar hotel in another town, Titanic and six or seven of his gambling buddies were enjoying a break from another big-time poker game. They were seated at random on the large front porch at the entrance of the hotel. One of the bellmen who had obviously been previously approached by Titanic came through the doorway toting Titanic's golf bag.

"Mr. Thompson, do you want these put in your car? If you'll

hand me your keys, I'll be glad to oblige you."

"Thanks, young fella." Titanic handed the bellman a five-dollar bill.

Titanic knew from the earlier poker conversations that one of the participants was particularly proud of his expertise in golf, especially his short game around the greens.

"Roger, I remember last night you telling me about your golf game. Are you really as good a golfer as you say?"

"I can beat you, Titanic, my boy! Shall we try to find us a golf course?"

"Suits me, but how about a friendly little exhibition right now, here on the front porch?"

"What ya got in mind?"

"How about me puttin' a couple of napkins down on this hardwood porch floor, and pitch a golf ball into a glass of water – say from ten to 15 feet away?"

"Get your sticks. I can damn sure make more than you. I'll go get a couple of glasses."

Titanic went to his car that was parked right out front of the hotel and withdrew four golf balls and two clubs – a pitching wedge and a sand wedge.

"Okay, Titanic, who goes first, and for how much?"

"How about ten dollars for every ball hit into the glass – you gotta fill the glasses with water so they don't fall over when the golf ball hits in them."

"Okay, I'll put some water in them. You pick the distance, and you go first. Ten dollars a ball, and each guy gets 20 chances."

At approximately ten feet, Titanic placed two cloth napkins – one on top of the other – on the porch floor. Then Titanic chose his pitching wedge. He waggled it several times while eyeing the water-filled glass. Titanic opened the blade a bit, made a slow and short backswing, then a crisp and quick downswing with his hands always slightly in front of the clubhead, and plop – the little white ball was in the bottom of the glass.

"Roger, you want me to continue through my 20 chances, or do you want to take turns?"

Roger was stunned at Titanic's obvious skill, so he decided

rather quickly that he wanted to break up Titanic's rhythm and feel. "My turn. Let's alternate."

At the end of the 15 minute match, Titanic had drowned his ball 12 times, and poor Roger had one rimming shot that finally fell in. Net gain to Titanic Thompson: $110!

****

From a single experienced loser to Titanic Thompson – even in losing, he recalls one of his most memorable moments in golf, and an always-to-be-cherished true story about how he lost to the greatest gambler of his time:

On the same cross-country gambling trip that saw Titanic win $110 in 15 minutes pitching golf balls into glasses of water, Titanic perfected a special, full-swinging golf shot to be used during an actual round of golf.

The scene was a northeastern country club that had a famous, short par four that was just over 300 yards long. It was the 16th hole, and by the time that they had gotten to that hole, Titanic had thoroughly waxed his three opponents. As he strode to the tee box, he offered the threesome a chance to get some of their money back. All were low-handicap golfers, and with this short hole, they were all looking forward to a hole that Titanic didn't hold a huge advantage on with his extra-long length from the tee.

"I'll continue with our other bets so you all have a good chance of getting back in the game, but I'll add a new one if either of you want to add another bet – I'll play the entire hole with my nine iron."

The threesome jumped all over the offer. Not only was another bet added to the wager, but two of the three players asked to play the nine iron bet for double or nothing on all of their existing bets. Titanic was playing on their money, so he readily agreed.

Because Titanic had birdied the last hole he had the honors, and the threesome all wanted him to fire first so they could size up what they needed to do off the tee to seize the advantage.

Titanic took a normal backswing toward the high-teed ball.

His desire was to hit the ball right in the equator – to intentionally blade the shot. The ball shot off the tee at a trajectory reminiscent of a perfectly hit three wood. Titanic knew the shot carried well over 200 yards; leaving him a perfect 100 yards to the pin – uphill and slightly against the wind – a perfect nine- iron distance with average backspin.

The three trailing swingers were aghast. In fact, they were all so shook up that none of them found the narrow fairway. True, they all out-drove Titanic's nine iron, but they were in the rough.

Titanic's next shot landed six feet past the pin, and sucked back two feet. The three competitors had mixed results. One actually missed the green, but the other two might as well have done the same because they were both 30 feet away from the cup. Titanic patiently waited for the three to hit their next approach shots and long putts. Ti's ball was now still inside their third shots, and he lay only two. One opponent actually made his putt for par, while the other two missed and settled for bogey.

Titanic lined up his barely breaking downhill putt and intentionally bladed it with a closer-to-the-heal stroke than usual. It was in before he hit it – the ball had no chance of escaping gravity. It settled right in the bottom of the cup with a sound that two of his opponents heard every night for two weeks when they tried to go to sleep. More money for Titanic, and another beaten foe in golf – beaten both mentally and physically.

****

From an ex-professional boxer turned card player who was better at boxing than dealing cards – but he was a good-hearted man with sincere respect and love for a man he just couldn't beat:

Titanic was involved in one of the highest-stakes poker matches in Kansas City, Missouri history after which, one of Titanic's classic stories emerged.

It was a nine-man game with one man rotating every second deal except when the dealer won his own game; then the dealer could keep the deal until he lost a hand. The game was short by the traditional length standards: this one broke up about ten hours after the first hand was dealt. One of the participants was a burly ex-heavyweight boxer known for his unusual pleasant disposition, but if he ever got riled, watch out! Titanic had pretty much cleaned everyone out of his original stakes toward the end of the tenth hour, and the big boxer was no exception.

"Titanic, why do you seem to win almost every poker game you're in? I don't think I've ever heard you lose. The cards are the same for everybody, but you seem to manipulate them better than anybody else. You gotta be cheatin'! I don't usually go around making crazy accusations in front of others, but the facts are: you win every goddamn time!"

The game came to a screeching halt with the big man's claims. Yet, Titanic seemed to always be prepared for any eventuality. Titanic just sat there and smiled.

"I know you guys are with me on this. You can't keep losing all your dough and not wonder why. Now let's either handicap this fella, or let's invite him to play somewhere else. I'm telling you, I ain't going to sit in on another hand until we get this straight!"

All the players now looked to one another for the first move. Titanic, sensing trouble brewing, rose to his feet and addressed the ex-boxer.

"Look, all of you boys have been playing poker a long time. You're good at it. None of you came in on the turnip truck, so every one of you has had experience in getting cheated – me too. All of us can spot a cheat or a rigged game a mile away. What do you want me to do? Blindfold myself? I've just had a good run of cards. All of you have had the same thing. I've always told every one of you that gambling is how I make my living. I'm good at it, or I'd be down in the soup line right now. I admit, on a lot of situations I use my talents to set up the odds in my favor, but I ain't figured out how to do that with a group of professional poker players like you guys. You're wrong, big man, if you think I've never lost. I damn sure have, and I've lost aplenty. But I know it's going to happen every once in a while, and I'm ready for it. I don't like it any more than y'all do, but I take my medicine and go on. Now, I don't care if y'all want to call it quits for the night or not. Many of you are pretty big losers, and I would think you'd want to get your money back – at least part of it. So it's up to you. I've had a good run, and we all know it can't last forever, so I'll do whatever everybody wants."

The boxer now looked a little ashamed at his accusations, but everyone knew he was still peeved at being cleaned out so early. The rest of the crew played right into Titanic's hands; they wanted more chances to get their money back.

"Tell ya what I'll do, big man. I'll stake you with 2,000 of my winnings here for a 50 - 50 split for the rest of the evening – how `bout that?"

"I don't want any of your money, Titanic. I just want to go home."

"Look, I don't want you to go away mad, so here's what else I'll do. I know you used to have a pretty good right hand in the old days, and I bet you didn't know that I have probably the solidest jaw that ever was. I'm goin' to give you one punch at my jaw, and I'll bet you $500 that you can't knock me out. You can count out your winnings from my pot right here if I'm wrong – I trust you. But if you don't knock me out, you'll owe me 500 the next time I see you."

"Well, maybe this evening ain't such a loss after all. I'll take your bet – can't wait!"

"Now hold on a bit, partner. I don't want you to take advantage of me, so we gotta set some rules – like I don't want you to get no running start or stuff like that. I'm going to put this newspaper down on the floor. I'll stand on the far edge of the paper, and you gotta stand on the near edge. The width of the paper will be between us."

The highly skilled boxer was now imagining his reach compared to the width of the newspaper.

"One more thing. I get to pick where to put the paper, and you got one swing, but you have to swing as soon as I say I'm ready. I'll set my jaw, then say 'go'."

"Place your paper, Titanic. You got a bet."

Titanic picked up yesterday's newspaper that was thrown all over the couch on the far side of the room. He unfolded a double page, and flattened it out. Then Titanic went over to the middle of the doorway and laid the paper down on the floor between the sides of the door.

"Okay, big fella, you stand there in the hall on that edge of the paper," Ti said as he motioned exactly where the one-time champ was to stand.

The ex-champ did as he was told, and he started loosening his arms and shoulders for the punch of all punches. Titanic placed his toes on the edge of the paper just inside the room.
"Now, I'm getting my jaw ready. When I give you the word, I'm gonna close my eyes and set my jaw. Are you ready?"

"Yeah!"

Titanic reached back to the doorknob to his right, grabbed the knob, and slammed the door. At the same time, he yelled "GO!" Good thing Ti also locked the door with the same motion he used in closing it. The whole place erupted in laughter while Mr. Ex-boxer banged on the closed door.

"I ain't going to open up until you promise me you won't come in here and hit me, or do me any bodily harm. I'll let the bet go if you'll come on in here and act like a good sport. You gotta promise me, though, that you're going to be nice!"

Titanic slowly opened the door. There was the big man bowled over in his own laughter.

****

From a "hangers-on" poker player who followed the golf hustlers from town to town in hopes to pick up some of the winner's loose money in an after-the-match poker game:

Titanic had just finished a prearranged, huge gambling exhibition with three of northern California's greatest amateur golfers at Pebble Beach. One of the golfers had participated in that year's U. S. Amateur Championship and had come out victorious against the best-known American golfer of the day, Bobby Jones. The other two were not only superlative ball strikers, but each had one of the wealthiest entrepreneurs in the country as his money backer.

Reportedly, the two money-men were Howard Hughes and Walter Chrysler. Unfortunately, the game didn't come off quite as it was supposed to because Howard Hughes had a sudden conflict, and Sir Walter Chrysler bowed out for some other unexplained reason. Rumor had it that Walter didn't want to risk being known as the only big loser to Titanic Thompson since Howard could not make the date.

Nevertheless, the game went on, but without the monstrous stakes that Titanic was hoping for. Still, Titanic cleared more than $5,000 from the other three participants and numerous side bets. Professional poker players of that day frequently followed the big golf gamblers to host or sit in on card games held after the golf match. After all, most big winners on the links were not so talented on the felt table, but they couldn't resist the temptation of another gamble. It was usually good pickins for the pro poker player over the pro – like-to-be – poker players that traveled the gambling golf circuit.

As soon as the sun went down, and all of the payoffs from that day's golf match were made, Titanic and the two resident California golf hustlers were whisked off to one of San Francisco's finest hotels for a marathon poker game.

The game lasted for just over 48 hours, and surprise, surprise, Titanic more than doubled his golf winnings.

When the game wound down, and all of the gamblers had regained their rest, all were ready for the next event on the gambling agenda - another golf match down the coast from Carmel, this time in Los Angeles at Riviera. The two northern California golfers were invited to participate along with two southern California hustlers. Hopefully for Titanic, Howard Hughes had gotten word of the match, and he would be enthusiastic to bet against Titanic. Six of the floating poker players had previously booked reservations near Riviera to cash in on the almost- certain poker game that would follow the golf. It was then quite natural, that the small group rented a small bus and a driver to drive them from San Fran down to L.A.

Titanic had opted for the four-seated back row of the bus so he could lie down and get some more rest. Since most of the other passengers were only card players and didn't have to be in good physical shape to play golf, they were wide awake for the whole trip, jabbing each other and cracking the newest jokes. As the bus was nearing Los Angeles, it passed a road sign that clearly said, "Los Angeles 51 Miles." Within a minute after passing that sign, Titanic awoke from his slumber and asked the driver, "How much farther to L.A.?"

Immediately, two of the alert passengers turned around to Titanic and told him that they had just passed a sign less than a minute ago that said that LA was 51 miles.

"Well, boys, it's been a couple of years since I've been on this here highway going to L.A., but I'm telling you, it ain't no 51 miles to L.A. If memory serves me right, we gotta be at least 70 miles to L.A.'s city limits."

"You wouldn't want to bet on that memory of yours would you, Ti?"

"I ain't that wrong that often, boys. Yeah, I'll take your bets that L.A. is further than 51 miles. In fact, I'll go so far as to bet you that L.A. is over 60 miles from this here point where we are right now."

One of the gamblers-to-be on this sure-to-be wager asked the driver to call out the odometer reading on his speedometer. The inquisitive one wrote down the odometer reading and passed it to Titanic.

Titanic took the slip of paper and said, "Okay, fellas, what's the bet?"

"I can't speak for everybody else, but I'll take a thousand." Three of the others dittoed the same thousand. And then one said, "Titanic, you're a fool on this one. You don't know what you're doing, but I don't mind taking your money."

"Well, boys, you might be smarter than me, but I'm willing to bet I'm right. The bet's on; the way I'm figuring it, it'll be about 60 plus minutes from now when each of y'all are goin' to owe me a thousand apiece."

The laughter in the front of that bus grew like a beanstalk. No one could contain his jubilation that they had finally outsmarted the king of the unusual gamblers.

Soon the mathematical calculations had the bus coming up on the 50 miles or so when they expected to see the city limit signs of L.A. The smiling and laughing faces were turning to scowls. Miles and miles passed without a hint of a city-limit sign. Finally the odometer told the true tale of the actual mileage they had just traveled since making the bet: 61!

"Time to pay up, boys. You know you shouldn't doubt ole Ti."

Ole Ti had had the "L.A. 51 Miles" sign moved a little further from town!

****

From an assistant golf professional who had witnessed and talked to Titanic Thompson about his undying thoughts on just how to separate another golfing gambler from his money:

Practicing one's golf game is often pure drudgery. The gambling circuit in the `40s and early `50s found a remedy for this necessary consumption of time that yielded no income. The putting green was the choice for gambling at the golf course without having to be on the golf course. There seemed to be an equality on the putting green that transcended size, strength, club-head speed, and pure ball-striking ability, plus the wind factor was minimized. Money won and lost on the putting green often was greater than the sum total changing hands on the actual golf course.

Titanic Thompson was by any standard a great putter. He won far more money than he ever lost on the "moss." However, Titanic faced two serious problems: he was a constant winner on the putting green, which led to minimum bets or no bets at all from scared foes, and there was virtually no romance or vibrancy in over and over just putting a golf ball into a hole that was less than 20 feet away. Imagination within the contest was lacking, and the contest lacked style. Titanic invented a solution to this non-income time problem.

The putting contests switched to the "pitching green." There,

Titanic would take four clubs from his bag – a putter, a pitching wedge, a sand wedge, and a five iron. He would bet all comers that he could get a dropped ball "up and down" in two strokes from any position – except in water - within 20 yards of the green – EITHER RIGHT-HANDED OR LEFT-HANDED!

Titanic's capabilities astounded everyone. It was an honor to participate in this bet and to lose to such a talent. However, the pigeons soon were mere watchers instead of donators. Even though Titanic usually failed in one out of every four tries in this scheme, the intrigue soon couldn't carry enough bettors. Soon, the gamblers who wanted part of Ti's action figured out predicaments to put him in that Houdini himself couldn't get out of. So, Titanic added a couple of new wrinkles: once the ball came to rest after a drop, he would then state the odds of him getting the sphere "up and down" in two strokes – never less than a one-to-one bet in his favor. The wager was never complete until the odds were agreed upon.

Time after time, pitching green after pitching green, regulation green after regulation green, mountainous terrain or desert sand, Titanic exposed his unbelievable golf skills around the putting surface to win hundreds of thousands of dollars betting on his skill and touch. Many golfers could come close to his short-game skills, but none then, or none today, could do it right- handed or left-handed – competitor's choice!

****

From an early Texas millionaire who lived and golfed in a little town in central Texas, he remembers well Titanic's now famous visit to see him and negotiate oil leases – but the visit turned to golf, then it turned to another one of Titanic's improbable feats that even a smart businessman had to bet against:

In Mexia, Texas – just east of Waco – Titanic made a special trip to accomplish two things: to try and buy some new oil and gas leases from one of the best-known horse traders in this business in the world, and to try and trap the same gentleman into betting on his hobby – golf. Titanic had been thrust into the oil and gas business by accepting some leases as payments from his betting schemes in the petroleum areas of the northern mid west – Illinois in particular. As could be predicted, he analyzed the business in every way: he forecast the futures, and he preyed upon those in need of cash where bidders didn't really know what was being offered for sale.

In less than two years, Titanic was a multimillionaire in free-and-clear oil and gas leases – not to mention an exorbitant inventory of coal leases. The business was extremely profitable; it was reoccurring, and it held a special mystic charm to all other types of businessmen and investors. It introduced Titanic to a new crowd. This crowd was full of pomp and circumstance. The parties in every city were extravagant, notorious, and bawdy, and Titanic never missed an invitation. In this new arena, he curtailed his poker playing and dice tossing, but he continued his hustle on the golf courses. He was pure double-barrel trouble to deal with in the oil and gas business – he was going to get you on the swap, or he was going to get you in the celebration golf game thereafter.

When Titanic's wife at that time simply got tired of all the traveling and partying on the oil-lease circuit, she asked for a divorce. Titanic wasn't about to change his life-style for anybody, so he protesteth not. Instead, he wished her well and gave her a number of his prized oil leases that would provide a monthly stipend in excess of $15,000 per month for the rest of her life.

J. K. Hughes was the intended victim in Mexia, Texas. He was a wonderful man by all sorts, and everyone that came in contact with him viewed him as tough, but always a gentleman with a giving heart. He loved his new hobby of golf, and he was a fixture at the newly renovated Mexia Country Club course. When he wasn't there, he journeyed 20 miles west to Ridgewood Country Club in Waco. Titanic called J. K. from Illinois one afternoon and made an appointment to talk to him about some new Texas leases in J. K.'s area that were coming available. The appointment was gladly given.

Titanic arrived in his freshly washed Pierce Arrow sports car. He checked into the remodeled Mexia Hotel and awaited a call from J. K.

Old J. K. didn't get rich without doing his homework, and this day was no exception. He pretty well knew all he needed to know about the leases that were to be discussed, but J. K. wanted to know all about the man he was about to do business with. He made phone call after phone call to everyone he could think of that had previously done deals with Titanic. Titanic wasn't stepping into a world of the unknown, but into a world where everything about him was known.

For four hours the two tycoons discussed the new offered leases. They decided to buy six or seven of them jointly, then they began discussing each other's present holdings to see if any deals were plausible between themselves.

After less-than-fruitful discussions about individual leases, J. K. suggested the two continue their new-found friendship on the golf course. They adjourned to the fairways and greens of central Texas.

Titanic couldn't get J. K. to commit to any bet above a gentleman's wager. At the end of 18 holes, Titanic had won just over a $100, most by trick shots that caught J. K.'s fancy.

J. K. dropped Titanic off at the hotel, and suggested that he would go home, take a shower, and come back for dinner around seven o'clock.

Titanic dressed leisurely and tried to focus his thoughts on what he could do to win another bet from J. K. Having made a half dozen oil deals was not enough for Titanic's blood, he had to satisfy his gambling fever. To that end, Titanic began practicing an old trick.

Titanic was waiting in the dining room at the hotel when J. K. arrived. The service was superb because of J. K.'s recognition. Dinner lasted an hour and a half with J. K. quizzing Titanic about all of his past golf exploits. After dinner, the two adjourned to the bar for a nightcap. While sitting in the overstuffed, big leather chairs, Titanic looked over to one of the closed entry doors and began to laugh. J. K. inquired about his sudden humor.

"J. K., I was just reminiscing about several years past when I was out at Bel-Air Country Club in Los Angeles. Some high roller out there challenged my gift of touch with my golf game and my card playing. I offered to demonstrate to him just how good a touch I really had. I offered to bet him that I could pitch a skeleton key into its door lock from three feet away in three chances. I did it! See that closed door over there J. K.? It's been a long time, but it would give you something to talk about if you bet me that I couldn't duplicate what I did years ago in L.A."

"Titanic, you're a hustling dog. I'm smart enough to know you wouldn't be offering me any kind of bet that you didn't know you were going to win. But, seeing you came all this way to be in my company, and seeing that you really didn't reach your quota on the golf course today, I'll play your silly game for a $100."

"Damn J. K., you're a hard nut to crack. I don't do much of anything for less than $500."

"Okay, Titanic, you've got your bet – $500."

Ti barely missed his first pitch, and that gave J. K. a little hope, but then he suspected Titanic was only trying to set him up for another bet. When J. K. extended his silence, Titanic lined up his second pitch, and in it went – a three-inch skeleton key softly thrown into a hole in the door barely bigger than the flat part of the key itself. Amazing!

****

From a fellow neighbor in Phoenix, Arizona who just happened to be in his favorite pool establishment on the day when Titanic had a birthday:

At age 50, Titanic celebrated with a hustled pool game in Phoenix, Arizona. Of all Titanic's skills, pool was his least favorite, and it was his least proficient, but he was certainly better at it than 99 percent of the people who thought they were good at it. Nevertheless, when there wasn't an available golf, poker, or dice game, he thoroughly enjoyed positioning himself for his best advantage with pocket billiards. He preferred a partnership match, not because he always wanted the best partner, but because he somehow provoked the best play out of all his partners. Maybe there was a mystic shadow that seemed to be cast over his opponents in pool, or maybe all of his partners tried extra hard to please Titanic, but something always seemed to work in Ti's favor.

On this day, there were three other players, and all voted for a round-robin tournament – each would partner with every other player for three different games. Titanic won all three. Then Titanic decided to reveal his age. He chided the younger players that they had just been beaten rather soundly, by a 50-year old. Pretty soon the chiding came back around to Titanic, and then he issued another challenge. He challenged each player to jump – flat footed from the floor to the top of the pool table. The young guns could hardly refuse a physical performance bet with someone ten to 20 years their elder. The bet was further described as unfair if anybody used a hand to help himself in any way – no hand could touch the table. Titanic reserved his performance for last. The first three youngsters didn't even come close. In fact, one fell right on his posterior. Then came Titanic's chance – at six foot three, tall and lanky, with not an ounce of fat on him – HE DID IT! It only netted him a few more dollars, but it was another notch in his belt of unusual wagers, unusual feats, and an unusual record of winning. He was so proud of himself he spent the rest of the evening buying the guys drinks to honor his birthday, at a cost that far surpassed his net winnings.

Chapter 3

Jeanette Thomas, Titanic's fifth wife, filed for divorce in 1973. It was financially necessary. In the last few years of their marriage, Jeanette had gone through all of their meager savings to keep her husband in a reputable nursing home in Hurst, Texas, just outside of Ft. Worth. Complying with the advice of their long-time attorney, it was a necessary move to preserve what money was left in their joint custody. After the transfer of half the assets of the couple to Jeanette, she would be able to live out the rest of her life without monetary assistance from anyone. Titanic's remaining years of life would then be the burden of the U. S. government. So, after 19 years of marriage, the certificate of proof for such companionship was destroyed because of the silly laws of government assistance. When Jeanette and their lawyer friend explained the options to Titanic, Ti was in complete agreement. In fact, he was ashamed he hadn't known what to do years earlier.

Hanging on as long as he could, with a deck of cards and a pair of dice in the top drawer of his dresser in his nursing home room to tease its patrons, Alvin Clarence Thomas, alias Titanic Thompson, gave up the ghost. He died in his sleep from a stroke in the month of May in 1974.

Jeanette and the family lawyer had already made predictable arrangements at a modest funeral home in Ft. Worth. The least expensive burial plot at one of the community cemeteries was picked solely because of costs, and the closest one available to the funeral home offered the least expensive hearse ride.

****

Dwayne Douglas was a second-year sports reporter for the Ft. Worth Star Telegram. As soon as Dwayne checked into the office on the second Monday in May in 1974, he saw a note attached to his typewriter. "Before you do anything else – come to my office – Ben." Ben Winkleman was the editor of the Telegram; not the sports editor, and not the obituary director, but the big boss. Dwayne had never had a private audience with Ben, and Dwayne was concerned about the obvious urgency of the message.

Ben was seated at his desk with the glass office door closed. Dwayne gently knocked, and Ben motioned him in. "Dwayne, you ever write anything about Titanic Thompson?"

"No, sir, but I've read a good deal about him – mostly fiction, I'm sure."

"I wouldn't be too sure of that, my son. I knew Titanic, not a close friend, but I knew him well enough for him to remember my name and of course I could always remember his."

"Sir, you're talking past tense; is that by accident?"

"You're right, Dwayne. The world's greatest gambler, and certainly one of the world's greatest characters, died last night at a nursing home in Hurst. His legend will live as long as there's golf."

There was a protracted pause in the conversation that let both gentlemen gather thoughts.

"I want us to take the lead story on this. I'll get the AP to pick us up, so it will be a big reflection on our abilities. There may be nothing there – with the funeral. But, I want you to get down to the funeral home and pitch a tent. I want you to stay there through the actual burial. Take whatever files we have here on Titanic, and do your writing somewhere in the lobby. I don't want anything negative, yet I want a real-life portrayal of his life. I have a sneaking suspicion that we're both going to be surprised by some of the people who might make it by there to pay their respects. Without embarrassing anyone, I think it only appropriate to include them in your piece. I'll be at the office all day, and here is my home number if you need to reach me." Ben passed the phone number note to Dwayne.

"I'll do my best. I appreciate the opportunity."

"You better get going. I don't want you to miss a thing, and by the way, I've called one of my funeral director friends – John Lewis – there. He expects you, and if you need anything in the way of expenses there, he'll take care of whatever you need."

As Dwayne was opening the door, Ben had one last thought. "Dwayne, I don't want this in your article, and I don't want anyone else to know: the paper is picking up all of the funeral expenses."

"I got ya, it's safe with me, but I gotta tell ya, it's a wonderful thing."

It took Dwayne just over an hour to gather all the pertinent material he needed on Titanic from the Telegram's files. He purposely excluded any pictures from the file in case someone might see them and get a wrong idea. It took him 40 minutes to drive by his house, change into a suit, and drive to the funeral home.

Dwayne told the greeter in the foyer his name and that he was from the Telegram. He indicated that he was to see Mr. John Lewis if he was available. While waiting to meet Mr. Lewis, Dwayne read all of the announcements for the upcoming funerals and viewings that were scheduled. None of the other deceased had any part of their name that resembled Titanic Thompson, so Dwayne deduced that Alvin Clarence Thomas was the legend's real name. The two other deceased, who were already in separate rooms, were to have their services later that day. Alvin Clarence Thomas was to be buried early Tuesday morning. The family had obviously not seen it necessary to prolong a visiting schedule. After all, Dwayne suspected that Titanic hadn't had any contact with his friends from his earlier life in years.

From 9:30 that morning to two o'clock that afternoon Dwayne assembled past newspaper articles in chronological order as references for his story. Only two visitors had come by to pay their respects to Titanic. One was obviously Jeanette, and Dwayne didn't feel right in disturbing her thoughts. If the story progressed, he could have a word or two with her at a better time. The gentleman who came by signed his name in the book, but there was no clue as to if he was a relative or anyone remotely famous.

Shortly after two o'clock, three well-dressed, thuggy-looking gentlemen strode into the foyer and asked the soft-spoken greeting director where Titanic Thompson was. Dwayne's ears perked up as the director asked them to kindly put their cigars outside on the ash-tray container. Their accent was obviously Italian, obviously north-eastern, and obviously Mafia-connected.

Dwayne put down his writing pad and deliberately met them around Titanic's casket. No one else was in the viewing room. The men didn't say a word. Two of them held their hats in their hands, and all just stared at the open casket. Dwayne took a chance and broke the ice.

"Did you gentlemen know Mr. Thomas, I mean Mr. Thompson?"

"Why do ya think we're here? Course we knew him. He was a great friend of the family."

Dwayne was dying to ask what family, and further dying to ask where is the rest of your family, but discretion was the better part of valor – for sure in this case.

"I'm a reporter for the local newspaper, and I'm doing a story on Mr. Thomas. Care to add anything?"

"Look, creep, we don't got no stories to share with you; we don't want our names in no newspaper – understand?"

"Hold on, Tony, you know Titanic wouldn't want that kinda attitude. You apologize to that young man."

Then the gruffiest of the three turned to Dwayne.

"We're sorry, young fella, but we still don't want our names in the paper. We flew down here to pay homage to a real good friend of the family. This was one straight-up guy. He was da best at what he did in da world. We all loved him. Our daddies loved him, and all the other guys loved him. He was a livin' legend when he was among us. Need to know anything else? If you do, we're sticking around for the funeral, but we don't know where we're staying – do we, guys?"

"Sir, if you don't really know your way around here, I'll be glad to suggest a hotel or something around here close. I'll even be glad to make reservations for you."

"No thanks, fella. We saw a couple of nice hotels down there by the freeway a mile or so back that looked pretty good to us. We'll probably catch you later here for the evening viewing.

They're a couple more of our friends that haven't made it in yet; we're gonna meet them here this evening."

Dwayne had made his first contact, but it hadn't amounted to much, although it had some promise. He had noticed that none of the three had signed the guest book, and he doubted that they would, even when their friends arrived.

Two more slow hours passed before any other visitors appeared. The other two caskets that were opened for viewing were now moved to their special chapels for their respective services, so it was reasonably certain that anyone new who lingered in the foyer was there to pay his or her respects to Titanic.

The next visitor was a woman, pretty young for someone of Titanic's age. Dwayne thought it might be Titanic's daughter, but Dwayne made a confession to himself that he had a lot of work to do; Dwayne didn't know if Titanic even had a daughter. Curiosity about to kill him, Dwayne moseyed over to the guest book to take a peak at her signature. It read Maxine Thompson, fourth dedicated wife of Titanic Thompson.

"My God," Dwayne thought. "She is beautiful. Well-tanned, and not a day over 45. That's nearly 40 years younger than Titanic is supposed to be." Dwayne quickly checked his math from Alvin Clarence Thomas' birthday in 1892. He was right – Titanic died at 82!

Dwayne reverently approached the casket when he had given the beautiful ex-wife enough time to get through her initial grieving.

"Mrs. Thompson, I couldn't help noticing your signature on the guest book. Were you really married to Mr. Titanic Thompson?"

"Sure was young man. Who are you?" Maxine was afraid she had failed to identify one of Ti's children by a previous marriage.

"My name is Dwayne Douglas, and I'm a reporter for the Ft. Worth Star Telegram."

"Is that the newspaper in this town?"

"Yes, ma'am. I've been assigned the privilege of writing a story about Mr. Thomas and his life. We hope to syndicate it through the AP – the Associated Press. No disrespect ma'am, we want to honor Mr. Thomas. You know he was somewhat of a legend around here. It would be a big help to me, and an honor, if you'd find some time to talk to me about some of the great things that Titanic did – particularly during your marriage to him. I know I'm catching you at a bad time, but I really don't have much of a choice if I'm going to meet my deadline. I noticed that you took a taxi here alone. I'd be glad to give you a lift somewhere if you'd like. Maybe we could talk along the way."

"Honey, you don't have enough paper to write all the great stories I know about Titanic Thompson. He was a great man, a great teacher, and the most fun-loving human that has ever been born. I'm here for the funeral, and it isn't until tomorrow, so I just might adopt you as my official caretaker. Why don't you drop me by a hotel close by, let me freshen-up, and then come get me for the viewing tonight. I'll give you so many stories your fingers are going to fall off."

"That's a deal, Mrs. Thompson, I'll be waiting in the foyer."

"You call me Maxine, young man. I don't want to hear something that makes me feel any older than I am. All right?"

"Sure, Maxine."

Dwayne didn't have to wait long in the foyer. Maxine came calling in five minutes. But during that time, Dwayne was saying his prayers of thanks because he had gotten his story source. At a funeral, he was the happiest person alive.

Dwayne returned to the funeral home after dropping Maxine off at the Holiday Inn, and then dropping himself by a local Seven-Eleven for a soda and two packages of cheese and crackers. It was now almost four o'clock, and the guest register didn't show any new names. He then resumed his spot on the smaller of the two sofas in the foyer and rekindled his thoughts about what he needed to ask Maxine. But his thoughts occasionally drifted back to his new "Mafia" acquaintances – at least that is what they sounded like.

No sooner than he had gotten his brain back in gear for his story than in came another young figure. This young man looked much too young to be a friend of Titanic. Somewhere he had read that Titanic had two sons; this had to be one of them. He waited for the young man to sign the register. When the casually dressed potential son entered the viewing room, Dwayne made his way to the signature book.

"God Almighty," Dwayne thought. It is Tommy Thomas. Next to his signature was a proud association spelled out in steady and beautiful printing, "Son of Titanic and Joanne Thompson – Proudly announced by Walter Winchell."

Dwayne had grown up hearing his parents listen to and rave about the broadcaster and writer, Walter Winchell. "Why did Titanic's son write such a thing in the registry?" Dwayne's thoughts were running wild. He had to go to the restroom; that soda had gone straight through.

Dwayne didn't have to wait long for Tommy to exit the casket-viewing room. He had a smile from ear to ear as Dwayne moved closer to him to pay his respects to an obvious family member.

"Mr. Thomas, I saw your name in the book there, and I wanted to pay my respects to you. I'm a reporter for the local newspaper, and I'm assigned your dad's story. I don't want to be rude, and I want to pick the timing right, but I sure would appreciate a few minutes of your time to get a thought or two from you concerning your father. Do you think that's possible?"

"That's fine. I'm going to be around through the funeral, and I can't think of anything better than to let more people know about my dad. I really didn't know him that well, but I am his son, and I know-first hand from my mom all about dad's wonderful generosities, and of course his legendary winnings. Whenever he had time, he always called me. He checked on me every chance he got. He provided well for my mom, even after their divorce, and of course, I benefited to having almost everything I wanted. I've just turned 30, and I'm just now growing to appreciate all that my father did. He was truly amazing. He was 53 when he had me – that's amazing enough. I came here straight from the airport, so I'm a little hungry. How about me meeting you here or somewhere later on? You know my mom's planning to get here a little later; I'm sure she'd like to visit with you as well. I'll introduce you."

"Oh, that'll be just fine. You name the time for anything. I probably should stick around here as much as possible to see if anyone else comes in who I might possibly talk to. But I sure do want to pick your brain a bit if you don't mind taking the time." Dwayne was careful not to mention Maxine because that Mrs. Thompson just might not be Tommy's mother.

"That'll be fine. I'll see you in a couple of hours or so."

Tommy departed, and Dwayne started digging through his material in search of family members. He knew he remembered seeing something about Titanic having had five wives, and had killed five people – but with absolutely no connection. Nowhere did he remember having seen anything about Titanic's offspring.

By five o'clock another older lady checked in to sign the guest book. She left her overnight bag just inside the front door as she entered. Again, Dwayne waited for her to leave the foyer before he checked her sign-in name. It was another wife – Joanne. Dwayne kinda figured it was Tommy's mom.

While Dwayne was waiting for Joanne to reappear, another young man walked in. He asked the present greeting director for help, and the director introduced himself and took him over to the guest book. During the two's introduction, Dwayne overheard the name Ty Wayne Thompson. "Must be another son," Dwayne thought.

Ty Wayne signed the book, and then studied the few names in front of his. As he was doing so, in walked Joanne from the viewing room. The two stood there just looking at one another for a full minute, before Joanne quietly said, "you must be Ty Wayne." Then she opened up her arms and hurried her step to him to give him a good hug. Had Dwayne not known who Joanne was, he wouldn't have become emotional, but this sight was more than he could bear. He quickly got up, went around the corner, and dabbed his eyes with a coat sleeve.

He came back and took up a position not very close to the private reunion of kin, but close enough to hear their jubilant comments. Joanne had recalled seeing Ty Wayne as a youngster on two occasions when Titanic had brought him by, but Ty Wayne was stretching the truth a bit when he said that he remembered Joanne as well. Nevertheless, they were extremely happy to see and hold one another.

When the moment presented itself, Dwayne came over and performed what was now his standard introduction. The two paid little attention to the reporter, but they agreed to have a family picture taken later that evening for a keepsake. Joanne asked about Ty Wayne's mother, Jeanette, and Ty Wayne said that she had gone to run an errand and would be back in a half hour or so. Ty Wayne indicated that she was a little emotional, and it was Ty Wayne's idea that he be dropped off at the funeral home before his mother paid her visit. Then Joanne mentioned that she had to go unpack and she would see Ty Wayne a bit later.

From five to six o'clock, business was slow – there were no visitors. But just after six, the floodgates seemed to open, and Dwayne had a hard time keeping track between ordinary folks and famous people who were obviously surprised to see others just like themselves.

Slammin' Sam Snead was one of the first notables to sign in. Then came an old but distinguished Damon Runyon, one of the most famous newsmen of all times. From his home of 40 miles away strode in none other than the professional golf tour's 11 straight tournament winner, Byron Nelson. Two more northeastern "Mafia" type Joes came in. Then in walked a nattily dressed middle-aged man who introduced himself to several of the crowd as the son of Nicky Arnstein, and of course, Fanny Brice. Then came an old man named Nick "The Greek" Dandolos, one of Titanic's favorite people to hang out with, and one of the few who rang a bell with Dwayne after reviewing Titanic's previous escapades. Then came another elderly chap. They said his name was Dempsey, the son of the famous heavyweight champion, Jack Dempsey.

The crowd was getting a bit older now. In walked Ed Duddley, the past resident pro at Beverly Hills Country Club in Los Angeles. From right here in town, one of Titanic's Ridglea Golf Club's partners, T. A. Avarello. Then a guy named Ralph Greenleaf. Then the former U. S. Amateur Champion, George Von Elm, who in 1926 beat Bobby Jones in that year's U. S. Amateur Championship, joined the crowd. Then came Joe Davis of San

Antonio – the hill country's best poker player. Then the double-doors opened, and in pranced the Fat Man – no one else but "Minnesota Fats" – arguably the best pool player to ever wrap his fingers around a pool cue. With the fat man came another American legend of pool hustling, Harry Moskevitz, from his home in Joplin, Missouri. From west Texas, still making his home in Lubbock, walked in the youngest phenom golfer of his time, Johnny Moss. The recognizable Chill Wills of movie fame then graced the doorway entrance. An oil businessman named Harry Sinclair was next to come in to pay his respects. Then came another businessman from New York, the previous owner of the New York football Giants, Charles Stoneham.

By now the viewing room, the foyer, and halfway down an adjacent hallway were filled with grateful friends and relatives who had come to say goodbye to an old friend. The greeting director opened the two other viewing rooms that were now vacant to handle the crowd. Coffee was being served, but the coffee and a few soft drinks weren't keeping up with the demand. Dwayne could sense his story starting to slip away when the guests would soon depart for more comfortable surroundings. He quickly went in search of a phone to call his boss.

While Dwayne was seeking an answer to the overcrowding by phone other guests arrived. Famous golf writer, Oscar Fraley, walked in and was immediately mobbed by all of the notable golfers.

Lamar Hunt, the the son of a notable billionaire, H.L. Hunt, was the only one who came to the viewing with a package--wrapped in plain brown paper. Mr. Hunt unwrapped his father's favorite checker set, a beautiful inlaid board and hand-carved checkers. He placed the set under the casket, said a prayer by himself, and slowly walked away. He was stopped by one of the guests who recognized him and was asked a question. The crowd quieted to hear him answer. "I wanted Titanic to carry with him this special checker set that my father cherished so much because he and Titanic had so many memorable games on it. My father used to say he was the second best checker player in the world, second only to Titanic Thompson. God Bless them both."

Eddie Merrins, another club pro from Los Angeles, came in to be counted by Titanic's family as a respected friend – he had played a few rounds of golf with Titanic prior to becoming the Bel-Air Country Club pro in 1962. Gene Shields from down the road in Waco, came in. The president of Ben Hogan and AMF came in with one of their representative pros, Johnny Arreaga, one of the first Mexican-American to ever be invited to join the PGA tour.

The former Nora Trushel from Missouri went straight to the registry to check the names and proudly sign her name. She recognized no one, and no one recognized her. But she was proud of her Titanic connection – she was a former Mrs. Thompson. When others around her read her signature, they inquired as to when she was married to Titanic. She replied, "That was too long ago, and the date isn't important. What is important was that I was stupid enough to have asked Titanic for a divorce because I didn't think I could take any more of Ti's lifestyle and being gone from home so much. The judge granted me a divorce on the grounds that I alleged. I want everyone to know I didn't know what I had. I jumped out of the frying pan into the fire! I then married a more stable man – to be known in banking circles as Pretty Boy Floyd. I'm here to tell Titanic how much I loved him, and I'm terribly sorry I didn't say that often enough. No way anyone could tell if the marriage could have lasted if I hadn't asked that judge for a divorce, but somehow I know. I made a big mistake not trying to make it work."

Titanic's old bodyguard, named Wes Billinger, barely fit his monstrous frame through the front door to get in to pay his respects. Then came Frank Jackson, the 1930s world champion of horseshoe pitching from Pittsburgh, Pennsylvania – until he lost the biggest match of his life to none other than Titanic Thompson.

Two of Dallas's best-known past golf hustlers, Bob Montgomery and Doug McClanahan, were the next to sign in. Former partners of Titanic's and past Masters champion Herman Kaiser joined Bob Hamilton – former PGA champion – and they were the next to join the crowded funeral parlor. Fellow Titanic poker player Herbert Cokes from Los Angeles showed, as well as

Ace Darnell, owner of Dallas's Redman Club on Ervay Street, and well-known for its around-the-clock card games.

Time was now running short for Dwayne on keeping this crowd together, and he knew it. Unless his boss, Ben, called him back quickly, his story was going to be buried in the same casket as Titanic Thompson. The greeting director was at his wits' end when the phone finally rang. It was Ben, and Ben had a great idea. All of the local country clubs were closed on Mondays, and he had had a difficult time getting someone at each of the ones he called to agree to open up their club for special entertainment for the evening, but he had succeeded at one.

River Crest Country Club was an in-town club that was one of Titanic's favorite tracks in the world – not only because of its length, its design, and its fast greens, but because it held the best gambling membership of any club in America. Ben was on the board there, and he had just moved mountains to do the impossible. Ben had also arranged five limousines and two vans to provide back-and-forth transportation to the club from the funeral home. Arrangements were made for there to be heavy hors d'oeuvres and plenty of drinks with three bartenders to serve them. Ben was excited, and he couldn't wait to make the announcement.

He asked the greeting director to help him assemble and quiet the crowd so that he could make his pitch. By the time Dwayne finished summarizing the much-appreciated generosity, the vans and limos rolled into the parking lot. The funeral home agreed to furnish two more limousines when they became available from the other two completed funerals. Counting a dozen or more cars that were already there with the friends and family, the procession was over 20 vehicles long – each car packed full of dignitaries and just plain friends.

Dwayne made sure that one of the funeral directors remained at the parlor to greet the expected remaining guests and to ask them to please join the family and other friends at River Crest. Assurances were made to Dwayne that such a plan would be carried out – including the necessary transportation, if needed, to join the other guests, and then Dwayne accompanied the crowd to the club.

Chapter 4

Dwayne's was about the third vehicle to arrive at the gorgeous River Crest Country Club. All of the other scheduled cars and limos arrived within the next ten minutes or so. Dwayne was immediately greeted by the head of the service staff when he entered the main clubhouse door, and all Dwayne could do was just listen to all of the accommodating efforts Ben had made arrangements for. He was really impressed. Being slightly on the bashful side, and always in the past being able to hide behind a pen and newsprint, Dwayne wouldn't like what he was about to hear.

"Dwayne, I think it would be a good idea if you stepped up to the podium and made an announcement about all of the food, drinks, and service these people can expect. Tell `em that they are the guests of the Ft. Worth Star Telegram, and anything the club can do to make their stay with us more comfortable, please don't hesitate to ask. Then whatever else you think appropriate, because I understand this is some sort of an overflow from a funeral, I think you should speak from your heart. But you better get with it, `cause we've already got a bunch of people here."

"Yes, sir. We sure do appreciate your response to a totally unpredictable situation. I know everybody down at the paper is very grateful. I'll go do my duties now. Thanks again."

Dwayne hurried into the main ballroom where members of the staff were still setting up the bars, the tables, and the food line. It was a push, but he made it to the slightly elevated podium stand and tapped the mike to see if it had any juice.

Tap, tap – the sound echoed a positive mike hookup and power.

"Ah, hah, ladies and gentlemen – welcome to River Crest Country Club. There is no doubt why we're here, and in spite of the festive surroundings, I will not lose the thought that we're here for a very somber occasion. My boss and the board of directors at the Ft. Worth Star Telegram are pleased to be able to provide you with the best of drink and food under the circumstances. The cars and other vehicles that brought you here will also be available to take you back to the funeral home or your hotel when you are ready to leave. I can see that most of you know many of the others that are here, and we realize that everyone should take this occasion to visit with and get to know the other wonderful people that have come to Ft. Worth to honor a true American legend and hero – Alvin Clarence Thomas, better known to all of us as Titanic Thompson.

"There is nothing I can say here that you all don't already know about Mr. Thompson. It's my belief and my paper's belief that more people would like to know more about him. That's why I've been assigned the task of creating a journalistic article about his life. Maybe you all noticed me sitting in the foyer back there at the funeral home with my notes and my research from other publications about Mr. Thomas's life. Well, from what I've already heard from a number of you, those publications don't say anything about the true man. Nobody paid y'all's way to come here, and a lot of you came from a long way away. I know every one of you had other plans for today and tomorrow, but you thought enough of this man to show up here today to honor him. Not any of us would be disappointed to have this many folks show up at each of our funerals. It is a great testament of friendship and an appreciation for Titanic, his family, and all of his friends.

"I hope all of you will tolerate me listening to some of your experiences with this legend. I would greatly appreciate all of the input you can give me. I never knew the man, but with all that I've read about him, and with all the stories and experiences I've heard thus far from you, I feel that I knew him. Now, if there is anything any of us here at the club, at the paper, or at the funeral home can do to make your stay more pleasant, please don't hesitate to call on us. Oh, please remember that I can write fast if you see me lookin' over your shoulder trying to get a story or two from you. Thank you for being here."

There was a small smattering of applause, but, as with any crowd, attention to the person at the microphone doesn't last very long. Drinks were constantly being filled, and plates of food were already being consumed during every word of Dwayne's address.

After those few words, Dwayne headed straight for the table where he had rested his briefcase. He took off his coat, wrapped it around a chair, loosened his tie, grabbed a couple of stenographer's pads and four pencils, and started to mingle. The stories, the facts, the figures, and other dialog were just too much for a note-taker to reduce to anything comprehendible at a later time. He was getting frustrated at the chances of stories passing him by. Every clique of two people or more was engaged in rapid-fire conversation about "remember when." Every table had its seated participants glued to a new storyteller every five minutes. It was fast becoming a no-win situation for Dwayne as he saw story after story begin and end without being able to jot down a word. He had to do something!

After seeking out and having a short conversation with Titanic's two boys, and Titanic's two ex-wives that he had been introduced to, Dwayne headed back to the podium. "May I have your attention one more time? Please, may I have your attention one more time?" Dwayne and a few crowd members joined in tapping their silverware on drinking glasses to draw attention to the podium.

"I've just had conversations with Titanic's family, and they collectively feel just as I do – we all feel we are being left out of so many stories and experiences. So I've come up with an idea. Given that this certainly isn't a normal situation, and given that so many of you are eager and anxious to tell a Titanic story, why don't we have a Titanic Roast. This in no way is disrespectful – now a days, most remarks given during the funeral are from the heart, a bevy of experiences that are meant to provoke memories – some happy, some sad, some good, and some bad – but a microcosm of a life, life we are here today and tomorrow to honor and celebrate, to retrieve and to relive." Spontaneous shouts and clapping pierced the air. Dwayne had a new chance.

"I don't want to scare anyone off. The smallest and seemingly trivial story may touch someone else's memory, or give life to another valuable experience to be told. Just like writing a newspaper article, the first sentence is the hardest part. Can I ask for a volunteer to get this thing going? Who'll be the first to break the ice, and let us relive some of the experiences of the man we are gathered here to praise?"

From two banquet tables back came a shout. "Here I come, young fella, here I come. Ain't anybody gonna believe what I'm about to tell ya."

****

The Rambler was a paddlewheel riverboat that ran up and down the St. Francis River in Arkansas. It was owned by a professional gambler and game maker named Joe Green. Joe and The Rambler resided in a small river community named Marked Tree, Arkansas, a little country town known for religion and its unsavory characters. As a secondary income producer to help finance his operations, Joe Green pulled a produce barge behind his famous gambling boat bartering and selling all types of fresh produce gathered from his boarding and exiting stops up and down the river.

Alvin Clarence Thomas was 19 years old and feeling his gambling oats. Marked Tree wasn't far from his hometown of Rogers, Arkansas, and Alvin was running out of "pigeons" to take money from near his home. He had heard about Joe Green, and the big-time dice and poker games that were being held on his boat with a welcome for all comers – regardless of age. With his pockets full from his recent home town winnings, Alvin decided to parlay those winnings into something special, something that would get him away from the small-town atmosphere and into the limelight of big-town gambling. Alvin packed his small worn and torn suitcase his mother had given him, gathered up the tools of his trade – a .38 long-barrel revolver, his small- bore rifle, a pair of horseshoes, his two-piece pool cue, four pairs of dice, six decks of cards, his well-rubbed throwing rock, and a bowling ball – and began his hitchhiking journey to a world of dreams.

Joe Green relished new gambling blood on his boat, and he prided himself on knowing just how to part a new guest's money from him, and making him think that he really had a chance. Alvin had done his homework once again, and he knew how to make Joe Green notice him. Alvin was quickly invited to join in a small poker game with three other guests and Mr. Green. By the time the boat had reached its turnaround point, Alvin had pretty much cleaned out all of the guests. The young man was now the apple in Joe Green's eye. At Joe's insistence, the game switched to dice. It took two more up-and-down trips on the designated river path for young Alvin to take every ounce of cash Joe Green had--$2,000.

That's when the big-time began for Alvin Clarence Thomas. With a score of witnesses looking on, Joe Green acknowledged his unlucky losses, and offered Alvin a deal. "This boat has got to be worth upwards of $2,500, right here, right where it sits. I'll give you an IOU for that amount backed up by the title to my boat, The Rambler."

The dice game continued, but Joe thought his luck would be better enhanced if he upped the bets and played fewer rolls. He was dead wrong. It took Alvin less time to win all of that IOU than the first $2,000. Joe Green was now down to only one remaining asset, the barge and its contents. He offered Alvin another IOU for $1,250 for the barge and the floating produce. Alvin had no idea what the barge and the perishables were worth, but he had the fever, and greed was overrunning any thought of losing or comparing risks. In eight rolls of the dice, Joe Green was broke; he had lost it all to a bootstrapping kid of 19 years old. Then to add insult to serious commercial injury, Alvin admitted that he knew next to nothing about the mechanics and art of running a paddle wheeler, so he offered a job to Joe Green to be his straw boss. But from now on, the passengers and the games, and the ports of call, would be of Alvin's choosing.

Alvin Clarence Thomas slept well that night in the only decent hotel in Marked Tree. Alvin's reputation swirled on the winds of gossip around the community. At every store and every eatery, Alvin was recognized and heralded as the man who broke old Joe Green. One of the people that he met, and one that took a special fancy to him, was the most beautiful girl in town, Nellie Harris. Within a week, they became a regular scene. On the following weekend after they had met, Alvin announced a special party for his new sweetheart on board his new paddle wheeler.

The party was well attended with all of Alvin's new acquaintances, one of which was an old, ugly, weatherworn friend of Joe Green's. His name was Jim Johnson. In earlier days, Jim was the chief bodyguard for Joe Green when he traveled outside the community on gambling excursions. He was the burliest, stinkiest old codger in town, yet Alvin welcomed him on his boat because of Joe.

The friendliness of the party took a nosedive an hour or so after pulling up anchor. A dice game got under way, and of course Alvin and Jim Johnson were participants. It didn't take long for Alvin to get up $50 or so on burly Jim. That fact, and the fact that Jim had been drinking rather heavily since morning, led to a preordained scuffle. Jim pulled a knife and challenged Alvin as a cheater.

"You already cheated my friend Joe out of everything he owned, now you're trying to do the same thing to me. I'm gonna teach you a goddamn lesson. I'm gonna cut your head off and throw it in the river!"

Alvin tried to play the circumstance cool, but Jim threw back his chair, turned over the table, scattering dice and money everywhere. Then he drew his knife and headed for Alvin. With the long blade pointed at Alvin's throat, Jim backed Alvin to the rail of the port side of the rear of the boat. As Jim withdrew the blade and took a swing at Alvin with the knife, Alvin dodged and fell overboard. As Alvin bobbed to the surface, he heard big Jim roaring with laughter, and he heard him yelling that he "done got Joe's boat back for him."

The boat was heading upstream, and moving at less than three or four miles an hour. Alvin scrambled up the bank, ran down the boat, waited till it had to come close to the shore to make a bend, and then jumped back into the water ahead of the boat. He knew the docking ramp had a place for a good grip, and he knew he could pull himself up. This he did, with unsuspecting help from

Nellie and her friends who recognized his plight in the muddy water. Once on board, Alvin then worked his way to the back of the boat where Jim and Joe were shouting and celebrating.

As Alvin neared the two men who were draped over the back rail, Jim turned to holler. "Where's that pretty li`l gal who used to belong to the kid who went swimmin'?" Then Jim turned and saw the wet and haggered Alvin. "Want more of my knife, kid?"

As Jim advanced on Alvin, Nellie screamed. Alvin looked down and to his right, and grabbed a mechanic's hammer. Jim swung wildly with his knife. Alvin ducked, and as big Jim was turned around by the force of his own swing, Alvin crashed the hammer into the side of Jim Johnson's head. Jim crumbled to the deck. Everyone watching went into dead-silent shock. Then Alvin picked up Jim and rolled him over the four-foot-high rail. The aggressor made a bloody splash into the muddy water. Then Alvin ordered the boat turned around and to shift its course back to Marked Tree.

The first person off the boat was Joe Green. He pushed and shoved his way through the crowd to hurry to his friend, the sheriff. Joe and the sheriff were close. It happens that way when one pays graft for protection of one's illegalities. Joe Green swore out a complaint that said Alvin Clarence Thomas wantonly and without cause killed Jim Johnson.

Alvin was locked up, and an immediate trial ensued. It was an orchestrated one-man verdict. The sheriff only allowed Joe Green as a single witness, and a jury trial was out of the question. Alvin was railroaded, but there was a somewhat silver lining. The sheriff offered to grant Alvin clemency, with no criminal record, if he would give back all of the money he had on him when he was arrested, and if he would give back the IOUs and title to The Rambler, the barge, and its present cargo.

Alvin had little choice; he agreed, signed the paperwork, and he and Nellie were on the next train out of Marked Tree – never, ever, to return. It was a good thing that Alvin had hidden almost $2,000 in his hotel room when all the ruckus had started. Alvin Clarence Thomas had – for a few moments – been a rich man. He had killed a man. He had learned about the claws of justice. He had a new traveling companion, and he had ten times more money than he ever had before – all before he had met his 19th birthday!

****

Ironically, from the same table as the previous storyteller came another elderly gentleman who hurried to the podium to add a connective story to the previous one. He didn't have to be called by the host, Dwayne. The mike was positioned for a much taller gentleman before him, and as he fumbled with the apparatus to try and get it adjusted to his stature, Dwayne did bounce up the stand to help.

The gentleman introduced himself to the crowd and acknowledged everyone at his table. "I was the most surprised person in the world when I got to the funeral parlor this afternoon. I had plenty of time to gather my thoughts on the way here from Missouri, and I never dreamed there would be so many of us here. I expected five or six old-timers like me, but, my God, we've got nearly a seated congress here. I haven't seen my old friends at my table in ten to 20 years, and I've only heard about most of the rest of you. It's my honor to be among you. Titanic was my friend, and he always spoke so highly of all the people he had the pleasure to encounter – whether he kicked your brains out in golf, or just sat at a gambling table with you. He was truly one of a kind.

"At the end of the last story, Alvin and his new girlfriend had just gotten on a train headed for Joplin, Missouri. I didn't meet him on his first trip to Joplin, but many of my friends at that time did. There was an old but famous pool hall in the area down south of town, and that is where the big gambling games of that era were held. Somehow, Alvin made his way to that dim-lit joint, cue stick in hand. I know this story is right because I've had a dozen friends tell me the identical version. Do any of you really know how Titanic got his name? Well, I'm about to tell you the truth.

"There are many legends of untruth about this subject – Alvin Clarence Thomas escaped the sinking Titanic ship disaster by posing as a woman in women's clothes to assure himself a seat in the last lifeboat – rubbish, bullshit – not so, nor are any other stories so except what I'm about to tell you.

"Alvin Thomas entered the pool hall in Joplin, Missouri, obviously intent on finding a pick up nine-ball game. He watched the other players on the two tables there for almost three hours before asking to join. When he was invited, it was to take the winner of the two best players in the bunch. Alvin wore his opponent out. The defeated shark then asked for an immediate rematch. Because of the one-sidedness of the previous match, no one objected. The second game was more of a slaughter than the first. Two young lads looking on at the bar began some cat calls regarding the new renegade pool hustler. When the second game was over, Alvin asked either or both of the well-built youngsters if they wanted a piece of the action. They answered with, 'football's our game, we ain't much for non-contact sports.'

"Alvin took no further issue with them, but he did offer them a bet utilizing their apparent strength. 'Just to be sporting with you two, I'll give you a chance to prove your strength. I'll make you a small bet – you pick the amount – that one of you can't pick up two of those bricks outside, walk down the road carrying one in each hand for two miles, then walk back here and put those two bricks up on the bar. Now you can't dilly dally. When you pick up the two bricks, you can't set them down until you get back here and put them on the bar.'

'I don't know who you are, boy, but I'll take that bet for all the money I got in my pocket.' He then emptied out his pocket on the closest table. 'That'll be $11.'

"Alvin smiled and said, Okay. You know a spot down the road that's at least two miles away? I'll trust you for that amount of money to be honest about the distance.'

'There's a general store east of here, to the right, down the same road that this here pool hall's on. Will that do?'

'Yeah, that'll do. Now I wanta watch you pick up those bricks and get started. I'll be right here when you get back. I figure you're goin' to walk three to four miles an hour; you should be back in a little over an hour. I've got to put a time limit on you. You gotta carry those bricks pretty fast. You got one hour to get back here and put those bricks on the bar.'

"The young athlete had had just enough beers to be invincible. 'Come on, I'm going to make $11 in one hour!'

'Okay, I'm puttin' my 11 bucks right here with yours. We'll let your buddy watch over the money. Winner takes all.'

"Alvin excused himself from the other pool players to go outside and watch the football player pick up his bricks and get under way. Then he returned to the table and asked, 'Who's next?'

"Everybody wanted to play the new stranger, but everybody was also a bit scared. Finally, one of the original players who was playing when Alvin walked in picked up a cue and said he'd play two games of nine-ball for $10 on the five and $20 on the nine. Two games were not enough for the challenger. He stretched it to four, and he lost every money ball except one five – a net loser of $100.

"One more challenger spoke up and agreed to play one game for the same stakes. He, too, lost. Then the dog outside let out a familiar bark,' sounds like your buddy's returning,' as Alvin turned toward the other football player. No sooner than he finished his observation than the brick toter walked in. He was a lot more whipped than he thought he'd be, but he had a smile on his face that silently said he was a winner. He stepped up to the bar, looked over his shoulder at his audience, and gave a mighty heave – NO LUCK! Try though he may, he couldn't get those bricks above his elbow. He tried a dozen times with every try worse than the one before. Finally, he dropped both bricks and stormed out of the place with his buddy in hot pursuit. In a few minutes the two returned.

'How about a fight to give me a chance to get my money back?'

'No way, my friend. I ain't very good at fightin,' but I'll give you another chance to get your dough back if you can come up with something to bet.'

'My buddy's got five dollars. Will you give me two-to-one?'

'Yeah I will. I'll bet I can stand flatfooted and jump on top of that pool table, and I'll bet you can't. A do and a don't bet – five dollars if I do it, and five dollars if you don't.'

'Okay!' The football player had to be the better physical ath-lete, so Alvin was offered several side bets. He took them all.

"Alvin pushed back the pool players and took his flatfooted stance about two feet from the table. 'You can't use your hands!' And then he jumped, with his knees fully bent, and landed right on top of the felt and wooden edge. Then he stood up, turned around and jumped down.

'Your turn.' Alvin motioned with his hand toward his foe.

"The opposition looked to be much stronger, much more agile, but he had never tried such a stunt before. He tried four times, but he was never close. Alvin collected all his money, wished everyone inside a happy rest of the day, and then he walked out the door. He had won nearly $500 – in pool, on a weird brick-toting bet, and jumping on a pool table. One of the regular patrons then said, 'What's that guy's name, anyway? It ought to be TITAN-IC the way he sank all of y`all's dreams.'

"Two days later, Alvin came by the establishment again to hustle some more action. The same old patron was sitting at the bar when Alvin came through the door. 'Well boys, looks like the Titanic has come to shatter more of your dreams.'

"Alvin was able to entice a few players to play him in pool, but not much money was available. Alvin then left, got in his recently purchased used car, and went on down the highway.

"Titanic told me that he could think of nothing else on his drive back to the hotel. He went to bed thinking about his new name. He said that it didn't seem to ring well as Titanic Thomas, so he decided himself on Titanic Thompson. That's the truth – so help me God!"

The entire ballroom roared with laughter and applause as the elderly gentleman sought back his seat at the big banquet table with his long-lost friends. He received a standing ovation!

Chapter 5

Dwayne Douglas was in hog heaven with just the beginning of all the stories and experiences he expected to hear. The booze was flowing and that usually meant less inhibitions and more conversations. The food was being replenished at somewhere near a tray a minute, and there was no sign of anyone becoming restless or wanting to leave - not what anyone would have predicted at a funeral, but everyone there was having a wonderful time recollecting the life and experiences of Titanic Thompson.

To keep order, Dwayne regained his stance periodically at the speaker's podium. "Isn't it great to hear these kinds of happenings – to hear how Titanic really got his name? Now, who's gonna top that?

"Who's next?"

****

"Good evening, ladies and gentlemen. My name is Johnson Walker, III. I am the grandson of the 1920's World Champion of Checkers. My family is from Detroit, but what I'm going to tell you about happened in Kansas City, Missouri.

"I hope you dislike loudmouth braggers as much as my grandfather did, and I want to tell you about who my grandfather says was the worst. Seems there was a guy named Lock Renfro that lived in Kansas City who thought he was the absolute best at the game of checkers. Truth is, he was pretty good, but he didn't have the best of worldwide competition in Kansas City, and that fact certainly played against his self-proclaimed license to make his claim as the best in the world. His loudmouth bragging caught the attention of a visiting Titanic Thompson when Titanic was there to play pool and poker. Somehow, Titanic got the name of my grandfather from a fellow checker player who wanted someone to put Lock Renfro in his place. The gentleman furnished Mr. Thompson with my grandfather's telephone number, and Mr. Thompson called him. My grandfather was then the true World Champion of Checkers, having proved himself against all comers and in every tournament he could find, including an invitational-only Worlds Championship.

"Titanic told my grandfather that he knew this guy was good, and he could probably beat him, but there was no sense in taking chances, so he voiced a plan. Lock Renfro had put out the word that he would pay $10,000 to anyone who could beat him. Evidently, Titanic Thompson was fond of making braggarts eat their words, and he was especially fond of making money at the same time.

"Titanic told my grandfather that there was no way Lock would play grandfather – he was bound to know of his reputation. But Titanic told my granddaddy that Lock only knew him as a pool hustler, so he'd jump at the chance of playing Titanic in checkers. Titanic said he had stayed at a relatively knew hotel in Kansas City a while back, and he had remembered a poker room there that had a false ceiling. Once Mr. Thompson got my grandfather to say that he was interested in Titanic's plan, Titanic said that he needed a little time to check out the ceiling, then he would call my grandfather back to finalize the deal. In the first conversation, conditioned on the ceiling and a proper fix, Titanic offered to split the ten grand with grandfather if he'd crawl up in that ceiling and signal to him if he were about to make a wrong move. After confirming that a set-up could be accomplished, the next morning, Titanic called my grandfather and told him to get to Kansas City as fast as he could – the match and the fix were on!

"Turned out that the challenger was expected to put up show money of $1,000 to have some risk by the challenger and weed out the novices. Titanic argued about the late stipulation, but in the end he agreed to the put-up money.

"The plan was for grandfather to be in place above the designated checker table an hour before the match. Titanic warned my grandfather that a restroom break was impossible, so he suggested that my grandfather fast without any liquid for at least three hours before his climb. Titanic was able to drill a hole through the ceiling two days prior to the match, and he actually tested the setup the day before the competition. Titanic was to hold onto the checker when he was in doubt about a particular move – kinda hesitating after he pushed the checker to the square of intention. He would hold onto that checker while it was on the new square for five to ten seconds. If grandfather thought the move was a bad one, he'd signal Titanic by putting his finger down through the drilled hole just far enough for Mr. Thompson to see his finger tip. Grandfather said that the cramped quarters in that ceiling were just about the most uncomfortable thing he had ever been through, but it was worth $5,000 to him. Titanic told my grandfather that without him, he probably would have lost – Lock was a better player than Titanic anticipated, but he said he hadn't any qualms about picking Lock Renfro's feathers because he was such a braggart.

"Just thought you all ought to know that Titanic stood for no un-official braggin' – he'd do just about anything to put someone in his place if he was a loudmouth and made claims that were not deserving. Someday, if any of y'all happen to get to Kansas City, and if you want to take a few minutes out of your day, I'd be happy to show you that old hotel. It's still there, and I've seen the hole in the ceiling!"

****

Ralph Greenleaf was an 80 year-old man now, but he zipped up one of the aisles to tell his story.

"There was a big-time pool hustler around Joplin, Tulsa, Carthage, and Kansas City named Jim Buford. He challenged everybody that he thought he could beat. He was smart. He never played a soul until he saw him shoot pool under pressure. Then he loved to chide that someone into a big bet. Titanic had played with him on past occasions and had held his own, but everybody that knew Ti knew that he wanted better odds than 50-50.

"Just like the checker champ's grandson that preceded me, I was a world champion in my own right, but at a different sport – my game was pool, any kind, any time, and any place. I never had a chance to play the Fat Man that sits here with us tonight, but he's heard about my game, and he'd tell you it'd be a close match." The crowd erupted with laughter and applause again, and it wouldn't die down until the "Fat Man" stood up to be recognized.

"Okay, back to my story – Titanic knew me, and he was dying to set up a partnership match between Jim Buford and Buford's partner and the two of us. He put a lotta' thought into this setup, and it came off like a dirty pair of boxer's trunks." The crowd liked that!

"There was a hard-luck pool player in the area who was well-known. He had better than moderate skill, but he had no cash to back it up, and besides that, Titanic knew that Buford knew he could beat this one-time hustler anywhere he would light. This all worked into Titanic's plan.

"On purpose, Titanic made a point to run into this guy named Johnny Littlepage. He offered Johnny some quick money, and a chance to play Jim Buford and his partner in a big pool game. He slipped Johnny a $100 and told him to go buy himself some new clothes, to shave, shine his shoes, and go respectful lookin' to challenge Jim Buford to a big time partnership pool match. Buford was to set the time and place within three days. Johnny Littlepage thought he had gone to Heaven. He was so excited that he did everything that Titanic had ordered, and he had an agreed game with Buford within four hours.

"Titanic reached me in New York, and I jumped at the chance to be his partner. Titanic gave me specific instructions as to where to be and when to be there. I follow instructions real well, and I was where I was supposed to be when I was supposed to be there! Titanic showed up at the gambling site almost a half-hour late – an intentional ploy of his to set the stage in his favor – it gets the competition on edge. Already there was his good friend – me, blending in with the crowd, and dressed as inconspicuously as I could dress. Titanic slowly walked around the place, inspected the table, bent over and checked the lighting, and then hung up his coat like he was going to stay awhile. Jim Buford, couldn't hold his enthusiasm any longer, and told Titanic that he wasn't used to being stood up or made late, and that he was ready to start the match – $10,000, three games, winner take all. Titanic was in no hurry to speak. He just stood there looking at all of the kibitzers. Finally, Titanic said the game was fair, but he had to have a partner. Immediately Johnny Littlepage started to screw together his cue and get himself ready for his certain inclusion. However, a man from the crowd spoke up and said he'd like to be Titanic's partner – that was me. Titanic looked at me with amazement. He asked if I could play. I told him loud enough for everyone to hear that I wasn't scared. Then Titanic turned to Buford and said it looked like he had two partners, and he'd have to pick one for the match. He then asked me if I had enough money on me to take care of my share of the wager. I said that I didn't have much cash on me, but I'd give him an IOU or a personal check before we played and he could fund my portion with my guarantees. He then turned to Johnny and asked him the same question. Of course, poor Johnny didn't have a dime, and everyone knew it. Then Titanic told Johnny that he was sorry, but he'd be a fool to risk the whole bet to win only half.

"Then he turned to me and said, 'Mister, I hope you can handle a cue, because these guys are good, and we're goin' to have to play our butts off to win against them.' I just smiled and said hand me a cue.'

"Titanic floated the whole $10,000 in cash and put it on the table to match the opposition's cash. I asked the waiter at the joint to give me a piece of paper and a pen, and I wrote out Titanic my IOU. He looked closely at my scribbling, folded up the IOU, and put it into his pocket.

"The first game was no contest; they hardly had a chance to shoot. And true to the circumstances of the setup, Titanic looked more surprised at my game than any of the spectators. The second was almost as bad, but they did threaten us at one point, but of course we prevailed. I told Titanic that had we not been so good that day, we might have enticed them into another bet, but as it was, they took their whipping, congratulated us, and never knew what hit' em. Johnny Littlepage got another hundred-dollar tip from Titanic for setting the match up, and then we both left town. I have to say, I've been in some of the greatest pool matches the world has ever seen, but that one match was the thrill of a lifetime for me. Titanic and I were more acquaintances than friends before that match, but afterwards, we became the best of friends, and we had a few more chances to partner up with each other a few times thereafter, but nothing like that match with Jim Buford and his partner. That match will go down as one of the greatest setups is history."

****

"My name is Wes Billinger. I'm a rather simple man who enjoys seeing everyone perform and do his best. Although I did a right amount of boxing in my past, I never had the desire to hurt anybody, so that profession went begging. In fact, I never really settled in on one profession. But I'm proud of my life, and I'm proud to have so many friends that know I'm an honest, hardworking man who always gave my best. I've always prided myself on giving back to everyone who hired me a good, honest effort, and a real value for his money. I've worked for more than a hundred people doing everything from common labor to entertaining. But the reason I'm up here right now is to tell you about the best employer I ever had. I wasn't with him long, but we hit it off just right, and our friendship grew and grew. When I finally decided to head to California to seek new fortunes, Titanic Thompson rewarded me with some extra money for my past dedication and loyalty, and the warmest handshake anyone could give. I loved that man, and if I were ever in a tight, he's the guy that I'd want at my right hand. Titanic and I went through thick and thin together, and I want to tell you about one of those thin moments.

"I met Mr. Thompson in St. Louis, Missouri, in 1917. I had just given up my boxing career, and I was looking for a job where I might use some of my intimidation skills – as you can see, I'm a pretty big fellow. Because I'm such a big man, I guess my greatest skill was intimidation – outside of the ring, I would never want to hurt anybody, but my appearance never showed that.   Mr. Thompson picked that up right away, and after he hired me, we became a notorious team. He'd do all the money-making with all sorts of gambling games, and I'd make sure the people he played with were always on the up-and-up, and that they were always hesitant about not paying their losses. God, he made us lots of money! And to tell the truth, I rarely had to intervene to hasten someone into paying up.

"However, there was a time in Missouri where we both complimented each other with our special skills. There was this big crap game that Ti and I had heard about that was held almost daily in the back room of a tailor shop down in East St. Louis. Saying that that area was tough was a severe understatement, and the guy who ran the game was double tough. His name was George Dalton – a tailor by profession, but a crap game organizer for his real income, and he had plenty of criminal ties to back him up. Of course, it was my job to be Titanic's bodyguard, and to make sure there was no trouble on Titanic's behalf.

"As I recall, we entered the shop around four o'clock one rainy afternoon. By five, I was watching everybody watch Titanic run away with all the marbles. I'm not lying when I tell you that Titanic won over $40,000 in that first hour! How or why he knew it was time to leave, I don't know. But Titanic suddenly got up from the table holding his stomach, and said he wasn't feeling real good. You could tell that nobody was buying that, and that's when I stepped in. I asked him if he was all right, and then I shook my head and explained to everyone that this wasn't like Titanic to just get up and leave to protect his winnings. By that time, Titanic was playing the script real well. I couldn't even tell whether he was puttin' on or not. Anyway, George Dalton said that he was sorry for Ti's sudden illness, but he better make an appointment to let everybody have a chance to get their money back. I knew our plans, so I spoke up and told them that we'd be back tomorrow at the same time, unless, of course, Titanic was still under the weather.

"Titanic never told me why he pulled out of that game, but it wasn't my job to ask why. Before we drove over to the tailor shop the next day, Titanic packed his .45 in his shoulder holster, and I did the same. Titanic rat-holed half of the day-before's winnings, and we went in with a $20,000 wad. Every single person that was there the day earlier was there, and most were accompanied by some questionable friends. Titanic's luck wasn't as good as the day before, but he managed to know when to up the stakes, and to simply play the odds. After about two hours, we were up somewhere around $1,500. Evidently, the drunken host named Dalton knew better than we did about how much Titanic was winning.

"All at once, Dalton slammed down his fist on the table and challenged Titanic to a one-on-one game. They set a time limit of one hour, awfully short for a typical Titanic game. Nevertheless, Titanic obliged because he thought he owed any loser a chance to get back his bait. At the end of that time limit, Ti had doubled the $1,500 – all from the famous Dalton. Dalton began to accuse Titanic of cheating, and the drunk reached across the table and retrieved his previously issued IOU's. At nearly the same instant, the phone rang in the back portion of the shop. Titanic grabbed me and motioned me to have a word with him over in the corner. He said that I should follow Dalton to the back and listen in on the call. I did just that. I couldn't hear both sides of the conversation, mind you, but I could feel something was up, and it wasn't going to be good.

"I came back and whispered to Titanic that I thought we were in for some trouble. Like a plague had just set in, all of the other gamers got up and left. Titanic watched them all leave, and then he asked Dalton to make good on his IOUs. Dalton said that Titanic was to come back the next afternoon to get his money, and Titanic politely agreed. It was dark outside when we gradually opened that rear door to leave. We expected something really bad, so we had our hands on our under cover pistols. I was the first one to exit, and I immediately noticed a cop leaning against a light pole across the street. I sensed that we were lucky, so I reached back and grabbed Titanic and told him we needed to get out of there fast. When Titanic started that car, I could envision us being blown to bits, but everything was all right, and we made it back to our hotel without any further trouble.

"I suggested to Ti that we leave well enough alone, and to get out of town while we still had plenty of winnings and our healthy skin.

"Titanic looked me straight in the eyes and told me, 'Wes, we're in the business of gambling and collecting. We won fair and square, now we have to finish the rest of our occupation – we gotta go there tomorrow and collect.'

"The next day, just after noon, we headed back to the tailor shop. We entered through the front door and walked past all of the steam presses back to Dalton's office. He had obviously been warned that we were coming, so he was half-way out his office door to meet us as we got there. He said he had our money, but he wanted to know more about Titanic, and he wanted us to sit down and have a drink with him. Titanic didn't drink, so we had several cups of coffee. Finally, Titanic said that we had to go, and he wanted to collect on his IOU. Dalton never winced; he rolled off 30 new $100 bills from his rubber-band wad in his pocket and paid Ti off.

"Dalton then made a quick move going over to the back door – a conspicuously quick move. Titanic and I saw him flip the outside light-switch twice – most unusual in the daytime! Titanic and I acted like we were putting our hands in our coat pockets and began to walk to the door. We were really wrapping our fingers around some cold, hard steel and walking to the door. I was about to go out first, but I was pulled back by Ti. He said that this was his idea, and for me to back him up. Dalton pretended not to hear a thing, and he half opened the door for us. As Titanic stepped out, there were two thugs standing there with pistols drawn. I swear I've never seen anything go so fast – Titanic had his .45 out and aimed at the first guy before they could swing their already drawn guns to their target. Ti blew the first guy away, and then shot the next guy right in the heart before he could react. There was nothing left for me to do but to turn and cover Dalton. That sleazy tailor was on his knees bawling like a baby, and begging for mercy. Titanic turned to Dalton and grabbed him by the front of his shirt and raised him to a standing position, then he just shook him. I in turn grabbed Titanic by the arm and told him to leave well enough alone because we were getting out of there. Titanic dropped that crying weasel like a bag of potatoes - I mean he crumbled to the floor like a limp dishrag.

"The next thing I knew, we were in the car. So calm it was scary, Titanic turned to me and asked a question. Which way to the police station? I was dumbfounded. I asked him if he was crazy. He said we were in the right. It was self-defense, and we were going immediately to the law and tell them our story. Of course, in hindsight, he was right, but at the time, I thought he was crazy!

"We walked right into that single-story police station and went straight to the complaint counter. Titanic told me to give him my gun. He took it, un-holstered his, and placed them both on the countertop. He then told the policeman in charge that he had just killed two people down at the tailor shop in self-defense. He suggested they check his gun and the two empty chambers. Then he suggested they check my gun, which had obviously not been fired. The policeman looked as if he were in shock. He called in three or four other officers and asked a couple of them to stay with us while he took one of them with him to go investigate. We waited there, seated, without saying a word for nearly an hour until the captain returned.

"The serious-minded captain pulled up a straight chair and sat down right in front of us. The captain looked at us right in our eyes and asked if we had gun permits for those guns. We said, 'no sir.' He then got up and walked over behind the counter and pulled out some permit papers and asked us to sign them. He said that we had just killed the two most wanted criminals in Missouri. Turns out that the two had been wanted for kidnapping a mother and kids, and had molested the mother and then killed her. We were suddenly heroes.

"Titanic was a gambler that no one could match, he was a talent in every physical activity he tried. But his real talent was his thinking. Time and time again, he always thought about things quickly, and he always made the right decision – not just at gambling. I don't want to leave the wrong impression of my friend – he was gentle, yet he was tough, but he would never hurt a flea if he had a choice. At the end of this story, he was a public protector –

he had killed two gangsters that were literally on Missouri's most-wanted list. He was an amazing man, and I was proud for him to be my employer and my friend."

****

Dressed in his World War II U. S. Army uniform, Captain Lee Wilson struggled to make it to the podium. Earlier war campaigns and constant training had obviously taken their toll.

"My name is Lee Wilson, and I am a proud veteran of the United States Army from 1917 through 1937. I am the recipient of the Purple Heart – on three occasions – and other special commendation awards. I love my country, and every man that served with me or under me loved their country equally as well – if the truth be known, I'd have shot them if they hadn't." A smattering of applause and laughter greeted those remarks from all over the ballroom.

"I was with Private Titanic Thompson from 1918 until he was honorably discharged seven months and 20 days after his induction. My man, Titanic, was a proud American. I'm not saying he wanted to be there - in the Army - and go through basic training and what all, but he was willing, able, and glad to serve. It took less than a week for his pistol and rifle marksmanship to come to the forefront. He was special. He told me that he learned to shoot from an old-time barn-busting carnival man called Colonel Adam Beaugardus of the traveling Buffalo Bill Show back in Arkansas and Missouri and the rest of the mid west. Titanic said that after about six months, when he started to out-shoot the colonel, he was promoted to head marksman, above the colonel, and from what I'd seen, I sure as hell didn't doubt him! He was with the show for almost two years, before his 18th birthday, and whatever he learned about firearms, their deployment, and their use, he learned it damned well.

"I'm here to tell you that he never lost his edge from his wilderness-show experiences. As far as I'm concerned, he could outshoot any man alive with either his company-issued pistol or his well cared for rifle. You know how I know? I was in charge of keeping his winnings. That's right, I held his cash for him. He came to our unit as a rich man – he had almost $6,000 on him when he undressed and put on his fatigues for the first time. I'm not saying that I was responsible for his taxes, but I guarantee you that he left my post with an excess of $60,000 – all won fair and square on a rifle range or a turkey shoot. I've heard hundreds of stories about his prowess on the golf course, in skeet shooting, in horseshoes, and with cards, but there is no way that he wasn't the best man that ever squeezed a pistol or rifle trigger in the U. S. Army. Thank you all for letting me tell you about a proud American who I admired very much."

There were a lot of great stories about Titanic that had preceded Captain Wilson's, and there would be a lot to follow, but his commentary gained a standing ovation with many clicking their heels and awarding him a well-deserved salute!

****

Frank Jackson was the 1930's World Champion of Pitching Horseshoes, and he was seated at table number five, two tables deep from the small stage on which the podium was located. He was seated with one of the most notable Hollywood actors of the recent past, Chill Wills. During the last army story, Frank begged Chill to be the next person to take the soldier's place on the rostrum and tell about Titanic being only the second person ever to beat him in horseshoes. Chill obliged, and he strode to the podium.

Chill Wills was recognized by everyone, and he got the heartiest of welcomes by the now-unbridled, appreciative crowd. Chill bowed in appreciation, and then he addressed his admirers.

"I was asked by none other than the person who lost heavily to Titanic in a horseshoe- pitching incident to come up here and tell the story. Of all the Titanic wonders, this is my favorite. So, if I get a little carried away, you, Frank Jackson, sitting right there next to my vacant chair, please correct me.

"When visiting the house that Titanic had bought and paid for in full for his mother, back in Monett, Arkansas, Titanic cured his boredom by pitching horseshoes. He got damn good at it. In time, he heard about a guy named Frank Jackson of Minneapolis, Minnesota – the then declared champion of the world in pitching horseshoes. When Titanic thought he was good enough, he approached his new wife with a suggestion that they take a trip. He was married to a young free-spirited girl from Pittsburgh named Alice Kane, and at that time in her life, she was game for just about anything that Titanic would suggest. Titanic was always trying to think of new ways to gamble and win in the companionship of his beautiful new wife. Golf was not yet his bag, and poker and dice games were mostly off limits to decent ladies, so Titanic was ever looking for something wide open so his pretty wife could feel like she was participating. When he read in the newspaper about Frank Jackson for the second time, he immediately thought about challenging this newly crowned world champion of horseshoe pitching. To Titanic, there was a special enticement, Frank's backers were offering a ten-to-one bet with any challenger willing to put up a minimum of $1,000 to $10,000 to anyone that could beat him.

"Now, let me tell you some statistics about a horseshoe pit. A regular horseshoe pit is 40 feet from pole to pole. The poles must be driven into the ground in a vertical position to withstand any jarring from a thrown horseshoe, and there is no limit to weight on a horseshoe. There is a requirement that the horseshoe must conform to a certain size, but to tell you the truth, it is so mathematical, I can't remember the formula." That got a huge laugh from the audience.

"Titanic was good enough to ring regularly 80 out of a 100 throws. He knew that might not be good enough to beat a world champion, so he cleverly devised an angle to improve his odds.

"He notified a couple of his gambling friends in Chicago who had ties to Minneapolis that he needed an introduction to Frank Jackson. The invitation to compete was quick in coming, and Titanic and Alice set off to the state of 10,000 lakes. Upon their arrival, Titanic cased four or five gambling houses and hotels that were known to include horseshoes in their gambling repertoire. He found an ideal place for the match. He then knew he'd have to doctor up the place a bit and then entice Mr. Jackson to come to his suggested place to stage the match. Of all the things he did best, maybe his silver tongue persuasion was his most talented possession. Somehow, he convinced one of Frank's friends that the match had to be staged at a neutral site just to make it competitive. He was able to influence the friend by telling him how much the side bets would be if the match were publicized to be at a neutral pit. Titanic got word back that Frank had accepted his proposition, the place was booked, and the word was quickly spread.

"Over a 100 people turned out to view the spectacular event – they even had an official scorer and a paid announcer with a megaphone to call out instant ringers and the score. Unfortunately, Frank was a little too trustworthy; he forgot his tape measure. Titanic and Frank have often joked about the match since, and Ti would always say that he had moved the poles back to 41 feet the night before the match to make Frank feel better about his loss. Maybe that did happen, because Frank lost only two times in his career as a horseshoe champion, but one of those was in Minneapolis to Titanic Thompson. Titanic and Alice left the city with $10,000 more than when they came. Titanic was never behind in the contest. He led early at 15 ringers to 12, and then Titanic rolled off 51 straight ringers – not even Frank had recorded that kind of feat in big-money competition. Despite Titanic's claim of fixing the pit – which Ti just might have done, given the stories that have been following him around all these years – he and Frank became true friends, and I'm sure the Ti-man is looking down from upstairs right now, being very grateful for Frank Jackson's appearance here tonight to honor his longtime buddy. Frank Jackson: stand up and take a bow – the former World Champion of Horseshoes!"

****

Dwayne Douglas' attention was suddenly moved to the main double doors at the entrance to the banquet room. Dressed in typical casual golf attire were two of the most famous of the day's new breed of tour professionals – Lee Trevino and Ray Floyd. Whispers among the guests were suddenly louder than the normal rumble of conversations between stories. Byron Nelson, no less, rose from his table and motioned Lee and Ray to join his group. Bryon asked the neighboring occupants of the next table if he could have one of their vacant chairs to make enough seats available at his table. When the twosome arrived at the living legend's table, the crowd became hushed. Mr. Nelson extended his hand to Lee first, and the whole house felt the warmth of that handshake; then ditto for the same feeling when the flesh of Ray's and Byron's right hands met.

"Ladies and gentlemen, I've told everyone here tonight about my lack of real personal knowledge concerning the life of Titanic Thompson, but I, too, recognize our two new guests, and I know they both knew and respected Mr. Thompson. Being a sports reporter, I do have knowledge about some of their time together. Hopefully, we'll hear them individually tell us some of those memorable moments. Until then, I've been instructed by the clubhouse management to ask each of you if there is anything else in the way of food that you might want. The kitchen is going to close right away, so make your orders known to your waiter if you want some more food. The drinks will, of course, continue.

"Before we invite our next honored guest to share some more of all of y'all's life experiences with Titanic, let's give a big hand to all of the personnel that has come here so willingly to make this gathering possible." The applause was appreciative, but the hoots and hollers gave a better understanding of the appreciation.

"All right, I believe the gentleman over at the table to my far left had his hand up in the air to be our next speaker." As Dwayne pointed to that table, the next contemporaneous speaker pushed back his chair and made it to the podium.

Dwayne had seen the hand raised, but hadn't really paid any attention to the person at the other end of the arm. It was one of the Mafia-type three that had been some of the first to arrive at the funeral home. From a table of five, the burly resemblance of a big-time "hit man" that one might see in the movies paced his short-stridden walk to the speakers stand.

****

"I'm Tony Ryan. My daddy used to own a gambling joint and restaurant in Toledo. People used to call it the Get Rich Quick Club. Of all the stories I've heard from my old man and all of his friends, there is one that really stands out as something special – something that Mr. Titanic Thompson did at one of the big poker games at my dad's place when it was the biggest and best action place in the east. My dad wasn't in the game, but he was seated at a table next to Mr. Thompson's game, and everyone in the room was watching the outcome. The game had gone on for hours, and every once in a while, one of the players would have to go down-stairs – down some old, rickety wooden stairs--to go to the bath-room. Well, just after Mr. Thompson had won one of the night's biggest pots, Mr. Thompson pushed back his chair and said he had to go relieve himself. The game continued with one less player. Now I know this whole story is true because Mr. Thompson told my father in private how it all came to be. My pappa laughed so hard every time he told it. So, I'm gonna give you all the chance to laugh at it as well.

"When Mr. Thompson got about halfway down to the bottom of those rickety stairs going to relieve himself, a rat – that's right, a rat ran right across his foot. Now we had a respectable restaurant there, so it must have been some of our clientele or one of our next door neighbors that caused us to have an occasional rat or mouse there." The place erupted with laughter and clapped hands.

"Anyhow, using his well-known quick reflexes, Mr. Thompson instinctively grabbed a small vegetable crate that we stored down there and slammed it toward the fleeing rat. He must have led it just right, 'cause he hit it square. Mr. Thompson said the rat was stunned – it was alive, but it wasn't moving. He seized the moment with his mind, and he thought of a gambling gimmick. He wedged the motionless rat under a bigger crate with his foot and headed back up the stairs to the game.

"He came back, sat down as if nothing unusual had happened, and then he kinda' shuddered so everyone could see him shake.

"He said, 'men, we gotta get a better place to play, or we gotta get a better place to go to the bathroom. That basement down there is full of rats.'

"Then one of the players answered with, ' I ain't never seen a rat down there, you must be scared of the dark or something.'

Mr. Thompson then made his pitch.

'I'll tell what I'll do. If you give me three minutes down there within that rat infested place, I'll come back with a still-warm dead rat.'

"The guy played right into Mr. Thompson's hands.

"Another player then joined in."

'How you gonna catch this here rat, country boy? Shoot him with a shotgun?'

"Mr. Thompson had another answer.

'Naw. I ain't got no shotgun with me, but I do have a neat little .38 special over there in my coat, and I ain't such a bad shot. Anybody wanna bet that I can't come back in three minutes with a warm rat?'

"My daddy said that everybody in Mr. Thompson's game and half of the other table that was just watching bet $500 each on the proposition. Mr. Thompson then slowly got up and fetched his gun from his hanging coat. He checked it to see if there was a round in it, and then he told everyone to set their watches. All the patrons were laughing at each other as Mr. Thompson opened the stairway door and headed down the stairs. Mr. Thompson said he didn't trust his watch, so he counted to sixty before he fired at the bottom of the stairs. He then went into the bathroom and grabbed a hand towel to wrap his prize in.

"The laughter of all the bettors died when they heard the shot, but one of the guys who still believed there were no rats down there, said that Mr. Thompson was just trying to scare them with a shot of some sort. However, when Mr. Thompson opened the stairway door and came out with that bloody hand towel and a smokin' pistol, everyone reached for his wallet. My father said that Mr. Thompson was the fastest-thinking man he's ever seen. We all know how talented he was in his many fields, but in every field he played in, he was the quickest thinker. I thank you, and my family thanks you."

All but a very few stood and clapped at this one-of-a-kind story.

****

As Tony reached his table, his brother got up and headed to the podium. Everyone knew better than to challenge his right to speak – he might get mugged right then and there.

"Thank you all very much for coming here to honor one of my family's finest friends. My brother there did a right good job with that rat story, huh?" The crowd roared its approval.

"Mr. Thompson wasn't really a member of our official family, but he was as close to being so as anyone can get. From Chicago, to Philly, to New York, he was idolized by every member of the family. You're right, my brother did a good job telling you one of the best setups I've ever heard about. I've heard that story a hundred times, and I get the same picture every time. Mr. Thompson was an artist. But he was also a very funny man, a man that had a wonderful sense of humor. I gotta add another good story to the one my brother just told.

"This also happened at a big poker game, but this time it was in the back room of one of the still-open speakeasies in the subs of New York. We're talking about a game where every hand was worth at least a $1,000. There were seven guys, and about as many bodyguards. It was a dim-lit room, and one of the notable players had a habit of sometimes falling asleep when he was not in the hand.

"Well, that's exactly what happened on about the hundredth hand that night, Mr. Albert Anastasia nodded off. Real quick, Mr. Thompson asked Mr. Capone to reach up behind him and click off the lights. Of course there was a quizzical look on everyone's faces but Mr. Thompson put his finger to his mouth and motioned for everyone to be quiet. Mr. Capone turned off the lights.

"Then Mr. Thompson slapped his hand on the table and said, 'Albert, it's your play. You're holding up the game. Come on, it's your play!'

"Honest to God, Albert woke up and rubbed his eyes. He rubbed and rubbed, then he began hollering and crying – 'I'm blind, I'm blind!'"

It took almost five minutes for the crowd to quiet down before Tony's brother could give his salutation.

"I was just a little bambino when most of these things happened, but I do remember meeting Mr. Thompson at my father's house one evening. He picked me up and hugged me – and I was 14 at the time–I bet I weighed almost 110 pounds. Ive gained a few pounds since then–Italian cookin'. Anyway, he gave me a kiss on the cheek, and I could feel the warmth in his blood and spirit. He paid me a lot of attention that night, and I will never forget how sincere he was. But he was a funny man too. I'm sure glad that I was asked to represent my family here. May God be with you, Mr. Thompson."

Chapter 6

"My name is the "Greek." My name at birth was Nicholas A. Dandolos. I don't know what the A stands for, but I bet it is Greek for something! I am a little younger than the person we are here to honor. But our age difference was never a barrier for either of us. We were hard and fast friends. We gambled and played against each other and we were partners with each other. It has been said that I have won and lost over $500 million; whatever the number is or was, Titanic Thompson put that number to shame. The real difference between my gambling winnings and losings and my friend Titanic's was that he didn't lose very often. He loved to spend his winnings more than I did, but he very seldom lost them in a future game.

"The wonderful people who have taken the stand here tonight have told some marvelous stories – from horseshoes to checkers to poker, but Titanic had a few more talents that he liked to bet on. If I were a betting man – ha! ha! – I'd bet that most of you didn't know that he was a National Champion at Skeet Shooting. That's right, after he semi-retired in the desert air of Arizona, he and his wife took up the sport. It wasn't long before his wife became the Arizona State Women's Champion and he went on to be the American National Champion. He was the most multitalented human being of all time with his hand-to-eye coordination. Pure and simple, the world has never seen a human being with as much talent in as many skilled things, who could face the very best competition in the world and never choke. Even if he were behind, it was only temporarily. He would never let his mind get down on his belief that he was the superior player, and he was going to win.   If he were ever in a losing mode, his only enemy was time – he knew he could always turn things around from a losing posture to a winning one. I couldn't get inside of his body to see if he ever got scared in competition, but the evidence is there in all the sports, with and without throngs of spectators, he always had an answer to the competition – in the end, he seemed to always be on top. Of all his sports and other gambling challenges, his most talented enterprise was golf – golf by far.

"I'm standing up here now to tell you about the greatest gambling golfer the world has ever known – present company excepted – ha! ha!" As The Greek pointed to Byron Nelson, Lee Trevino, Ray Floyd, and a few others. "No offense to the greats of the game who are here, I guarantee you, Titanic would find a way to take your money from you on a golf course whether he beat you in score, or on a particular hole, or on some other side bet. I guarantee you! I know most touring pros are out there for the competition – not for the money – ha! ha! But in Ti's days, he made more money in a week than the top pro made in a year. He'd have had to have taken a hell of a pay cut to have gone on the tour. Granted, he didn't have the day-to-day competition that was present on the tour, but he had individual pressure every day that few pros experience. I've heard Lee Trevino say that the most pressure he ever felt was when he was playing a $100 Nassau when he didn't have a $100 – Titanic Thompson had almost that same pressure every day – because he had to pay up if and when he ever lost. Like poker, in a match play golf game, second never pays a penny – on the tour, the consolation place always pays something. Titanic's life was molded in a motto of winner take all, and he personified that quote and that lifestyle to its fullest.

"I know there are going to be a lot of golf stories that'll be told here tonight about Titanic's golf experiences, and I want to be the one that starts that subject off.

"In 1922, when Titanic celebrated his 30th birthday, I personally introduced golf to the greatest match-play player that ever came down the slope. One day at the Kingston Club in San Francisco, I asked the lanky Mr. Ti if he'd ever considered playing golf? He wasn't very complimentary of the sport. He admitted that it had a minimum of exercise built into it, but he saw no use in wasting his money-earning time chasing a little white ball around a cow pasture. I then reminded him of his last few hours of winnings that had to amount to somewhere around $20,000. I told him that surely he has noticed that those same gamblers went directly to the golf course after they had finished their card game. I told Titanic that someday he was going to be banned from the card table because he virtually never lost. Just like a guy that invests in the stock market, he needed to diversify. I'll never forget that smile that overcame his almost serious previous expression. No doubt, he thought that I had issued him a challenge. Thank God I did, because over the next 30 years or so, I had to make several millions of dollars partnering and watching Ti play golf. There ain't no IRS agents in here are there?" The room broke out in laughter.

"Titanic was no different than anyone else when it came to taking up golf. He wasn't a pretty sight. But, he worked at it – mostly privately – but he really worked at it. He was so mentally sound that he immediately put his finger on the most important part of the game, and that is what he concentrated on first. He developed the best short game in the business – both right and left-handed. He gradually perfected a swing, and then he added distance. Then he turned it around to the other side – he wasn't satisfied in any part of his game until he could do it well from both sides. He was a thinking machine. He set out to be the best; he made a plan. He stuck to a schedule, and he developed the best understanding of the game of anyone I know. In 18 months after picking up the game, he had won two new automobiles and just under a million dollars. He and I sat at a bar one night – all night long – and figured out how much he had made by following my golfing suggestion. I was so proud of him, and I was proud of me too, `cause I made at least a tenth of that amount betting on him.

"It wasn't long before Titanic was known as golf-by-day and cards-by-night!

"No one had seen Titanic practice his golf game because he intentionally planned his practice sessions in the mornings. Every time he hit a good practice shot – and there were plenty of those – you could see him already planning a hustle just in case he became as good a golfer as he thought he was going to be. He knew how people folded in physically proficient games, and he prided himself on developing a game that wouldn't fold under pressure.

"One day, a golf professional came by one of the Kingston Club poker games – he was a really good golfer – and a guy that can still hit the pill pretty good – he's here tonight – Buddy Brainer. Stand up, Buddy, and let everybody see the man that was the first victim of Titanic Thompson on a golf course." The crowd roared, and Buddy rose with both hands clasped above his head just like a statuette of a winning prizefighter.

"I'd let Buddy tell this story, but I'm afraid he'd leave out some important details." The crowd was in the palms of his hands as they all laughed and squirmed to the edge of their chairs to listen more intently.

"When Titanic was introduced to Buddy, Titanic was kind in his assessment of Buddy's golf profession, but he more or less ridiculed the skill it took to play the game. Of course, it wasn't ten minutes until a challenge was issued and accepted. To keep this story short, I'll tell you that even after Titanic took a putting lesson during the match from Buddy, he lost miserably. Titanic lost $500. When the twosome trudged back to the card room with the predictable story of how Titanic was taken to the cleaners, Titanic pretended he was ever so embarrassed."

'Look,' Titanic said, 'I had a rough day, but I learned a lot. The problem was that we weren't playing for enough money!'

"God, did that get the rumblings started. Everyone wanted a piece of Titanic as everyone was dying to jump on the Buddy Brainer bandwagon.

"Titanic had a plan. He said that he'd replay the match at a $1,000 a hole if Buddy would give him three shots a hole. Titanic knew that everyone present knew that he had lost an average of four shots a hole on the earlier game. The chiding reached a fever pitch until Titanic finally agreed to play the match with only one shot a hole. I forgot to mention that the first match was only nine holes. Now, everyone in on the new bet demanded an 18 hole match – Titanic reluctantly agreed. The match was set for the next morning, and Titanic and Buddy agreed to post their $18,000 in advance. All of the side bets that Titanic accepted – and he accepted all that were offered - were written down and initialed by both parties.

"On the first hole, Titanic out-drove Buddy by fifty yards. Titanic won eleven holes, and they tied five. Honest to God, Titanic won just over $56,000."

As The Greek pointed over to the blushing-red Buddy Brainer, The Greek shouted, "tell `em it's true Buddy; tell `em it's true!"

"It's true; I hate to admit it, but the whole damn story is true." The crowd gave them both a standing ovation.

"All right ladies and gentlemen, I've opened the grab-bag on Titanic Thompson's golf life, now it's time for others to take up my beginnings. The night has just begun on the life and history of my great friend, and his unbelievable golf escapades."

****

"My name is Ed Dudley, and I'm the retired resident golf professional at Hollywood Country Club in Beverly Hills, California. This trip to Texas has been an arduous one for me. I had serious trouble in getting an airline ticket that I could afford, and I had all other types of logistics problems, and I've just gone through some rather serious health issues. Nevertheless, I'm here. Titanic Thompson meant so much to my life that I wouldn't miss his funeral to honor him with my effort for anything in the world. Not only did he provide friendship to me, he single-handedly proved my method of teaching golf was and is the best methodology in the sport. Three months after his game with Buddy Brainer, he sought me out in southern California and thought enough of my teaching abilities to move his wife, Alice, and home to me. He was one hard worker. You know, he was always thin in statue, and I always thought he had some high metabolism or something, but after watching him practice at the game of golf, I've decided that he stayed thin by always working hard – that and constantly using that little evil mind of his. I say evil, but I mean evil in two ways: he thought out every proposition to such an extent that he knew he was never being taken advantage of, and then he flipped the tables and made sure that if there was an advantage, he was the one that was going to get it. All that thought and his work ethic made him thin." The crowd appreciated that wisdom, and gave Ed an unmistakable humorous ovation with its energetic applause.

"Anyway – to the story I'd like to share with you. I helped Titanic find a house that I thought he and his wife, Alice, would enjoy. It was near the club, and it had beautiful flower beds that Titanic knew would help entice his wife to willingly come to California. In short order, Titanic had moved everything to sunny California - lock, stock, and barrel. While waiting for his wife and his possessions to arrive, he made application and was quickly accepted at the Hollywood Country Club. Every morning he was at the practice tee waiting for me. He instructed one of the bag boys to always leave out two extra buckets of balls when he left at night just in case he needed some late night or early morning practice when the facilities were closed. I have no idea what he'd do almost every afternoon, but he would show back up every evening around sundown to take his rightful place in the traditional poker game in the men's locker room.

"After lowering his handicap from about a ten to a legitimate two, he asked me to always keep his game and preparation a secret. He didn't want anybody to know how good he was. Finally I saw why. About a block down the street from him lived a rather loud-mouthed member of our club that had a fancy for picking people's pockets on the golf course. Mind you, he was pretty damn good, but he was in for a rude awakening thinking he was the club's best.

"Ed Jones was a lightweight at the poker table. He didn't win much, but he always limited his losses. His game was golf. During one late-night game, Titanic decided the moment had arrived and asked Ed for a friendly golf match at a hundred a hole. Not only Ed broke down with laughter, but all of the other players and kibitzers did as well. Titanic, for the first time in his life, wasn't interested in side bets – said it would break his concentration. The game was set for the next day – mid-morning.

"Word had spread, and there were at least a 100 people waiting for the match to begin – I was one of those 100. Everyone was betting each other, but Titanic could not be chided into a single side bet. I was afraid to bet on Titanic because I could feel he had something up his sleeve. The two golfers hit the practice tee around the same time – Titanic practicing right- handed, and Ed practicing left-handed right next to each other. The practice tee soon gave way to the putting green, and then the match was on. Titanic won the 17th hole to save a little face, but he had to pay Ed Jones $1,600 in cash. Titanic made sure everyone there saw him pay.

"That night at the poker game, all of the regular studs were there, and predictably, Ed Jones showed early to accept plaudits about his morning win on the golf course. Mind you, I never saw Titanic take a drink of alcohol in his life, but occasionally he would act as if he were drinking. That is what he did that night. Two hours into the poker game, and after Titanic had been highly ridiculed for taking on Ed Jones on the golf course, Titanic stood up and issued Ed another challenge. In a manner that certainly bordered on having too much alcohol, Titanic said that if he got one shot a hole, he'd take Ed's left-handed clubs and beat him. The place went wild. Everyone wanted part of that action. Nobody in the history of the game could play golf anywhere as close one-sided as well as the other side. The bet with Ed was made for 18 holes for $5,000 – match play – by the hole. Then the side bets started to kick in – Titanic booked another $20,000. Again, the game was set for mid-morning the next day. For the first time in Titanic's notorious poker-game life, he was the first to leave early.

"The parking lot was full of cars an hour and a half before Titanic's and Ed's scheduled tee time. How that many people got the word of the match that quick, I can't imagine – but I'd bet Ed Jones stayed up most of the night calling everyone he knew.

"The practice routine was the same as the previous day except for two differences: both players were practicing out of the same bag, and Titanic was only practicing his short game. The previous day's gallery had swollen to 300 or 400 onlookers, and many of them were there for a piece of the action. Titanic opened up his wallet and took on another $20,000 or so in more side bets.

"Everybody surrounding that first tee nearly fell backwards when Titanic's left-handed tee shot rolled thirty yards past Ed's – right down Broadway. Titanic never needed any strokes; he beat

Ed seven of the first nine holes straight up and all but ensured the 18 hole match. Then just before he was getting ready to hit his drive on number ten, he backed off and asked if anyone wanted to try and get his money back – if so, he'd make the same bet on the back nine as he had made on the 18 hole match but without any strokes. He had no takers. The match was finished as scheduled, and since Titanic had nothing to gain from giving Ed a bigger whipping, Titanic settled for a draw on the back side. Titanic's left-handed swing was put to its first gambling test, and it came through for over $45,000.

"Unfortunately, the story doesn't end here. A week later, as Titanic exited the country club's grounds, he stopped to assist what looked like a man and a woman in distress with their car. It wasn't a man and a woman. It was two holdup men – one of them had dressed up like a woman. They asked him to empty his pockets at gunpoint. Money, house keys, a knife and I don't know what all hit the pavement. They gathered up close to $4,000 from his two front pockets and his inside coat pocket. As they were picking up the money that Titanic had intentionally dropped a little bit away from him, Titanic made a run for it. As Ti jumped the curb and headed down a steep embankment, he tripped over a root and fell hard. He was temporarily dazed from hitting his head on another root, and the robbers quickly caught up to him. They pistol-whipped him a little bit, and then they pushed him up the hill to their car. When they got to the car, they frisked him good and found another $8,000 hidden away in his back pockets. They didn't hit him again, but they made him get into the trunk, and then they drove off. When Titanic actually told me this story, he still had a fit of rage in his eyes. He thought he was a goner.

"For some strange reason, the two robbers stopped the car outside of town, got Titanic out of the trunk, and pushed him down another hill. Titanic was severely bruised, cut, and mentally tortured, but he was alive. He managed to make it back up the hill, and he flagged down an approaching car. He offered the driver $100 if he would take him back to his house. The driver was in need of another few drinks that night, and the $100 looked promising, so he obliged.

"As happenstance would have it, Titanic ran into Ed Jones walking down the street the next day: while trying to loosen his bruised legs. He told Ed the story, and Ed appeared most concerned and obviously felt very sorry for what Titanic had gone through.

"That evening, Alice's sister who had moved to California at the insistence of both Titanic and Alice, dropped in. Upon hearing the story, Alice told Titanic that she was seeing a policeman in the area and wanted him to look into the crime. Turned out, two days later, the policeman called Titanic at his house and told him that he had an idea of who might have been the robbers. Titanic immediately offered the young lawman a reward if he would catch them and let Titanic know where they were, but the nice young man said that he wasn't interested in money, he wanted to find them for Alice more than anything. He asked about Titanic's schedule for the next few days, and then said that he'd be in touch.

"Sure enough, Titanic got the policeman's second call the next day. He said he had the robbers and they readily confessed without an incident, and in fact they had several thousand dollars still on them from the robbery – in their car. Titanic was very grateful and told the policeman that he wanted to split the recovered loot with him. The officer reluctantly agreed when Titanic convinced him to spend it on himself and Alice. Then Titanic had a strange idea. He asked the officer if he could find out who informed them of when Titanic was going to be leaving the club the night of the robbery, and if they were advised as to how much money, if any, he was going to be carrying. The officer said that he would gladly try to interrogate them for the answers. To Titanic, that meant a pistol-whipping of their own from the police. He expected to get his answers.

"Two hours later, Titanic got another call from Alice's sister's boyfriend officer. He asked Titanic if he had ever heard of a man named Ed Jones? There was a prolonged pause, and then Titanic started screaming into the phone for the officer to hold them right there `cause he was going to come down to the station and kill them.   Alice overheard the commotion and ran down the stairs to try and calm down her enraged husband. Finally, between the young policeman on the phone and Alice, cooler heads prevailed.

However, that was not to last very long.

"The truth of the incident festered in Titanic's mind continuously until he went semi-berserk. Titanic grabbed his new, silver-plated Smith & Wesson .45, checked that it had all six chambers full of soft-nosed bullets, and headed down the street to Ed Jones' house. He calmly pushed the doorbell, but no one answered. He then tried the door, but it was locked. He banged on the door, but again no answer. He walked over to the garage and looked in. Ed's car was in the garage. Titanic crawled over the backyard fence and into the backyard. He tried the backdoor, and, to his surprise, it was open. With his gun drawn and his finger on the trigger, he walked into the kitchen area next to the backdoor. The house was devoid of sound. He then shouted:

'I know you're in here, you old son-of-a-bitch. I know you're in here, and I've come to kill you. You better come down those stairs and take your medicine like a man, or I'm going to make you suffer just like I did before I finally kill you.'

"There was still no sound. Then Titanic could hear a woman's muffled crying, like sobbing into a pillow. Titanic called out to Martha, Ed's scared-to-death wife, and told her that she had nothing to be afraid of if she'd just come down the stairs and tell him where Ed was. Titanic said that it took her ten minutes to navigate from her bedroom to the bottom of the stairs where he met her. She told Titanic that Ed had gotten the one call that the two robbers were allowed to make when they were apprehended. As quick as he could, Ed gathered up his immediate personal belongings, took his wife's car so that he wouldn't be recognized in it, and got out of town. Titanic believed Martha when she said that Ed had told her that he didn't know where he was going, but she was to wait for a phone call. Ed told her that they would have to sell the house and move out of California for good because he had done something real bad, and he was too ashamed to tell her what it was.

"Titanic said that he opened his new pistol, extracted one bullet, and rolled the empty chamber to one shy of the firing chamber. He then put the pistol in his belt and gave Martha a comforting hug. He said he told her that he had once been ordered to leave a town, and that wasn't a very pleasant experience – he was recollecting the time when he was run out of that Arkansas town when he had won that traveling water boat – the Rambler. He said that living a life knowing that someone was after them to kill them wouldn't be a very pleasant experience either, so Titanic gave his word that if Martha would indeed get Ed out of his sight forever, and if they moved out of town, Titanic would never pursue Ed, and in fact would let bygones be bygones. To this day, no one at Hollywood Country Club knows where Ed and Martha went. Their house was sold through a real estate Company with a promise not to let out where the Jones's were to be relocated.

"I want to end this story with a very important fact about my friend, Titanic Thompson, and it is well borne out here. Titanic very seldom lost at anything. When people get beat at something, they usually harbor grudges and hate from the experience, but for some strange reason, very few losers to Titanic Thompson ever felt hatred back to Ti. Look out among us here. I'll bet anything that there isn't a sole here that hasn't lost a bet, and probably a pretty good-sized one, to our friend, Titanic. And yet we're here to pay homage to this wonderful man. Respect has to be the word. He beat our brains out, but we all had respect for the way he did it. And, when he wasn't beating our brains out, he entertained us as a real comic, a conversationalist, and a real friend. We all know that he'd give his last dollar to any one of us if we had ever really needed it. May you rest in peace, Titanic Thompson."

****

It took five minutes after Ed Dudley had taken his seat for the applause to die down. Then it took another five minutes and many more drinks before anyone else had the guts to take the podium after such a story.

"Ladies and gentlemen. I'm one of you. I've taken my lumps in losing at golf to the man we honor tonight – just like you. I also am here like you to pay homage to one who entertained us and humbled us. As Ed just said, he usually beat our brains out. Nevertheless, we're all here to say to him, 'we'll miss you.'

"I know you can't tell how fit I was then by my present stature, but I was almost a Wheaties specimen when I was ten years Titanic Thompson's junior in 1926.   That was the year I was fortunate enough to come out on top in our National Amateur Championship.   In 1926, I had my finest hour on a golf course, and I came out victorious against one of the finest gentlemen that ever gripped a club.   I beat the famed Bobby Jones."

Whether the seated guests were golfers or not, they rose in unison with clapping hands to honor George Von Elm.   As the applause died down, George quipped, "that may be the only blemish on Mr. Bobby Jones' entire golfing record."   The crowd seated itself in laughter.

"After that memorial event for me, I returned to my stomping grounds in and around Los Angeles.   There I was introduced to a man named Titanic Thompson.   For some time, many of the betting crowd tried to get us together for a head-to-head match, but oddly enough, it never materialized. Although we occasionally socialized somewhat around the Hollywood Country Club and on other occasions around restaurant row, it was my doings that kept us from actually teeing it up against one another.   You see, as a typical brash youngster who thought I was better than I was, I really had nothing to gain by playing against a man who had no amateur or tour reputation.   My games in that day were with politicians, millionaires, and people who might be of value to me as a businessman in later years.   My most notable playing companion was the omnipotent Howard Hughes.   He loved golf – among many other things.   And he did like to bet a bit.   But I know of no one who really won a bundle from him.   For a man with women constantly on his mind, he was a better-than-average golfer, and he understood that one had to have a bet going to make the game interesting."   The crowd appreciated the humor, and clapped its approval.

"Finally, sitting at the same locker room table one day with one of our previous speakers, Ed Dudley, and watching Titanic out the window hit a few practice balls, something got into me, and I was brashly ready to issue Mr. Thompson a challenge.   At the time, I was playing the best golf of my life, and I was playing every day.

The challenge came after our pro had addressed my question to him of just how good a golfer do you really think Titanic Thompson is?"

"He replied. 'For my money, that skinny fella out there is one stroke better than anybody else in the whole goddamn world anytime he tees it up.'

"Well, that got my competitive juices flowing even more. I nonchalantly made my way to within talking distance of Titanic's practice tee. I told him that I didn't have a game scheduled that day, and if he wanted some competition, I was ready. He answered with a question: 'do you play for money?'

"I told him that I'd play for something interesting, but it was the game that counted for me. We settled on $100, and I'd give him nine shots. The way the scorecard set up, he'd get five shots on the front and four on the back. I couldn't believe what I was about to see on that first tee. Titanic was practicing right-handed, but for some strange reason, he brought his left-handed sticks to the first tee of our match. I was no novice about Titanic's abilities, and I had heard that he could play righty and lefty, but practicing one way and then immediately playing the other way was something crazy to me. Obviously, it didn't bother him!

"The game was set up so quickly that there was no time for a gallery to gather, so we were almost alone out there. We flipped a coin for the honor of striking it first, and he won. I expected him to go first, but he said the coin flip was for the winner to have an option, and he asked me to hit the first ball. Well, I caught it real good – right down the middle. Titanic then teed his ball and whacked it right by me by 20 yards.

"The first two holes were stroke holes. I had short birdie puts on both of them, but I missed, and I lost both to Titanic's pars. Titanic birdied the next two holes to go four up. I won't bore you with the rest of the nine, but I lost every hole on the front nine. That meant that I had to win every hole on the back side to break even, and I had to spot my competition four more shots along the way. This was not what I had envisioned!" The crowd was into the story, and they applauded his honesty.

"The tenth produced a great approach by me to within four feet. Titanic had some trouble getting to the green, and had a 30 footer for his par. I was lickin' my chops. Then the lanky man drained his par, and I missed my birdie – so we halved the hole. I was beat! I threw down my putter, picked it up, shoved it in my bag, and told my caddie to follow me to the clubhouse."

George Von Elm casually shrugged his shoulders, smiled, and said, "There wasn't any point of prolonging my beating!"

"Two important things happened after that match that forevermade Titanic a respectable citizen to me. First, he never told a sole about that match, other than I've heard him say that we've played against each other a time or two, and I understand he nodded his head in the positive when he was asked if he ever beat me. But, he never went around bragging about it. Secondly, I never paid the man his $100. I was so upset at my lickin' that I hadn't remembered the bet at all, and he never asked me for it. When I think about that, and what I'd said before our match about the game being what counts, I know he was kinda teaching me a lesson – the game was what counted, and he was clearly the winner." The crowd applauded as if it had never clapped before.

"A year or so later, I ran into a really good golfer from Omaha, Nebraska. He was an up- and-coming assistant pro who had tour aspirations, but no one knew about him – at least the folks in California didn't know about him. He had nerves of steel and a game to match. He was sending every gambler in Omaha home crying. I told him that I would get ten grand or so backing for him if he'd pay his own way to L.A. to play a guy named Titanic Thompson. Now it was my time to teach brother Titanic a lesson! The young pro didn't even ask about his competition, he just wanted to know the date. I told him that I'd inquire as to if Mr. Thompson would be available for a few dates, and after securing those times, I'd call and set the game up.

"I had little trouble raising the ten grand for him and a few grand for me. I really thought that the guy had a chance at Titanic if I could get him a round or two under his belt on the course where the match was to be scheduled. It all worked out just as I had hoped – except the outcome. Now, when I tell you that my horse tied the course record at 66, you'd have to think I won. Well, I didn't. That skinny fella that Ed Dudley was here talking about a while ago shot 65 and won just like Ed said he would – by one stroke!

"If I'd known that I would have had a chance to speak to so many of Titanic's friends and relatives here, I would've brought a hat to tip for him. Although we never hooked up again in the gambling arena, we talked many times by telephone and in person. I am proud to be listed as his friend and fellow competitor. May I propose a toast to the greatest unknown golfer that ever lived?"

Drinks were raised, and other toasts were shouted as George Von Elm made his way all the way back to his table. As he pulled out his chair to be seated, everyone there was still standing as the 1926 National Amateur Champion sat down. He waved to the audience, and the crowd quieted.

****

Extra light from the opening doors to the banquet room from the entrance lobby caused a few light-sensitive eyes to glance back to the open doors. There stood Ft. Worth's finest, one of America's finest, and certainly, one of golf's finest – minus his famous flat-topped golf hat – the Honorable Ben Hogan. Ben and his wife graced the doorway. Lee Trevino immediately dropped his napkin on his table and rushed to shake his idol's hand. The crowd became eerily silent, and all scooted out of their chairs and rose as one to salute golfing's finest. Lee led the game's finest-ever golf-ball striker to his talented table with Byron Nelson and his wife, and Ray Floyd. Two of the table's previous occupiers moved to the neighboring table to make room for the illustrious guests. On the way to the table, the Colonial King negotiated the aisle with a noticeable limp – he was never to regain the total use of his legs from his dreadful automobile accident in 1949 with that Greyhound bus.

Not being able to help resist a first time handshake with the immortal Ben Hogan, Dwayne Douglas rushed to the Hogan table.

"Mr. and Mrs. Hogan, my name is Dwayne Douglas, and I'm a sports reporter for your Ft. Worth Star Telegram. It's my paper that sent me here to cover Mr. Thompson's untimely death. When all of these people" – as Dwayne pointed in a circular motion around the room – "showed up, our editor made this club available. It would be my pleasure to have one of the waiters bring you and the Mrs. a plate of food, desert, and drinks."

Remaining seated, but looking up in a most appreciative way, Ben timed his insertion into the conversation like he would time a perfect swing, "Thank you very much. I'm familiar with your byline and I read you and your paper faithfully. We only intended to pay our respects; we certainly didn't expect to be a part of this wonderful group. We have to leave in a few minutes, so we'll just take you up on your drink offer."

Dwayne summoned the waiter and two drinks were on the way.

"Mr. Hogan, I realize that I am being a bit presumptuous, but many of the people here have taken this opportunity to say a word or two about Mr. Thompson. I wonder if you would like to say a word? Everyone here is doubly honored that you have chosen to be with them."

Ben was obviously taken by surprise by such an invitation, and being a man of very few words, he started to decline, but as he quickly looked around, he could see it in the faces of all that were still standing that everyone wanted to hear a word from him.

"Young man, if you would get everyone's attention, it will be my pleasure to make a statement."

Dwayne reached down and picked up an unused spoon from beside the table setting of Mrs. Hogan and tapped it against a half-full water glass. It took several attempts to get everyone's attention.

"Ladies and gentlemen, if we can be quiet for a moment or two, Mr. Hogan would like to say a few words."

As the crowd responded with deathly silence, it was apparent that Ben was not prepared, so it took at least 30 seconds for the first words to be uttered.

"First of all, the Titanic Thompson that I knew would be ashamed to be called Mr. Thompson – even at his funeral." That eased the crowd and promoted appreciative applause.

"I had only two or three occasions to see Titanic play in a game that really meant something. He was a special golfer. Watching him practice, anyone could see his imagination, his devotion to the short game, and his unbelievable skill at swinging from both sides. I only regret that I played only one round with him – no, we didn't bet, and I don't remember who finished with the best score because I'm usually always trying to have the best score possible on any given day on whatever course I'm playing – I rarely keep up with the other player's score. But I will tell you this: I wasn't always the one teeing off first, and I wasn't always the last to try my first putt on all the greens.

"True to his reputation, Titanic always had some type of match-play action going, and that usually doesn't bode well to having a good score. Maybe that's why I'm prepared to say Titanic Thompson was the finest shot-maker I ever saw. In match play, one can take more chances than in medal play – the risk and the reward only lasts for one hole, and for that reason, Titanic's expertise in imaginary golf shots had no peer. For those of you who do not play the game regularly, you just cannot imagine the skill that man had. Thank you very much for being here."

Maybe it wasn't the loudest applause for any one person or any particular remarks during the evening, but everyone gently clapped for five solid minutes. They had heard the most wonderful assessment of Titanic's golf game by perhaps the greatest golfer-to that day-that ever lived.

Chapter 7

"I know you folks have already seen me once, but my table keeps prodding me to tell you all another Titanic story." The Greek was on a roll.

"The last story told about my friend Ti left him back in the country club life of L.A. Up until about 1928, Titanic won a couple of million dollars in the southern California area. As he predicted on many occasions, he was going to run out of mullets pretty soon. Being that Titanic didn't fit well as an investor or living within his means, his itchy feet were obvious. Although he loved the beauty and the climate of L.A., he thrived on action, and action in those parts was slowing down. The same applied to me. Now I hate to say it, but I didn't spend money like water the way Titanic did, so I managed to rat-hole a little over a million in my winnings – I should have saved a lot more than that! Anyway, I thought that both Ti and I needed a change of scenery, so I began to resurrect some of my old ties in New York. This was easily done, and I invited Titanic to come along with me. I packed a month's worth of clothing for every occasion and I put a $1,000,000 cash in a separate old suitcase and headed northeast. Titanic accepted my offer, but he loved to drive, and after he informed his wife that he was going to New York for a few months he was to join me at Lindy's famous gambling house in The City.

"Alice, Titanic's wife, decided not to accompany Ti, and opted to remain in the comfort and sunshine of L.A., and meet him later if things proved to work out right. On the drive to New York, Titanic told me about several of his three-day-to-weeklong stops. One in particular was in Milwaukee, Wisconsin. While there, he got involved in several big poker and dice games and left town with more than $200,000 in cash winnings, another new car, and the title to a restaurant named The Golden Pheasant. He won that restaurant by cashing in on all of his side bets on a single hand of five-card stud.

"Now don't ask me how he got to New York from LA by going through Tulsa, Oklahoma, and Milwaukee, Wisconsin, but he did. I told you about his profitable stay in Milwaukee, but ya gotta hear about his week in Tulsa.

"For two days, he passed himself off as a mediocre amateur golfer from California who had won some small local tournaments, and he was looking for a game or two. The games were not easily horned into, but Titanic loved the course he had seen, and he was determined to play it a few times with money riding on it to test his skills. On Titanic's third day there, the young pro who was known for having a good game set the course record. Titanic took the occasion to meet him and congratulate him. During the conversation, Titanic mentioned his fondness to gamble for some pretty high stakes. The pro was all ears, but he lacked a bankroll. So Titanic told him loud enough for a good many of the pro's associates to hear that he'd play him even-up, and give the pro three drives per hole on every par four and par five – at a $1,000 a hole. People went berserk scurrying everywhere to find a phone to raise betting money. The bet was set and the match was to be the next day at noon.

"Titanic never told me about any side bets, only the grand per hole, but I've never seen Titanic Thompson turn down a side bet unless he was up to a set-up somewhere. No telling how much he really had on that match.

"The first seven holes were a disaster for Titanic – they halved two holes, and the pro won the rest. Then the pro got arm weary, and the game was over. Titanic won all of the remaining 11 holes. That was certainly not the most money I ever heard of Titanic winning on a single golf outing, but it has to be the most thought-out hustle I ever heard of. He later explained to me that after a guy warmed up on the practice tee, he should have about 25 good swings at a driver left in his bag. If you bunched them together close enough, you were pretty much guaranteed that the swing was going to crumble after that. He was right, and he won a bunch of money proving it.

"By the time Titanic got to New York, I had run into unbelievable bad luck, and I was almost totally busted. I told Titanic as soon as he found me at Lindy's that every game in town was fixed. I told him in no uncertain terms that we better get out of there right then and now unless we could beat them at their own game. I was ready to leave, but what I told Titanic seemed to be a challenge to him. He told me that he wanted to sleep on it that night, and we would talk the next morning. We both took a cab to the Mayflower Hotel and went to bed.

"At breakfast the next morning, Titanic was all smiles. He said that he had a plan. First, he asked me how well I knew the top players, and he asked me if I thought they would trust me to set up a game with me and Titanic. Almost all of the guys knew Titanic by then, and they all new they could trust me cause I'd already lost damn near $1,000,000 in all of their games. When I told Titanic that they would trust me, and that a game shouldn't be hard to set up, he outlined his plan.

"I was to introduce Titanic to a couple of the main players, and tell them that Titanic wanted to sit in on a big game, but he had heard that the town had gone into a fix, and he wanted to pick the site. They bit on the bait - hook, line, and sinker. They said that they would get the other players together, and Titanic should secure a site by the following Friday night – preferably in a remote warehouse location where the boys could exert their union security. No offense to anyone here, but this was a mob game if ever I saw one." The house rolled with laughter.

"Titanic used three full days of searching for a suitable site before he found the ideal location for his plan. He never informed me of the exact details until the game was over, but he told me that he would stake me in the game and give me 50 percent of my winnings, but if I ever reached a showdown with him on a single hand, I was to back off. Of course, I agreed – hell, I was halfway broke!

"Finally my cards changed, and I won a hundred grand or so,

but Titanic won nearly a million dollars! The next day, Titanic let me in on his secret to retaliation against the game fixers that had bilked me out of my million.

"Because Ti knew that I was telling him the truth about the fixes against me, and because he knew that I was too good a player to lose so much so fast unless something was up, he wanted very much for me to get even with those guys, and he wanted to be a big part of it. He had carefully picked out an old warehouse with a lighted stockroom that was perfect for a poker game. It was secure, and the parking lot was dark. The lamps hung down to a level where there used to be rolltop desks, and Titanic rigged a poker table that fit just under two of the lamps. It was perfect. However, it was more than perfect. The old water piping system in the place must have had a ton of leaks – not where we were, but somewhere in the system, `cause every minute or so you'd hear the water run, and invariably you hear the pipes clank like somebody was smacking them with a wrench or something just as often as you'd heard the water running. The sounds made for a good break in the usual silence, and nobody had any idea that the clanking was part of Titanic's strategy.

"What Titanic had done was hire one of the bellmen at the hotel to hide above the tables on the roof. He was dressed in black and was positioned in the ceiling well before the game was to begin. Titanic had drilled a small hole in the roof just big enough for one tube of a set of binoculars. He tore the binoculars up and made a single magnifying glass out of them. The bellman had two water pipes of different lengths next to him, and he practiced with Ti for a full day on how to mimic the sounds of the true water pipe clank and yet clearly send a prearranged signal to Titanic about a single card in a final player's hand. The spy was not to relay any signals unless the pot was a certain size, and then only if Titanic was one of two or three remaining at the end of the hand. However they did it, Titanic was unbeatable. I don't know what Titanic had on that kid who was the spy, or how much he paid him, but if I had known what was going on, they'd have had to treat me for heart failure by the second hand. These people we were playing with had no scruples; they were tough, and they'd had us killed in a New

York minute if they had found out what we were up to. It was really a very dangerous situation. However, the scheme was the most perfect thing I ever witnessed. Till this day, no one knows what happened that night, and I'm sure none of those players are still livin' so I'm not scared to share this sting of all stings with you."

****

"Dwayne Douglas is it?" The new speaker pointed to Dwayne with a grin.

"You're a sports reporter for the Telegram?" The speaker heard a soft, "yes," to both questions.

"Well, son, you're probably not old enough to know who I am or anything about my columns, but I want to tell you what a lucky fella you are. You're sitting here with some of the finest sports figures that ever lived on this earth, and most of them operated behind the scenes; that means you're getting the real stories. If I had been blessed with such an opportunity in my early days, I would have bowed down and kissed the earth. Congratulations to you for putting this together, and congratulations to Titanic Thompson for having such a loyal following.

"It's been said that when a fella dies, if he has five close friends that would stand up and be counted for the life he lived, he or she was a fortunate individual worthy of the utmost respect. How many people are here this evening? None that I know are here for publicity, because not one soul thought there would be anyone else here when they got here. None of the people here came for entertainment or self-gratification; no, everyone here is just as surprised as everyone else – to see everyone else – we're all here because this man we came to honor and give respect to was a part of our everyday lives. He taught us all something – one thing or another, and we are all richer because we were all associated with him. In all probability, we have all derived different riches from Titanic Thompson, but there is one common denominator – respect for some special individual who used his brains, his wits, and his physical prowess to outshine his fellow man in every endeavor he chose. He would have been a success in any line of business he chose. He had a brilliant analytical mind, and he wasn't afraid to work at what he believed in, and when he made a commitment, he pledged all of his resources to it.

"My name is Damon Runyon. I have authored more sports stories about sporting individuals than probably anyone who ever lived – at least the stories have been read by more people than any other like author or reporter. I have been very fortunate. But this moment tonight – shared with all of you – will live in my life until I am no more. There has never been a more mystic sporting hero than the man we call Titanic. It is true that we would - in all probability – not want our children to follow in the footsteps of Titanic Thompson, but let's face it – no one alive can do or could do what this wonderful man could do. His profession might not have been noble, but no noble man could have matched Titanic in any of his professions.

"I say all of this with one single regret: Titanic and I planned some day to co-write his biography. Unfortunately, I was too stupid to pursue the quest. After hearing these marvelous stories tonight, I know that I cheated myself for not accepting the task, and the American people have been robbed of a life adventure that stings the imagination.

"I say to you, Dwayne Douglas, take your time, choose your words carefully, and write your story about tonight with fervor and heart. Try to convey the intelligence that went into every bet by our man; try to convey the admiration of everyone who lost to the master of so many thought-out schemes and athletic brilliance. I look forward to your piece.

"Now let me add a little story that I know about that happened in my own backyard, so to speak. I wrote a column one weekend about some of the theatrics of Titanic's shenanigans in New York. It probably did a disservice to Ti, but it wasn't so intended. He later told me that he depended upon sudden exposure, not advance publicity. I told him that there were some people who would consider it an honor to lose a wager to him, but he replied that there were not enough of those people to keep his spending habits alive. He literally depended on his unique style of suiting a bet to a certain individual or group, and made them think they had the advantage. Prior publicity killed that opportunity.

"Nevertheless, my column provoked many gambling opportunities for Titanic with the local pros and hustlers in their own right. Unfortunately, most of these competitors didn't have the money that Titanic liked to wager. So, if Titanic was going to up the pot, he had to entice backers of his competition.

"A noted underworld character named Blackie Varsetti, a partner in crime with the late Lucky Luciano, through a friend named Leo Flynn – the ex-manager of former heavyweight Jack Dempsey - agreed to back Titanic for up to $50,000 in a match with the club pro at one of New York's more famous golf clubs. The pro and his membership thought they had a cinch. Titanic carried a five handicap that I had unknowingly included in my column about him, and no five handicapper could stay with their pro on the pro's own tough course. Well, the bets swelled beyond anyone's imagination. In the end, Titanic shot the round four strokes better than his worthy opponent, but more importantly for the side bets, Titanic beat the pro 11 holes, lost four, and halved three. It was said that Walter Chrysler lost $50,000 individually. Leo Flynn's backing came with a 50-50 split, but everyone on Titanic's side had a huge payday.

"After Titanic and Leo finished collecting their due, they arranged a meeting that night with Blackie Varsetti to pay him his share. The payment was made followed by a couple of drinks, and a cordial goodnight until the next gambling possibility surfaced. After a comfortable night's sleep, Titanic awoke late, and barely got to the hotel restaurant in time for breakfast before it closed. While he was waiting for his coffee, Titanic picked up his newspaper and glanced at the front page. There was a picture of a blown-up limousine. The headlines referred to the underworld character named Blackie Varsetti killed by the infamous Murder, Incorporated. Titanic could hardly drink his coffee from his shaking cup.

"To my knowledge, after taking only a few sips of his coffee, Titanic skipped the ordered breakfast, ran up the stairs to his hotel room, hurriedly packed his suitcase, came downstairs, grabbed a cab, and headed straight for Grand Central Station. No goodbyes for anybody. He left two notes at the counter for Leo Flynn and

The Greek saying that he would get in touch later, but he was on his way to Texas. Titanic thought he had just used one of his nine lives. Thank goodness my column didn't provoke a hit on the wrong guy."

****

"Let's have another Titanic golf story. My name is Bob Montgomery. I live about 40 miles east of here in a little city named Dallas." The crowd laughed and applauded.

"I met Titanic Thompson in southern California, and later, after moving to Dallas, Titanic and I became fast friends. I happened to be the first person who Titanic looked up when he vacated New York in favor of Texas, obviously, right after what happened in our last story. Titanic Thompson was a new commodity in Texas; Ti knew that, and I knew that. So it didn't take me long to introduce Ti to the real golf gamblers on the wagering circuit – in hopes, of course, to set up some very profitable encounters.

"There was a well-known long hitter named Doug McClanahan that played one of our fancy country club courses. On that course, there was a creek running straight across the first par five on the front nine. McClanahan was the only man in town, on a regular basis, who could carry the 280 to 290 yards to reach the other side. He was long, and he was good. He held at least five course records in the area, and he carried with him a contingent of willful gamblers who dearly loved to bet on him. I arranged for a casual meeting with Doug at his club for lunch. I had told Doug earlier that Titanic was in town from California, and he was a creditable golfer in the past, but I really wasn't sure how he was now playing – all I really knew was that he loved to gamble.

"During the lunch conversation, Doug invited Titanic to join him in a game late that afternoon. I got in touch with Titanic within the next minute – surprise, surprise – he was sitting right next to the phone! Ti said he was grateful for the opportunity to play and indicated that his afternoon was free. I then relayed the message to Doug. After hitting a bucket of practice balls, Ti met the foursome on the first tee.

118

"Titanic duck-hooked his first tee shot terribly. He did the same on the second hole, and announced that he was putting up his woods and going only with his irons. All of the players were somewhat astonished at Titanic's game and his purported single-digit handicap. One of the group said that it was obvious that Titanic was having a bad day, but if he wanted a little action, he would bet him a thousand dollars that counting his two double bogeys on the first two holes, he couldn't break a hundred. Titanic was quick to take the bet. Titanic scored a seven on the last hole for a cool 103.

In front of everyone on the 18th green, Titanic unrolled ten new hundreds to pay off his loss. He told them that surely they knew from his swing talents that he was a better golfer than what he had shown that day. He also said that he wasn't much of a player at medal play, but he'd beat anybody in Dallas at match play on this course. The group had now grown to 15 people or so, and, almost in unison, they all wanted to know how strongly Titanic felt about his ability to beat today's playing companion, Doug McClanahan, in another match – medal or match play.

"The question of the day from all was, 'What are your limits, Mr. Thompson?'

"Titanic indicated that they should make it light on themselves, as long as the total reached $50,000 or so.

"The match was scheduled in two days, at noon – to cooperate with the local weather forecast. At least 200 people amassed around the first tee and fairway to follow the game. Heading into the famous par five, crossing-creek hole, Titanic hadn't missed a shot and was already two up. Titanic had the honors on the fabled par five, and he crunched a drive that landed more than 20 yards past the cross creek – right in the middle of the fairway. Poor Doug knew he had been had, and he smothered his drive short and left of the creek. Not taking a thing away from a super golfer in Doug, Doug was no match for Titanic that day as he lost five and four. Rumors have it that Titanic won more than $400,000 plus a Pierce Arrow sports car that day, but I'm here to tell you that it wasn't nearly that big. The car part is true, but the cash won was just over a hundred grand. My share was ten percent for setting up the match.

"As fate would have it, later in their lives, Doug and Titanic teamed up at various golf events to win several two-ball tournaments and a lot of money. If there is any doubt as to the finest golfer that Doug McClanahan has ever seen, just ask him – he's sitting at my table. Stand up Doug – take a bow."

****

"Y'all ever heard of a name, Ky Laffoon? Sounds Cajun, doesn't it? Well, it ain't, but it's my name, and I was a proud traveling partner with my friend, Titanic Thompson, for several years. I think I was more proud to play golf with Titanic Thompson than to have played in the 1935 Masters, and that, my friend, is saying something because I really love that Augusta track!

"Taking up where the last story left off, you see, Titanic never sold his Hollywood mansion, and his wife, Alice, kinda got tired of traveling from city to city, so after his New York jaunt, Titanic gave Alice a hunk of money and sent her back to Los Angeles. She was glad to settle back down again, and Ti understood. The parting was amicable, and I was with Ti many times later on when he called to check on her. I can't say that I ever saw her again after Titanic sent her on her way, but I want to go on record as saying she was a beautiful, smart, and very sincere woman, and there was no doubt in my mind that they loved each other very much. A few years later, Alice went back to Pittsburgh – her hometown – and was tragically killed in an ordinary automobile accident. I happened to be with Titanic just outside of New York when he got word of her death and a description of the accident and the hurried funeral arrangements. It so happened that Titanic didn't have time to get to the funeral – he just was not notified in time to catch the next flight. Driving was an impossibility because there wasn't enough hours remaining to make the trip, although he really wanted to try. The funeral went on without him because no one knew how to get in touch with him in time for him to make the trip. He was devastated! It was one solid week before he uttered a word. He was the most remorseful person I ever saw. I don't think the guilt ever left him for not being able to attend Alice's funeral.

"But eventually, he realized that life had to go on, and he gradually stepped back into his old money-making ways. Because he was getting pretty well-known throughout the country, and especially among the traditional betting crowds in most major cities, he decided to let his individual reputation cool a bit, and he decided to start a partnership hustle. At the time, I had just resigned my post as a golf pro at a great little course in Joplin, Missouri, and he invited me to be his first traveling partner. For two weeks after we got reacquainted, he taught me the ropes of partnership golf hustling. Seems as if he had thought of everything, but his most important instruction to me was to always be patient – they'll always come to you once they know you're available for a challenge – if they know you've got the money to back it up – he'd always reminded me of that.

"For almost two years, we went city-to-city. I'd be the advance man. I'd go into town, seek out the best gambling course – usually a public facility – and I'd wrangle myself into quite a few games. The money I'd win was good, and Titanic never asked me for a dime of it, but I knew the big kill was right behind me. He always managed to win something after the set up, and more than likely, it'd be pretty big dollars – $5,000 to $10,000 minimum every couple of days. Of all those winnings, Titanic always handed me a third, and I never asked any questions – it was his game, his hustle, and his talent that put the money in both our pockets.

"The setup went like this. I'd go into town, play about three or four rounds, and get to know who could play and who couldn't, and how much they were willing to play for. Of course, I'd also check out their ability to pay. Titanic would come in a day or two later and I'd work him in a game or two. At some point, we'd get the big boys together, and Titanic would make a modest bet and lose – right-handed. Then he'd use his favorite ploy that no one could refuse. After he had paid off the small wager, he'd look over to a couple of caddies, say that he could play left-handed with one of those two caddies and beat the three of the guys he just lost to, for damn near any money they wanted to bet. Now they had to figure that nobody was going to lose on purpose like Titanic just lost, that nobody alive could play golf very good hitting the ball from both sides, that the two caddies couldn't be counted on to help a single hole, so the guy must either be rich and didn't mind losing his ass – pardon my French – or he was plumb crazy." The crowd was now worked up into a frenzy the likes of which had seldom been seen that particular evening.

"The bets couldn't wait to be placed on the table. Nobody ever turned down the wager once Titanic had them listening – it was a mortal cinch that they would bite, and it was a mortal cinch that they were going to lose. Time after time Titanic would blow away the cream of the crop in every city we lighted in – from Kansas City, St. Louis, Dallas, Waco, San Antonio, El Paso, Phoenix, Tucson, Oklahoma City, Tulsa, Amarillo, New Orleans, Memphis, and back here to Ft. Worth. The money he made was as legendary as his life. What a man!

"I'd be remiss if I didn't also mention another couple of front men who participated in some of Titanic's prearranged matches. They're sitting with us tonight, and I'll tell you a fact – even today, you don't want to get in a partnership match with these two. Please stand up – Bob Hamilton, former winner of the coveted PGA Championship of America, and Herman Keiser, the winner of the south's most treasured trophy, the Masters. Save my seat, you two, I've said enough. Thank all of you for being here. How in the hell did so many of us find each other without an invitation?" The crowd gave Ky a standing ovation all the way to his seat.

Chapter 8

"You'll have to forgive my nervousness, but I certainly didn't come here to Ft. Worth expecting to make a speech or tell a story. However, when I heard Mr. Laffoon – did I pronounce it right?"

Ky stood up by his chair, motioned, and said, "Any way you want to pronounce it is fine with me."

"Thanks. When I heard Mr. Lafoon tell that story about the big bets with caddies, I thought you all might be interested in my brief summer being Titanic's personal caddy."

The response from the crowd was, "Sure, sure, we want to hear it!"

"At the start of our college summer vacation in 1959, I got a call from our golf coach down the highway in Waco. He said that he had an acquaintance who wanted to offer me a high-paying summer job. I'm sure I don't need to tell you that a Mexican college boy from San Antonio, Texas, was always in need of a summer job. Most of the football and basketball players in school gobbled up most of the good-paying jobs, so we minor sports jocks had to virtually fin for ourselves. This call from coach was a lifesaver.

"He said that his friend needed a caddy to work for him from mid-June to the end of August. He said he was talking about a lump-sum payment of $10,000, and all expenses paid. He said I was going to come out of my summer vacation with $10,000 in cash! God, I thought I was dreaming – I couldn't believe my ears, and I had to pinch myself to see if I was awake. I asked coach if I could call this guy, get some details, and for sure accept the job. I didn't care if it was digging ditches; I had never imagined that much money at one time. Coach said that if I was truly interested, I should come out to the club – coach was also the club pro at the local country club – sit down with him, and he'd explain the deal. I was driving about a ten-year-old car at the time that my mother had helped me get the previous summer, and I bet I set all kinds of speed records for that car getting out to the club.

"I walked right into the pro shop and asked coach what was up. That's what we all said back then to get some conversation started. Coach motioned for his assistant to take over from behind the counter, and coach grabbed me by the arm and whisked me into his office. When he closed the door, I had a weak-kneed feeling. Coach never closed the door. He then said that he wanted to level with me.

'Johnny,' he said, 'I've known this man who's offering you this job for a long time. I've never heard of him saying something he was going to do and not doing it. He has a single source of income, and it is totally gambling. I've set up big gambling games for him here on this course, and I've actually played with him a time or two. He is a straight shooter. But – he always has an angle.'

"By then, I'm sure I looked like I swallowed the canary. I had to have a deep quizzical expression all over my face. Plus I was nervous as all get out.

'You know you're the first Spanish golfer to ever play for a major NCAA school in the Southwest Conference. You know that I wouldn't let you do anything that would endanger you from getting your degree or losing your scholarship.'

"Now I'm about to fall off the chair, and I'm really worried."

"Coach continued, 'so, I've got to tell you everything I know about this guy, and just what a chance you might be taking to work for him – your amateur standing could be in jeopardy!'

"Well, I could feel the dollar signs now slipping away.

'I've thought about this all night, and I called this gentleman back, and we both went over the rules that apply to your scholarship and your amateur standing, and I believe you'd be all right, but I want you to know that a lot of people don't approve of the way this guy makes his living, and I want you to be aware that there is some chance involved – whether you'd be strictly legal or not.'

"Tell it to me straight, coach. I'm a big boy, and I'll live with my intuition and my choice – always have, and I always will.

'Okay, let's go into the dining room, get us a quiet table, have a late lunch, and talk this thing over.'

"I had to stop at the men's restroom to relieve some of my pressure on the way."

The crowd was really into Johnny's story now, and everyone was at the edge of their chair.

"From the force of habit, I loaded up my plate from the big buffet-style lunch offering, but I was so engrossed with the thoughts of this summer job, that the last thing on my mind was food. When coach had filled his plate, we got our drinks and moved to an isolated table over in the corner.

'This is kinda an older man that doesn't necessarily think like we do today. I don't know for sure, but I don't think he has any prejudices, but again, I can't be sure. I know he only wants you to have the job – it was made clear that if you didn't accept it, I wasn't to offer it to anyone else. I can only figure that it's because you are Spanish. You're a smart guy, and sometimes we all have opportunities because we are who and what we are – that doesn't mean there are any negative prejudices at all. After all, I understand that he just wants a super caddy!'

"I don't understand, coach. There are lots of caddies around, and most of them – in this part of the country anyway – are white: school kids and bummed-out golfers that are just trying to pick up some change – how does being Mexican have anything to do with it?"

"Well, Johnny, he wants you to look like you've never been a player; he wants you to look like you are somebody who has only worked around golf courses –he wants you to play the part of being just a plain ol' pick-up caddy. Who knows, he might want to set up a bet or two with other caddies or somebody, and he wants the best of the deal – he wants you to be the best caddy golfer in the world, and I'm sure he wants to bet on you. Somehow, he wants to incorporate all of this in his daily gambling routine of going from city to city. But I know for sure that you'd never have to risk the money you are supposed to earn.'

"Coach, for $10,000 and no expenses, I'd be happy to be just that."

'The guy's name is Titanic Thompson, and he is not only one of the greatest golfers who ever lived, he can still beat almost anybody, and he's 60 something years old. He gambles for gigantic amounts of money, and, of course, he's susceptible to losing it all any day. When I talked to him, I asked him to pay you up front part of the job price to ensure you didn't walk away with nothing, and he assured me that he would take care of that. He wants you to travel with him throughout the upper East Coast, to Chicago, and some of the other big Midwest cities. You'll have a chance to see Washington National, Medinah, Shinnecock Hills, Winged Foot, Black Wolf Run, Pinehurst, Sugarloaf, Pine Valley, Oak Hill, Merion, Crooked Stick, Olympia Fields, and probably several others. It is literally a trip of a lifetime, and you'll be between the ropes on all of them. Evidently, he's put together a match at each of these famous places with their current club champion and their runner-up. He plans to play both players' best ball. I tell you, he can still play. The guy's a legend, but you've got to keep your nose clean traveling with him. I know you'll be all right if you only take money for caddying plus your exact travel expense as part of the job. You simply cannot fool around with bets, side bets, and other types of money-making. You gotta stay clean – it's going to take a hell of an effort and constant concentration from you all of the time. Besides, we're counting on you being here for next year. You know that I think we've got a chance at the SWC championship.

"Coach, I don't know how to thank you if in fact you recommended me. I promise I'll keep my nose clean – you won't have to worry about me one bit. How 'bout I call you every few days or so to check in?

'Johnny, that might be a violation, unless you paid for the call out of your pocket. You see what I'm telling you – you've got to be on your toes to determine if you're stretching the amateur standing rules. I want you to go back to the dorm and think about this. Every time you turn around, you've got to be thinking if whatever you're about to do is amateur perfect. It's a great opportunity, but your fate is only in your hands; you've got to be so careful.'

"Well, the trip back to the dorm parking lot was much slower than my drive to the club. Somehow, I trusted the situation, and I thought I could keep myself above board. But I was already feeling the pressure – not the pressure of doing my job or performing well if I was asked to play, but pressure that I had to make sure that I wasn't going to let anyone down – particularly coach.

"I only talked it over with two of my friends, my best friend who used to play on the same golf team with me before he transferred up north, and another good friend of mine who was a practical sort of guy that seemed to be all of us' athletes clubhouse lawyer. They both said that I was crazy if I didn't jump at the chance. So the next morning coach's phone was ringing when he stepped into the pro shop, and those of you that have been around golf near summertime know it was an early morning call. I told the coach that I had thought of every angle, and I thought it was too good an opportunity to pass up. I wanted the job more than anything.

"Coach got back in touch with Mr. Thompson, and the job was mine. I was to be out front on the dorm steps in two weeks, on a Monday, at noon, bags packed, and ready to go to work.

"It was hard for me to wait for that day, I was so excited. I didn't know what to pack – not that I had a lot of choices, but I really didn't know what to expect when I wasn't goin' to be on the golf course. It was one nerve-racking two weeks of waiting. I bet I lost ten pounds just being nervous.

"The day finally came, and I was on those steps an hour early. I waited and I waited, all the way to sunset, but no Mr. Thompson. I went back to my dorm room and cried. I couldn't imagine what had happened. Finally, I got enough nerve to call coach. He couldn't speak for a moment or two because he couldn't imagine what happened either. Our first thoughts were that Mr. Thompson had been in a wreck. Then coach took over the thinking alone and surmised that Mr. Thompson probably got held up in some type of poker game or other gambling event. Coach said that he would try to reach Mr. Thompson, for me to go to bed and get some rest, and we'd talk in the morning. Of course, I didn't sleep a wink.

"Hey, this is going on way too long. Shall I give you the short version? Otherwise, I need a glass of water."

"Get the kid some water, Mr. Host, we gotta hear this story!"

Dwayne Douglas was quick to the spot with a cold glass of water. After a couple of hefty gulps, Johnny was back on target with his Titanic caddy rendition.

"I was a miserable wreck for three days until Mr. Thompson finally called back coach. Sure enough, he'd been in a three-day and three-night poker game in Amarillo. He sent his apologies and he emphasized that I'd kinda have to get used to his kind of life. Coach spoke for me, and said that everything was quite all right, we were just checking to see if he was in any trouble. BS, I was scared to death that my job had fizzled out, and coach was just as scared. Mr. Thompson told coach that he better postpone my pickup until the next Monday at noon because he was surely going to need some long rest. Again, coach spoke for me and assured Mr. Thompson that I'd be on the steps waiting.

"I must have aged ten years waiting those next four days. Finally, the day and the hour approached, and I was glued to those steps. Just after noon, the finest looking convertible I ever saw rolled up to the bottom of the steps, and out strode one tall, fancy-dressed golfer. He was a golfer by dress, and obviously by practice. He grabbed my suitcase and threw it in the back seat. He said that we had a long way to go, and we had plenty of time to talk. But first, he handed me 50 $100 bills and a $20. He asked me how to get to a Western Union because he wanted me to wire my mother the $5,000 for safekeeping till I got back. The $20 was for the Western Union charges. That was my first exposure to the meticulous thinking that Mr. Thompson always did. He always thought of every contingency, and he prepared for it. If there hadn't been a windshield on that car, I'd have stepped out with bugs all over my teeth. There was no way I could have gotten the smile off my face.

"After we completed the wire transfer, he paid one of the attendants another $10 to use his phone for me to call my mother in San Antonio to tell her what was coming. He didn't want any surprises for anyone, and he wanted my money in the right hands.

Lucky for me, my mother was unexpectedly at home; she usually did some daily domestic work, but her job that day had fallen through. She was as excited as I was. Boy, I still grin when I think of that day.

"As we got back in his car, Mr. Thompson said he had one more thing to take care of. He told me that he wanted to get me a new wardrobe. I had just taken possession of more money than I had ever seen. I had just talked to my mother, and now I was going to get a new wardrobe. I thought this man was Santa Claus." Laughter had worked its way through the crowd constantly at some of the other comments, but Johnny's last line drew a chorus of laughter.

"The next thing Mr. Thompson said was – 'Where is the local Salvation Army?' Of course, I thought he was kidding – but he wasn't. He wanted me to look the part of a broken- down caddy that he just picked up off the road somewhere trying his luck at hitchhiking. On the way to the corner where I had remembered seeing a Salvation Army store, Mr. Thompson spoke over the high volume of the radio to tell me his ground rules. In front of every-one, I was to address him as Mr. Thompson or Sir. – nothing else. I was to wear clean clothes, but they couldn't match - not even the socks, and they had to have been bought by Mr. Thompson – that is all but my underwear." The crowd hooted again.

"He said that I was to be his personal caddy, and I was never to tell anyone – no matter what – where I was from or how I got where I was. He said that I was to keep his clubs clean, keep his shoes shined, and play when he said play.

"I understood everything very well except the part where he said, play when I say play. So, I asked him about that.

"He said that he was nearing his mid-sixties, that he had lost a little stamina, and that if those eastern and western hills got to him a little, he expected me to finish the match. I then asked him about the matches we were supposed to play. I told him that I presumed that he was going to play in some tournaments or at least be in some medal play championships. He tartly shot back at me that he rarely played medal play, he usually only played match play, and accord-ing to his ground rules, he could quit anytime he chose if he had someone to stand in for him.

"The Salvation Army attendant was a hoot. He thought both of us were absolutely crazy because of the clothes we picked out. Titanic wanted me to have nothing that fit, everything was to be too big. I don't know if any of you have bought anything recently in a Salvation Army store, but they don't have any dressing rooms to try on stuff!" The laughter was really getting big, now.

"Our shopping experience lasted only 30 minutes, then we stopped at a Seven/Eleven for some road candy, and we were off – for me – on a journey of a lifetime.

"Our first stop was in Memphis, Tennessee, at the Memphis Country Club. It took us three lackadaisical days of driving to get there. Seems like every time we passed a roadside pool joint, Mr. Thompson would stop and pick a match with the best player there. Sometimes the games were only for five dollars, but you could tell Mr. Thompson didn't care about the amount; he wanted to gamble and show me his skill. When there was no one to play, he'd ask me to fetch a cue. I thought I could play a little nine-ball, but I soon found out that my previous games were without much competition. No matter how big the table, no matter how level the floor was, or how worn the felt was, Mr. Thompson adjusted and whipped every soul in sight.

"When we got to Memphis, we headed straight to the country club. I took out his clubs, counted out enough new balls for him to use, and guarded his bag with my life at the caddy shack. That was also the first time that I had a real chance to look in Mr. Thompson's trunk. It was packed full. A bowling ball, horseshoes, two bags worth of playing cards, a pool cue case, a checker set, two small golf bags with clubs, a rifle, a shotgun, and two beautiful pistols. Ammunition was scattered everywhere among dress shoes, golf shoes, and hats. Good thing he kept his clothes in a suitcase in the backseat of the car because there was no room for anything else in the trunk.

"It was two good hours before I was summoned by Mr. Thompson to bring his sticks to the practice tee. He was laughing like all get-out when I set his bag down."

'We had a little problem back there in the clubhouse. Seems

like the whole group of those southern gentlemen thought we had a guaranteed match last week at this time. They were a week off, weren't they?' Mr. Thompson looked me square in the eyes and gave me the biggest wink of his life. 'I got `em straight though, we're on for tomorrow at noon. We're playing their club champ and the second in command. Ought to be interesting. We'll see how good a team you and I are going to be.`

"That night, I couldn't sleep a wink. I wasn't that nervous playing for the SWC Championship. I was petrified.

"Mr. Thompson hardly said a word all the next morning. You could tell, it was time to do business. We arrived at the gate, and we were greeted like royalty. He dropped me and the bag off near the caddy shack and he went into the clubhouse to greet the opposition and have a bite to eat.

"At 11:15, he again summoned me to the practice tee. I was dressed like the witch in The Wizzard of Oz. Nothing fit and nothing matched. True to his asking, I even had different socks on each foot. But I had my old golf shoes on – the comfortable ones, and I was ready to see my boss in action. It never dawned on me that the two sets of golf clubs in the trunk were for different occasions – one was for a left-handed person and the other was for a righty. I automatically figured he was right-handed because he shot pool right-handed, but he had me bring his left-handed clubs to the tee. That was really unusual for me because I never really saw a true scratch left handed player – but I did that day!

"He had a birdie putt of six feet on the first hole to win. I was astounded when he asked my help in reading the line. I told him what I thought, and he hit it right where I said – plop, right in the dead center of the hole. He asked my help on yardage more that green reading, and I prided myself on always being ready and up-to-date on whatever he might ask from me. I considered the wind, the terrain, the pin placement, possible hazards, and everything. I could tell he was pleased with my planning.

"After nine holes, he had his two opponents down three as they stopped to get a snack. Mr. Thompson won ten and eleven to make him five up with seven to play. They were dead meat, and they knew it. Mr. Thompson backed away from his teed ball on the

12th tee and approached his unworthy playmates.'

"I must have eaten something lousy at the turn 'cause I feel a little sick. I think it is fair to say that I could easily hang on to halve a few holes to win the match, but it can't be much interesting for any one of us, so I've got another proposition for you. If you'll concede the original bet, I'll bet my caddy can play out of your two bags and beat you both – just to let you get your money back. A seven-hole match – my caddy's ball against each of yours – double or nothing for the money you just lost – 50 percent on each of your balls. I'll sit back in the cart and ride along to watch. I've got no idea how my caddy can play 'cause I've never seen him grip a stick, but he sure seemed to read the greens pretty good. Now, I don't want to pressure you into another match that might cause your pocketbook to be depleted, so don't think you have to take my proposition. I'll be glad to struggle through for a few holes to win what I came here to win.'

"Well, you could have knocked me over with a feather. I had no idea what the stakes were, but I knew Mr. Thompson had to cut expenses some way, and it must be for a lot of dollars.

"The guys were only too glad to risk more money to get out of their first bet trap. They accepted with open arms. They even suggested that I could have a mulligan on the beginning tee. Thank God I didn't need it. I hit that ball better than any ball I hit all year. My game face was on, and I didn't want to let my employer down.

"I birdied the first hole, but so did one of my opponents – it was a par five, and I almost made eagle as it lipped out on my short pitch. That made me one up on one bet and even on the other. On the 13th hole I made par, and so did the other gentleman that had bogeyed the 12th where the other player made bogey. I was then one up on both bets. Both my opponents made bogey on the 14th while I barely missed birdie and settled for par. I was then two up with four to go. I made pars on the next two holes and so did both my opponents. On the 17th par three, I was fortunate to hit it stiff while everyone else missed the green. They both had gimmie pars with super pitch shots, but I managed to sneak a birdie in the side door. The match was over – three and one with me on top. I was never so happy in my life. I forgot to say that there were at least

500 spectators there to see the match. Man, I thought I had died and gone to Heaven.

"Mr. Thompson and I rode back to the caddy shack in the golf cart, and not a word was said. He let me out, asked me to put his clubs away, and pitched me the keys to the car. As he turned the cart away to head up to the clubhouse, he gave me another wink, and I knew I had done all right.

"That night on the road back to the hotel, I could sense that Mr. Thompson was worn out, and neither one of us brought up the day's activities at all. I kinda figured that this was a typical day for him, and, after all, I was there mostly just for the ride.

"As we got into the car going to our next destination the next morning, Mr. Thompson handed me 500 dollars for my out-of-pocket expenses. I cautioned him giving me money that could cause me trouble later if I were breaking any NCAA or amateur rules, and he just laughed and said he wouldn't tell if I wouldn't. Of course, I rat-holed it in my pocket, and never gave it another thought! Now don't laugh if you wouldn't have done the same thing." The whole house rolled in laughter.

"Pinehurst, North Carolina, was our next stop. This trip wasn't as leisurely as the first. Mr. Thompson intentionally wanted to arrive exactly a week late in Memphis because he knew he had missed the agreed-upon date with his extended poker game. If he arrived exactly a week late, he could blame it on some type of communication error. For his Pinehurst match, he figured he better make that one on time, and we had only a day and a half to make the trip.

"We stopped at only one roadside establishment along the way, and that was to try and hustle one more pool match, but also to get exact directions to Pinehurst. This time, when we pulled into the grounds, he instructed me to wait in the car until he checked in at the clubhouse. As usual, I was a guard dog that never barked and never left that vehicle.

"Soon Mr. Thompson returned with a gigantic smile on his face. 'Bring out the right- handed clubs, boy,' he said. 'We've only got an hour or so to get ready. I'm going to get a bite in the club-house, can you fin for yourself at the halfway house?' I told him that wasn't a problem to me. I'd meet him on the practice tee in 30 minutes.

"I'm telling you, the hamburgers and sandwiches they serve in North Carolina are pretty good, but nothing is better than their barbecue. Mixed with that coleslaw of theirs, a king couldn't want a better meal. Now I admit it ain't real comfortable toting a bag on a full stomach of that stuff, but I managed to get by.

"When we hit the first tee, I understood why Mr. Thompson had such a smile on his face – I could see the setup already, but first he had to gain himself an insurmountable lead. That happened on the 13th hole when he escaped a birdie putt by one of his opponents while he scraped in a tying par. That put him up four with five to go. I could feel what was going to come out of his mouth next.

"Here's what he said: 'You boys are pretty tough on your own home course, but it's hard to play a traveling old hustler that's been down the river a time or two. Surely you realize you haven't much chance overcoming the first wager, so how about me making you a better sporting opportunity. Mr. Roberts, how long you been playing with those left-handed sticks? Tell you what I'm aimin' to do. If you don't think I might break one of those suckers, I'll just add another equal bet to the mix and play both you boys through 18 with only your left-handed clubs – out of your bag.'

"He made that remark loud and clear so that every gallery person gathered round could hear the proposition.

"Mr. Roberts' playing partner looked at him for an instant, and then spoke for all parties. He said to book it! Mr. Thompson then turned to the gallery and asked very quietly if anyone cared to make a side bet or two. About six takers raised their hands and shouted their amounts. I still don't know what Mr. Thompson had going with the two players, but I heard a total of just over $10,000 being bet with side money on his left-handed outcome.

"You could hear his opponents squeal while Mr. Thompson's first tee shot was still in the air. He out-drove both his playing partners by over 70 yards each, and he was right in the middle of the fairway. Number 14 was a mediocre hole as distance was concerned, and Mr. Thomas ended up with only a wedge in to the elevated green whose front was protected by deep sand traps. The pin was cut just over the front trap, so getting it tight was all but impossible unless you could spin a short iron. Mr. Thompson was easily up to the task while one of his opponents went long and off the green and the other was left buried in the face of the front trap. There was no way to get the ball out of that front trap from a buried lie and hold it anywhere near the pin. For the ball that went over the green, that guy had a downhill pitch that would scare the warts off a frog. He had to keep it on the top of a hog's back all the way down a severely sloped green that was breaking straight away from him, plus he had to judge the distance perfectly – all from a half-buried, thick, grassy lie. Neither player had a chance at a par, and Mr. Thompson was only three feet away from his birdie. Both of Mr. Thompson's opponents picked up gimmie fives while Mr. Thompson intentionally left his birdie putt short and settled for a par. That hole closed out the first bet, and it put my boss ahead on the second one – one up with four to go. The next two holes were halved with pars, and then came the 17th. Mr. Thompson birdied that hole with absolutely three perfect shots, fading his drive intentionally for position instead of length, and then hitting a slight draw to the back pin location for a five-foot roll at a bird. The second bet was now closed out.

"Titanic turned to the gallery as he walked off the 17th, shrugged his shoulders, and told them that he was just lucky. He then asked if anyone wanted to try something else on the 18th to get his money back. He had no takers. The 18th hole was finished in a bogey by Mr. Thompson just to make his former betting buddies think what might have been.

"Mr. Thompson dropped me off again at the caddy shack with the keys to his car with specific instructions to load up and stay with the car. From the sound of all the laughter outside veranda where everyone had gathered, it looked like Mr. Thompson was giving them all their money's worth in past tales and experiences. For two hours I waited in that car. Finally the laughter and conversation dwindled, and Mr. Thompson came down the dirt path to his car – I thought he had raided the kitchen and put everything in his pockets the way they were bulging out. When I asked him what he had walked off with that made his pockets bulge, he just turned to me and said, 'You know, most betting people only carry small bills, thinking they're never going to lose.' I guess that answered my question.

"I was about to wet my pants just thinking about our next stop – Shinnecock Hills, the site of several former U. S. Opens and U. S. Amateurs. One of the oldest clubs in the country, built some-where around 1886 or something, it was some site to see. I kept praying all the way there that none of Mr. Thompson's opponents would be left-handed. I sure didn't want to get cheated out of a chance to maybe play a few holes.

"As it happened, I did get in a couple of holes, just like in Memphis, but the match and gamesmanship were much tighter than I'm sure Mr. Thompson had planned. He was going into the famous ninth hole all even. It was the strongest wind in a player's face I have ever seen. The par four was straight into that wind at over 400 yards. The green was elevated with protecting pot bunkers everywhere you looked. Titanic – I mean Mr. Thompson – knocked it on in two with two huge woods. Although he was 40 feet away from the pin, he up-and-downed it with no trouble. His two playing opponents didn't even finish the hole – they would have scored double bogey or worse anyway.

"Mr. Thompson managed to go up another hole on the 15th which left him two up with three to play. I could see there was no chance of me getting to test my game in that situation. However, on the next hole, Mr. Thompson won it with a par and the match was closed out. The guys who lost were real gentlemen, and they pulled out their wallets immediately to pay off. There were maybe ten side-bettors who did the same, and then Mr. Thompson looked over in my direction.

"I know you two don't want to quit now with 17 and 18 to go, but I'm a little tired. Not quite the youngster I used to be. I can't let you out of the trap completely, but I've been listening to this caddy I picked up from the side of the road a ways back. He says he can play. I know he's done a good job with me and the greens he's read have been right-on. Now I'm wondering about as much as you are if he can play under pressure. What do you say if I bankroll the kid for $100 a piece for the last two holes. He plays against each one of you – not your best ball, but individually.'

"Then Mr. Thompson made a sweeping look at the small gallery and asked the past side-bettors if any of them wanted a chance to get some of their money back. No one declined. I grabbed a driver out of Mr. Thompson's bag and took a few hefty warm up swings, and asked the gentlemen if they would like the honors. They both declined, and asked me to swing away. I didn't hit my best shot, but I did manage to keep it in the fairway, and being considerably younger than the two gentlemen I was playing, I did out-hit them by 20 yards or so. I had an eight iron in and they had a five iron and a four iron. My ball landed pin high just past the middle of the green, but 20 feet away from the hole. Neither of them hit the green, but neither of them had hard pitches. I two-putted, and for some strange reason, both of them missed short par putts. They were real gentlemen, and both smiled and talked with me going to the 18th tee. We all parred the last hole, and Mr. Thompson stuffed his pockets with more money. I wasn't invited in to the men's locker room for drinks, but I understood. I got to play two holes at Shinnecock, and there ain't too many people from where I'm from who can say that."

The crowd was still as intent listening to Johnny as it was during his first sentence. He had found a warm audience, and he was playing it for all it was worth.

"Our next stop was only a short drive away – 'bout a half day. It was in Springfield, New Jersey, and it was something special. Ever heard of Baltusrol?" Almost everyone let out a yell and clapped.

"They've got two 18s there – the Upper and the Lower courses. Both of them have hosted U. S. Opens, and boy are they something to see. The countryside was something I never expected - being from Texas, and I gotta tell you, it was so beautiful it made me want to cry. TV doesn't do it justice at all. It was something very special. Thank God, Mr. Thompson's two opponents weren't left-handed, so I knew I was going to have a chance at playing a few holes.

"You never know what gets into Mr. Thompson's head, but

that day I took out his left- handed bag like I always do, and I had it ready at the caddy shack waiting for his call to the practice tee. Instead, he came over, said he had been studying the Lower Course's score card and hole designs, and he thought his right-handed game was more suited to the course we were going to play that day. Isn't that amazing? Someone that could figure out which handed clubs he was going to use based on the configuration of the course? That was awesome.

"I wish that I could tell you about some great, unusual happenings that day on the finest golf course I ever saw, but everything went just like someone would draw it up. As I recall, Mr. Thompson closed his two opponents out on the 13th hole, and just like at Shinnecock, he backed me for five more holes at a hundred per man. There were a bunch of side bets, but I have no idea how many or how much money was involved. I'm sure Mr. Thompson wanted it that way. When the sun set, I had won by another single hole, but it was one of the most thrilling golf courses I ever played. I felt like I was playing golf in Heaven.

"We had a few days of leisure before we were scheduled to be involved in another match. So, I got a haircut, caught up on some phone calls, and read a book. No one knows where or what Mr. Thompson did. He checked me into a hotel in Pennsylvania, and told me to sit tight, and he'd be back in three days. When someone pitches you $500 and says sit tight for three days, in my case, you do it. I did just that.

"My next little slice of Heaven came at Pine Valley – just about 20 miles southeast of Philly. It was closed on Mondays, and that was when we were supposed to play their new club champion and runner-up. Unfortunately, we showed up, but it rained us out. The match was rescheduled the next morning at 9 A.M. Mr. Thompson wasn't very keen on early morning rounds, so I was a little nervous about how he'd play. I had read in one of my golf magazines that Pine Valley ranked number one as the best all-round private golf course in the country. From what I'd already seen, I couldn't begin to imagine how spectacular it must be.

"Mr. Thompson was up at six, calling me on the house phone

in the hotel. He wanted to meet me in the breakfast café immediately. I was afraid he was sick or something, but when I got to his table he was just fine. He just wanted some company.

"We made it to the golf course just before eight, and I got everything ready to go for his 8:30 practice time. This time, Mr. Thompson chose his left-handed clubs, and he made them walk and talk. I've never seen him play better. He absolutely drowned our hosts. They were both begging for mercy by the 12th hole. They complained about the wet fairways, the slower-than-normal greens, and everything else imaginable, but the truth was, no one in the world could have played Mr. Thompson that day. He had two or three six-footers that they told him to pick up because they were already out of the holes. If he had made half of those, he'd shot a 31 on the front – in really tough conditions, and on one of the toughest golf courses I ever saw.

"When his rivals were closed out on the 12th, seven down with six to play, he asked if it would be permissible for me to play the last six holes in his place. They said no. Mr. Thompson looked at me and shrugged his shoulders as if he couldn't believe his ears. I'm sure that I showed my disappointment as well. But they were kidding. They said I could join them and play, but they wanted to see just how low a score Mr. Thompson was going to shoot. We all had a big laugh of relief. So, we played five, all the way in. I had forgotten to say that we were joined by the club pro from the first hole. It was quite a treat to play that course, but if you'll recall the other stories, that was really the first time I ever had a chance to play with my summer boss. I was as nervous as all get out, but I think I managed to beat him by a hole. Of course, he was tired, and he didn't have anything else on the game. If we were back at the funeral home instead of here, he might roll over for me saying that, but I did beat him by a hole. But, I've gotta confess – I was the only one counting, 'cause we certainly didn't have a game against each other. That was the first time that I was ever invited to swing a club on our trip that didn't have any action tied to it. But of course, that was Mr. Thompson's call, and he never did anything without a reason.

"Back to the hotel that night, we went to bed early. Not even any ten o'clock news that night. The next morning, we were to tee off at my most anticipated golf course that I knew we were scheduled to play – Merion. The thing I wanted to see most were their flagsticks that are always topped with a wicker basket. I had done some research on the club, and it is obviously one of the hallow grounds of golf. Ben Hogan won an Open there, and that's where Bobby Jones won his last leg of his Grand Slam. All of that, and it still lived up to its billing. I will always remember Merion, and I will always remember those two long, tough par fives in the opening four holes. Both are around 600 yards, and there ain't a flat place on them. I had asked Mr. Thompson if he had ever played there before, and he said twice – both times with some gangsters out of New York. What a character!

"Mr. Thompson rolled in a 30 footer to birdie the first of those two monstrous par fives.

"When Mr. Thompson made his birdie on the second par five, both of his opponents said that was the first time either one of them had seen a player other than a pro birdie those two holes in the same round. They didn't look all that bad to me for no one else to have birdied them in the same round, but I surely wasn't going to dispute them on the matter. Maybe they were making excuses for themselves because Mr. Thompson had the twosome down two after those first four holes.

"On the way to the golf course that day, Mr. Thompson told me that he didn't want to thrust me into battle for money over at Pine Valley because word might get around that I was a stand-in for him to get an additional bet. He said that if he put me in – like I was a participant in a football game or a baseball game, he just wanted me to play and have a good time, but after he did put me in, he thanked me for the side bets I did manage to win for him. He obviously thought that Merion was too close in proximity to our last stop at Pine Valley to take any chances on future bets that he might need or might set up.

"He didn't need any help, I assure you. He waxed those guys. The match was over again on the 12th or 13th hole. Now I got another chance. Mr. Thompson challenged them with a statement that he bet they couldn't individually beat his caddy, so more bets were put on the board, and I was lucky enough to hold on to win both matches. For the first time during our trip, I felt like our hosts were uptight about Mr. Thompson's extra hustle, but no one twisted their arms to bet against me – the truth is, they thought they had a bird nest on the ground. Anyway, that eastern swing of a mix of coastal clubs and inland clubs was something I'll never forget. The courses, and the people for the most part, were terrific. Looking back, my experiences in being able to walk those courses, play a few holes, and watch the master at work were worth far more to me than all that money I made. What an experience!"

Johnny paused for another glass of water and then continued his obvious glorious experience – egged on by a very appreciative audience.

"On the road again, we backtracked next to what I call the feathered bird golf course – the fabulous Winged Foot Golf Club. We had three days to get there, so we weren't in a rush and we soaked up all the beautiful countryside. When we got there, we had a bit of a surprise, the runner-up that was supposed to be a playing partner with the current club champion was ill, pretty badly ill I was advised, so the earlier agreed-upon match had to be altered. The club pro – I forget his name, but he was a wonderfully nice guy – appointed another member to join us. He did himself proud with his appointment as the new guy shot one over par for the round. The champion wasn't any slouch either, and the two of them held off Mr. Thompson to the 18th hole before losing the match. There were a few side bets, but nothing spectacular. Thank goodness we got out of there with our shirts on – it was a hell of a match, and I enjoyed watching it, seeing the course, and being on the bag watching my boss still win when he didn't have his best game at hand was a real treat. He improvised and improvised. If he could have switched sides, he would have, but a 14 club limit wouldn't have allowed it. With all his adversity with his swing that day, he still managed to come out on top. He proved to me that day that he was the greatest competitor alive!

"Two days later we were at the Stanwich Club in Connecticut. It isn't as well-known as the others on a national level, but it is a super track. Mr. Thompson shot maybe his best pure round there, and of course it was good enough for a win, as I recall, four up with three to go. All in all, the two opponents were maybe the best we faced in the entire summer. I got to play along with the group on the last four holes, but only by alternate shots. Where Mr. Thompson came up with that idea, I can't imagine. But, when he closed them out, he said that he'd take his caddy, let me play out of his bag, and the two of us would play them on an alternate-shot basis through 18. He agreed to double the bet with them, and he gave them both a mulligan on the first hole. We won two holes and halved the other two – no contest. This was a new idea, a new bet, a new win, and more stuffing for my boss's pockets.

"Mr. Thompson had really planned this trip to the fullest. If he lived the rest of his life like he did that summer, I cannot understand how he lived past 50. Anyway, we took a long drive to our next destination, somewhere in Ohio at a neat little club called Scioto. I am a big fan of the golf architect, Donald Ross, and this was the second or third Donald Ross layout we had the privilege of playing, and although it isn't one of his most famous, he did a wonderful job of creation there. Mr. Thompson drew his worst set of opponents there, but they weren't slouches by any means, they just didn't have their games that day. I think they were more interested in watching Mr. Thompson than playing their own game. Mr. Thompson lost all interest in the match before the first nine was over. He claimed sickness, and offered to keep the bet alive by riding and watching me play for him. He reserved the right to break back in if things weren't going his way – kinda like a relief pitcher with an option for the starter to reclaim his position whenever he wanted to.

"Well, I didn't have my game together either as I lost the first two holes I played – numbers ten and eleven. I could tell Mr. Thompson was on pins and needles, and he was dying to get back in the match, but he let me go on because we still had a three-hole lead. Somehow, I righted the ship, and we went on to win by three. Mr. Thompson would have been an excellent coach because he coached me back to the winning side that day.

"Now, let me tell you about a challenging golf course that Mr.

Thompson literally brought to its knees: Muirfeld – also in Ohio. As soon as we drove through the gates, Mr. Thompson said he wanted to play this setup left-handed. For the first time on our little mini-tour, Mr. Thompson didn't concentrate on his match play, but emphasized his overall score. He still won, but he was a chance maker that day just to see what his best score could be, and all but one gambling shot paid off. He hit it in the water on a par five on the backside and still made par. I think he shot 68, and he refused any gimmies. It could have been 65 easily as he missed several make-ables. I've grown up hearing all about the Firestone Golf and Country Club in Ohio, and I really hadn't paid much attention to what else they had to offer, but for every square mile of golf courses in our country, Ohio may have the best around.

"We started our upper Midwest swing in Chicago. I've never sat in a car so long in my life as when Mr. Thompson visited every dive in town where he thought he knew somebody. I bet we made two dozen stops to see his old buddies. Some had fallen on hard times, but all went absolutely berserk when they recognized the legend, Titanic! While they visited, I was always a just-hired caddy whose job was to watch over the car and all the contents – which by now had to include a half million in cash or thereabouts. We stopped somewhere close to downtown Chicago at the Western Union there to wire most of that back to one of Mr. Thompson's safe havens, but I have no idea how much he sent back or to where. He did tell me that we were down to a hundred grand when he pulled away from that Western Union, and he said he had sent almost four times that back to his safe haven.

"Our club of distinction in the area that we were really looking forward to tackling was Olympia Fields. Bobby Jones had played there, and Mr. Thompson said that was one place he played almost every year with a group of his supposedly Mafia friends. As I look around this gathering, I want to make it clear that neither he nor I meant anything rude about that comment." The place went wild, and the five gangster types sitting at table number five jumped up to more than enjoy the comment and laughter. One even tried to draw his pistol from an inside holster that, thank goodness, was empty. Liquor was now free-flowing, and everyone was more than enjoying himself.

"On the way to Chicago, Mr. Thompson told me about many of the spectacular golf outings he had and would continue to have with his alleged underworld-type friends. They must have had one hell of a time. He told about one game where he gave one of those figures ten shots a hole, and he said he won over a hundred grand on that bet alone.

"From the outset, Mr. Thompson seemed to have a lot of pressure during his match at Olympia. I couldn't understand why until I recognized two or three of his mobster buddies in the gallery – they had walked Mr. Thompson to his car when we had dropped by to see them the day or two before. He finally got it together, though, and closed out his original bet with four holes remaining. He rather enjoyed showing off to his friends, so I never got to get in the game. I'm sure he gave his worthy competitors a chance to get even with another bet after the first one was over, but I never knew the details of the hustle. All I know is, after the match and all of the congratulatory drinks with other club members, he got into a big limo with his Chicago buddies and instructed me to unload the car at the hotel and go to bed. He said he'd see me in a day or two. I did just as he instructed, and I had a very restful two days. I'm sure the same wasn't true with my boss.

"It was a week before we had anymore of our scheduled action, and Mr. Thompson spent almost all of that time with his boys – the mob, and, of course, that wasn't any of my business! Our next stop on our little tour was west of Chicago at one of the three courses at Medinah.

"We played number three. What a famous setting, and how well it is deserving of all its accolades. All the courses we played were immaculately kept, but this one took the cake. Everything looked as if it had been clipped by hand. There wasn't a blade of grass out of line or over the desired measured height. The grass was cut below the waterline on all the manmade lakes – like they had to drain them a bit to cut the grass that low, then fill `em up again. The water in the streams and lakes looked like it was dyed. I've never seen anything that has to do with golf that was so beautiful.

"Unbeknownst to us, we got even a more special treat than the awesome course. We were matched with a left-handed champion! I couldn't wait to see the old right-going-to-left job that Mr. Thompson was bound to pull off. Only one small problem: Mr. Thompson had to birdie the very last hole to win the original. As everyone got out of our carts to go into the clubhouse, Mr. Thompson started to work his charm.

"'You guys are good, I want you to know I really mean that. I've been playing this type of match all summer at some of the finest places anyone can play, and the two of you have given me my closest match. I kinda hate to take your money after my lucky bird on 18, but I guess that's how it goes. Of course, if you're up to another nine, I've got a hell of a proposition for you if you want to try and get your money back.'

"The two former opponents stopped and turned around to hear more details. And with them stood a dozen or more potential bettors.

"'Mr. Club Champion, I'll continue the same format with a new bet for the same amount, but I'll play you both out of your left-handed bag.'

"The two losers looked at each other in amazement. They told the bar-tender to hold their drinks because they had another nine to play. Then the line formed with side bettors anxious to recoup some of their earlier losses, and in fact when the word spread to other club members, the gallery and the side bettors actually increased.

"You can imagine, the game was as lopsided as it could be. I really don't remember the partnership winning a single hole, and I know Mr. Thompson had three uncontested birdies for winners – it was a rout. And the money Mr. Thompson made on that extra nine – we call it a milk-run down here in Texas – he must have cleared a hundred grand – and that would not be a gross exaggeration.

"We left the Chicago area on a high note considering we almost had our first falter at Medinah. Nevertheless, Mr. Thompson got to see his old friends, and the champions at every stop got a little humility pie – we both always liked that. I don't know how much richer my boss was on that leg of our sojourn, but we sure made expenses!

"The old tarmac got a little hotter as we headed toward St. Louis. There we stopped for a couple of nights to bag our 12th win in a row at the main St. Louis Country Club. We were pitchin' a shutout on our whole road trip; I said we, but you all know what I mean. I had maybe five percent to do with our success. Regardless, we won our 13th straight there, and later that night we got to go see Stan – The Man – Musial play for the Cardinals.

"It was just a short hop over to Kansas City – another of my boss's old hangouts. I heard stories along the way about his life in those parts that would make your skin crawl with excitement. A lot of the stories have already been told here tonight, but believe me, you've only heard about half of 'em. The Kansas City course we played had a beautiful clubhouse, well manicured greens, and a bunch of super-nice people. But they didn't have two things going for them compared to where we'd been before: tradition and unbelievable rolling terrain with gorgeous hardwood trees. That's no knock on St. Louis and Kansas City because they did their absolute best with what they had, and it was quite enjoyable.

"The wider fairways and the now-hard fairways played right into my boss's game. He hit it long – at over 60 years of age, he could still cut corners with his hooks and fades that made everybody's eyes pop out. He was some kind of a show. Again, no contest with either match, and we rolled along with more fresh money in our pockets.

"Our last stop before we made it back to Texas was at Southern Hills, just inside the city limits of Tulsa, Oklahoma. I know all of you have heard about that phenomenal layout. It's got to be one of the oldest courses in Oklahoma, but I guarantee you, it is one of the finest anywhere. Men's and women's Opens have been played there along with a PGA and a lot more championships that I can't remember. It is terribly hot there at the end of the summer, and what wind there is doesn't seem to help much, but sweaty clothes are a small price to pay to be able to see and play one of America's finest.

"You talk about long and narrow, and a creek that runs

through the course that comes into play on 12 holes. You better have your game finely tuned to play Southern Hills or you are going to be embarrassed. We got hold of two really good players there. I say really good, because if you're going to play Southern Hills, you must shape your shots, and you must be able to knock them down when the wind tells you to. Mr. Thompson had all the shots, and he used every one of them in that round. The opponents knew all about the escapades of Mr. Thompson, and in fact one of the players had played in a game or two before with Mr. Thompson. His experience didn't quite carry him over the hump, however. My boss closed them out on the 17th hole, but not without a horrendous struggle. I was allowed to hit a few balls on the 18th as we were going back to the clubhouse, but I didn't get a chance to play when there was any action. I guess it was because Mr. Thompson had a reputation around there, but the side bets were few and far between. Mr. Thompson won every bet he made, but the agreed-upon bet on the match that was guaranteed by the club was 90 percent of his take-home pay that week. He didn't mind about the bets, though. You could tell. He was there for the challenge of the course one more time – and to be with the people he liked so much.

"Our last stop was in Texas, right here in Ft. Worth. Shady Oaks had just been built, and Mr. Thompson had agreed to play their champion and runner-up, as long as it wasn't Ben Hogan – we all know that is Mr. Hogan's favorite practice site. The owners of the club – the Leonards, I believe – wanted to be a part of the fray, so they actually played along with us – it was an ugly kind of five-some as far as golf went. There were three good players, and two that couldn't break an egg, but they were real fun folks. That kind of setup usually destroys the concentration of all participants, but Mr. Thompson was old and wise. Like he sensed the danger, he was never more into a game. His concentration was flawless. With or without his guaranteed bet, he was unbeatable on our mini-tour. I don't think much money changed hands at Shady Oaks because both players were calling Mr. Thompson by nicknames – they knew all about the Titanic reputation, and while they were extremely pleased to just be on the course with Mr. Thompson, they kept their bets well inside their pocketbook limits.

"The following day, we journeyed across town to Ridglea Country Club – the well- documented course where the match of 1934 took place with His Honor, Byron Nelson and Mr. Thompson. I haven't heard that greatest of all Titanic Thompson stories here tonight, so I'm not going to spoil someone else's fun by going into those details, but for Mr. Thompson, Ridglea was a second home. He knew everybody there, and there was no chance of sneaking up on someone with a strange bet. All the side money wanted to be on Mr. Thompson's side, so his opportunity for a big payday was slim. That didn't seem to be of a major concern to Mr. Thompson as he treated that match as if it were among friends. Sure, there was a sizeable wager involved, but it was business as usual within the boundaries of his second home. When the match was over, he had again won, but I believe Mr. Thompson stretched the match on purpose to the 18th hole. After the match and all the good-byes to his friends and cohorts, he gave me a choice of heading back to Waco, or playing a round with him the next day 30 miles away at the Dallas Athletic Club.

"I declined to go any further, and I told him I was itching to get back to school. My reasons were rather stupid. I couldn't wait to give my friends a blow-by-blow account of the trip, of Mr. Thompson's conquests, and the spectacular golf courses that I got to see and hit a few balls on. However, I was also truly homesick. I wanted to get out on a golf course and play for myself – to see if I had learned anything. I didn't know whether I could implement what I thought I had learned, but I was dying to try. I called it quits with my boss of all bosses, called my mom and coach, and told them both to expect me in Waco the next day, and on to San Antonio by the weekend.

"I'll never forget that goodbye with Mr. Thompson. He told me that he had a bunch of fond memories in San Antonio, and he wanted me to set him up with a match someday when he journeyed that way again. He gave me a warm handshake, and I swear he had a tear in his eye when he told me that he couldn't have done this trip with anyone else, and for sure he wouldn't have fared nearly so well. I'm afraid I lost it a little, and I had to wipe my eyes several

times before I could get away. Kinda like the way I feel right now.
He was a wonderful man. He counted out my money in hundreds
and put it into one fist; then he put both hands behind his back and
asked me – double or nothing if you pick the right hand? I laughed
and told him I'd hold the money and let him choose. He then let
out the biggest laugh I'd ever heard from him. – 'You did learn
something on this trip, Johnny, I'm very proud of you.' Then he
handed me the money. It was $5,000 and a good tip – another
$5,000. I couldn't say another word, so I grabbed his hand again,
squeezed it, and walked away.

"I've read every article I could find about Mr. Thompson
since then, and every time I've heard his name, I came a little closer to the conversation so I could hear a little better. Every time his
name comes up, I take my hat off, and I'd always say a little prayer
for him. Somehow, I guarantee he was doing the same for me.
Thank you very much for listening to my story."

For once, the crowd was totally silent. There wasn't a dry
eye in the room, and everyone was lost as to what to do. Finally,
as Johnny made it to his chair and started to sit down, someone
shouted "Long live Titanic Thompson!" And the crowd erupted
with "Johnny! Johnny! Johnny!" This time Johnny didn't know
what to do. Finally one of the table guests with him told him to
stand up and wave – he did.

"My name is Jimmy Haines, and I used to be the head club

Chapter 9

pro at the only country club in Tyler, Texas. One day sometime in 1931, a legend in those parts now – named Titanic Thompson – came to town to play a little golf. When he walked into the pro shop, I knew I had a little trouble on my hands. Now, I ain't no great golfer, and I ain't no prognosticator of future happenings, but something told me that this guy was something special in golf, and that he was going to be trouble in River City for me. As it turned out, this guy was as genuine as the morning sun, and about the best golfer that we've ever seen around the rose capital of the United States.

"I'm standing up here because I've heard it said that Mr. Thompson had had five wives and killed five people. Well, I don't know much about the five wives except that I've met a few ex's since I've been in town and they're wonderful – just like I would have expected, but I do know about one of Mr. Thompson's alleged killings. This one wasn't alleged, he admitted it; we all knew who done it, and although it was justified, he was the saddest person about it that I have ever seen.

"It happened this way: This guy rolled into my pro shop, said he'd been traveling for days, and had a hankering to play a little golf. There wasn't anyone in the pro shop on that weekday but me, and there was no one else there to play golf with him but my female assistant and a young boy who was a caddy that was waiting for a bag outside. This man proceeded to kinda praise and then berate my golf course. He said that it really looked beautiful driving by it, but he said it looked like it was a pretty easy course to score on. I told him that it was kinda new, but it was definitely one of the

151

toughest tracks around, and for sure it was the toughest golf course in Tyler, Texas. He had a couple of lady friends along with him – Yvonne and Joanne, sisters – if I remember their names correctly. I wasn't sure if he was trying to empress them, or just be a kinda hard-ass in regards to my course. Anyway, he got around to asking what the course record was on the course, and who set it. I told him that I set it, and that it wasn't likely to be broken anytime soon. Well, he challenged that, and said anyone ought to break par on this course because it didn't have very many sand traps, and it looked like every lie was a flat one. Then he continued on to say the course just wasn't rugged enough to be of much challenge. Obviously, I couldn't spot a set up if it hit me in the face.

"Being that this stranger came into my pro shop and started criticizing my golf course, I became protective and defensive. I told him that I'd put all the money I had in my cash register on the line if he could go out on that course and shoot him a 35 or better on the front nine, 'cause I thought the front was at least two strokes tougher than the back. He looked at me kinda strangely and asked how much money I had in that register. Now the thought ran through my head that he was a holdup artist, and I kinda backed off. He sensed my discomfort, and tried to make things a little better. He responded that he didn't mean any offense by making his honest observations, but he didn't see anyone else available to have a game with, so he figured that I was the pro, and that if he challenged me the proper way, I'd go play a round with him. He said he had noticed the caddy outside, and he'd be glad to pay that caddy to carry both our bags if I'd care to have a little competition with him. I looked over to my assistant, grabbed a few big bills out of the register, and said, 'let's go.' No practice, no anything – we teed it up from the first tee for a $10 Nassau, plus a mad bet of $500 even that he'd never shoot a legitimate 35 or better on the front nine – that meant never touching the ball, follow all the rules of the game, and putt everything out. I've never played golf with a nicer guy, and I've never seen anyone give the caddy as much attention and be as considerate to the caddy's job.

"Through the first four holes, my guest had it all even and we were even individually. I thought it was then time to needle him a bit, and I told him that the first four holes were the easiest part of the course, and he better watch out for the next five. Well, he proceeded to play them at two under – honestly, the man didn't miss a shot, putted our new greens like he lived on `em, and laughed all the way to the bank. When we got back to the clubhouse – I mean pro shop – his two lady friends had had themselves a couple of beers and were anxious to head into town. To tell the truth, I was kinda glad to get out of the trap. I'm no dummy, and I know if that game had gone much longer, I'd have lost my house and my wife." The crowd gave the old geezer a more-than-polite round of applause.

"Our caddy was all aglow about the greatest round of golf he had ever seen – even if it was only for nine holes. When the last putt was sunk, he put the stick in the hole and ran over to Mr. Thompson with his hand outstretched and offered his congratulations. Mr. Thompson was very grateful, and offered to buy us both a drink. We sat in the cool pro shop through one drink, and then the girls made it known that they wanted to go into town, NOW! The caddy asked if they would kindly give him a ride.

"It was in the next morning's newspaper that I read a full account of the story that happened next. Evidently, Mr. Thompson was to meet a prominent figure of these parts at the hotel they were staying at for dinner. Their dinner being completed, Mr. Thompson and one of Tyler's finest businessmen continued their business discussions out on the front porch of the hotel. The talks lasted well into the night, and finally Mr. Thompson went to bed. Mr. Thompson drove one of the fanciest cars I've ever seen, and he had it parked just off the corner of the hotel's front street and the intersection street that ran down the side of the hotel. The car had a burglar alarm on it, and about two in the morning, that alarm went off. The corroborated story shows that Mr. Thompson was waked up by his recognized alarm, got dressed in his flannel robe and house shoes, and sneaked out the side door of the hotel. Pressing his body tightly against the outside wall of the hotel to stay in the shadows and away from the light of the street lamp, he silently approached his car. It appeared that no one was in sight or left at the scene, but suddenly a shadowy figure rose from his crouch between his car and the one parked behind it and walked rapidly around the corner of the building out of the glare of the one distant street light. Mr. Thompson followed him with his hand tight around his concealed .38 pistol. As he came around the corner, the shadowy figure leveled a karate chop across the top of Mr. Thompson's ducking head. Titanic Thompson's reflexes took over, and he quickly thrust his pistol into the side of the assailant. Two shots were fired in rapid succession. The assailant fell face down writhing in pain and well aware that each remaining breath would surely be his last. As Mr. Thompson rolled the vagrant over, he lost his will to keep his supper down. The assailant was none other than the young caddy that had so joyfully worked for Mr. Thompson a few hours earlier.

"Someone just entering the hotel heard the shots and reported them to the front desk. The clerk immediately called the police. A police car was there in less than five minutes. When the officer came up to the scene, he saw Mr. Thompson holding the head of the young caddy. Mr. Thompson and the robe he was wearing were covered in blood from holding the youngster. The boy was still alive, but fading fast. He seemed relieved to tell the officer in blood-splattering gurgles that it was he that caused the whole thing. He had seen how much money Mr. Thompson had been carrying at the golf course, and he thought the money or something else of value would be in his car. He knew where Mr. Thompson was staying and he knew his car. He apologized over and over again in front of that policeman until his body went limp.

"I have had several calls from Titanic over the years about the incident. Needless to say, our local police had no intention of charging Mr. Thompson with anything, but that didn't stop the hurt of Mr. Thompson. He dropped by the funeral home before he left to pay for the young lad's funeral. He asked me to find out how he could help the boy's family, but they lived somewhere a thousand miles away. Still, for over a year, Mr. Thompson called me regular to ask if anyone from the boy's family ever showed up to visit the gravesite. He wanted to help them real bad, but there wasn't anybody to help. I never saw Mr. Thompson face-to-face again after that funeral, but I could tell what a man he was by his paying for and staying for the lad's funeral, and his dedication to try and help the remaining family – something that he sure didn't have to do. Mr. Thompson did nothing more than any of us in this room would have done, and I want to set the record straight, that I know it was self defense, and I know how sorry he was that it happened. The money, the car, nothing mattered more to Mr. Thompson than that boy's life, and I know he took a certain amount of undeserved guilt to his grave for that incident. For sure, he's being absolved of that blame right now in Heaven – God bless Titanic Thompson's soul, for he surely had one."

As Jimmy Haines exited the speaker's podium and walked to his table, among the light clapping of hands, many of the fellow guests reached out to shake his hand and pat him on the shoulder for the appreciation of sharing another side to the life of Titanic Thompson.

****

"My name is Johnny Moss and I'm from up north a bit – Lubbock, Texas. I met Titanic Thompson when I was 20 years old. I remember it well, and today I consider it a very distinct honor of having been linked up with that man.

"Through the gambling circles, Titanic had heard about a recent match that I had played with a gentleman from Roswell, New Mexico. The guy I played was a fair golfer, but I would categorize him further as kind of a rich pigeon. Mind you, he had beaten his fair share of amateur golfers – in fact, he held two city championships in Roswell back-to-back, and all the while being the present country club champ there as well – but the game that a traveling hustler played was head and shoulders better than anything he had ever seen. He was filthy rich, and no one near him was going to reach his choking point, so putting money pressure on him was out of the question. So, when I played him, I waited for him to make the first move as to how much we were going to play for. Per his suggestion, the game started off at $10,000 a hole; as the game went on, he kept doubling up to catch up, and it cost him just over a million dollars – in one game of golf. I had to share ten percent of that million plus with the group that set up the match, but at that time it must have been a world record of golf winnings for a single round. Plain and simple, this millionaire golfer wasn't about to back off from a brash, young, 20 year-old. Somehow, Titanic heard about that match, and he wanted to meet both parties involved. Evidently, he envisioned some easy pickins.

"By the time he had found me, in 1932, I was down to exactly $8,300. I had lost the proverbial fortune – just like I had made it – not quite just like I had made it, because I didn't lose all of it in golf, but in dice, poker, and other card games. Titanic's information on how to find me proved right, and he ran into me giving some ladies golf lessons on the practice tee in Lubbock. He waited patiently for me to finish before approaching me just outside the pro shop. He was very coy. He told me his name and that he would make it profitable for me to introduce him to this Roswell millionaire. He kept telling me how much he wanted to play the guy, and, quite frankly, he was so persistent that I got sick of hearing it. I wanted to play the new meat in town – him - and I sure as hell didn't want to share it with that Roswell golfer. I finally issued a challenge for Titanic to play me. He acted like he was scared to play me, and he said he wouldn't consider it until I showed him the color of my money. He made me drive back to my house, rob my little piggy bank, and bring him the money that I had told him I could come up with. When I proudly emptied my pockets to show him my stash, he said he'd play for all of it or nothing – the full $8,300 – on an 18 hole match. He knew it was all I had, and he knew that would work against me. He also knew that if I had it all riding on the whole match, I wouldn't have an opportunity to press the bet and try to get back any losses with another bet. I was too stupid to turn him down. He looked fit, but he reminded me of the older golfer in Roswell, and I figured I would wear him down – particularly on my own home course.

"As we walked up to the first tee, Mr. Thompson said that he had heard that I was about the best young golfer alive. He said the word was out, and that I had a big reputation to look after. He said that he had heard that no one hit their irons any better than Johnny

Moss. I was falling for whatever he was saying!

"'Tell ya what I'm goin' to do. I'm not going to play you heads up for anything, but I'll bet all of the $8,300 you got that you can't take just one of your irons out of that bag and go out there on that course and shoot yourself a 46 or better.'

"I hesitated a long time before giving Titanic my answer. I had played that course with almost every club in my bag at one time or the other – I just couldn't figure why I was getting what I thought was a cinch bet for me. Well, the course was closed on Wednesday – the next day – and that is when Titanic wanted to stage the play. He wanted nobody on the course but just the two of us and a caddy if I thought I needed one. My four iron was my choice of clubs, and I was hitting it flush every time I brought it back. But for some strange reason, I was missing all of my short putts with it.

"It took me three holes to realize that someone had all of the cups in the holes raised just above the putting surface level the night before – not much, in fact the naked eye couldn't tell, but the ball would just skirt the cup unless it was dead center. I never did know who at the club doctored those cups, but I suspect it was the greens-keeper that I had had some serious arguments with as of late. In fact, he told me a few days earlier that he was gunning for me because of my juvenile manner. I can't figure out how he knew about the match with Mr. Thompson, but something strange happened on purpose to get those cups at that height. The course would have killed me with that setup, but I spoiled the greenskeeper's, Titanic's, or whoever's fun when I paid my caddy to run ahead of us and tap down all of the cups. I parred the last hole for a clean 41, and I was grinning ear-to-ear. Titanic walked over to me, counted out my winnings, and told me they were mine – as soon as he introduced me to his Roswell friend. I said that he had a deal, and let's get rolling.

"We drove the rest of the day until we reached the pay dirt city of Roswell, and then we checked into a nice hotel – courtesy of Mr. Thompson.

"The next morning just before noon, we ran into Mr. Moneybags inside the men's locker room just before he was going out to practice for his regular afternoon game. Titanic indicated to him that he had driven all the way from Tyler, Texas, to try and make this match, and it didn't seem right that he would choose guys he plays with every day over a well-known out-of-town hustler, unless he was scared. Titanic said it looked more like he was choosing a hide-and-go-seek game to him. When Titanic offered him three shots on an 18-hole bet, he finally got Moneybags' attention. The game was set that afternoon, and everyone that was in the parking lot wanted to be a registered kibitzer. There were side bets galore, and although everyone knew about Titanic's gamesmanship to set up the match, some prophesied that he must be some sort of traveling pro, so a few opted for the new guy in town.

"Surprising enough, the match went down to the very last hole. The millionaire had used all of his shots and was sitting 12 feet away from birdie on the last hole with the bet all even. Titanic had the worst putting location on the green for his bird – a 30 footer, over a hump, and sliding downhill with an eight-foot break. Titanic later confided to me that he thought he had no chance at that putt, but you had that miraculous feeling when you heard the tap of that metal against the skin of that ball. It sounded right, it appeared it was on the right line, and the speed looked fantastic. Even from a weird angle, you knew the putt was in the minute he hit it. Mr. Millionaire went bonkers – calling Titanic lucky, cursing, and generally making an absolute ass out of himself. He had a chance to tie Titanic, but he didn't even hit the hole. He stormed all the way back to the clubhouse crying about his luck. After giving him about ten minutes to settledown, Titanic went over to his table to console the ugly bastard. Titanic readily admitted that he was awful lucky to make that putt, but that's the way it goes. He said that he hated to take $25,000 in cash from him on such a lucky stroke so he thought he should try and give him an advantage to get the money back.

"'Being that you're a pretty damn fair left-handed golfer with those sticks you have there, I'm willing to bet you double what you lost today on the same bet tomorrow, but with me using only your left-handed hardware.' Mr. Got-rocks and all of his entourage jumped at the chance. True to their natural thoughts that no one could play better left-handed than right-handed, particularly if he had originally chosen right-handed sticks to play, they couldn't wait for the match to begin. The game was set at 10:00 A.M. the following morning. The millionaire showed up late in an effort to rob Titanic of immediate prior-to-the-match practicing time with his sticks while he managed to practice at another course down the road. Titanic knew what was going on, and he never let anyone know that he cared one bit. He was ready to go on the first tee without hitting a single ball. In one of the fastest gambling matches ever witnessed, Titanic had closed out the millionaire country clubber four down with three to play. The day previous and that day had netted Titanic $75,000 less the appropriate fee that he had designed to lose to me just to get the match set up to his liking. That put him a net winner of $65,000 after he rounded out my take to ten grand as a tip for setting the whole thing up on the main bet, but Titanic really stole the show in his side bets. I didn't have a part of that so I'd be speculating if I picked a number in dollars that he won on those, but I know they had to total at least a hundred grand or more.

"I suspect that Titanic was truly good enough to beat every golfer he met by one up or so right-handed, but I would have bet anything that he could have beaten anybody left-handed by more. He had every shot in the bag with both hands, but he intimidated you all the more when he grabbed those left-handed sticks. I've had the pleasure of playing golf against and with a lot of you here, and I've paid my well-earned money to follow and watch the masters of our U. S. Tour that sit here with us today. And yet I have no hesitancy in saying that when I saw Titanic play a hard match on a hard golf course, I never thought for one minute that he could lose. He simply had the best game I ever saw, he never abused it, he was patient, he won most of the bets on the first tee, and then he was a master of execution from then on. When he felt comfortable, he encouraged side bets with such intimidating vigor that he made everyone ashamed if he didn't have a bet with him. He was the master of the betting golf game, and there ought to be a shrine out there about it!"

Johnny Moss made a special trip around all of the tables to

personally thank everyone who was there, and he was likewise thanked profusely for being there himself, and taking the stand to say some kind words about the man whom they were all there to honor.

****

"I'm Maxine Thompson – you guessed it – number four as wives go for Titanic Thompson. Ti and I were married when Ti was 54 years old in 1946. He had gone through a divorce with Joanne Thompson nearly a year prior to our marriage. Young Tommy – Ti's first son was then four years old, and a frequent visitor to our traveling home sites - he's here tonight, and he is one fine-looking boy. Tommy, I want you and your brother to know I am awfully proud of both of you." A natural response followed those remarks by the guests – a standing ovation.

"Titanic's and my first home was in Norfolk, Virginia, and then we moved from there to Virginia Beach. While in Virginia Beach, Ti was in the constant companionship of one of the most popular individuals I have ever known, and he too is with us here tonight. Please stand up and be recognized: the one and only Minnesota Fats. Ti and the Fat Man were inseparable for years, both at the pool halls and during normal socializing. The Fat Man wasn't much into golf, but he could sure roll another little white ball. He and Ti would partner up a lot in all types of pool games, traveling on three - and four-day trips to bring home the bacon. Thank you so much, Minnesota, for helping put bread on my table and for being here tonight.

"I've just told you a smattering of Titanic's abilities at the pool table – particularly in the company of his buddy, Minnesota Fats, but I want to share another talent that Ti possessed that most people here don't know about. In 1947, Ti and I moved to the desert town of Tucson, Arizona. There we were registered in the phone book as Mr. and Mrs. A. C. Thompson. Ti played a little golf there, but for some reason, he backslid on his golf in favor of skeet shooting. He got me interested in the sport, and he taught me how to bust those clay pigeons. For three consecutive years, both Ti and

I went on to repeat as Arizona State Champions in skeet shooting.

"We divorced in 1954 when Ti got that rover blood back in him and he began his past traveling routines. I elected to stay in Arizona at our house, so our marriage suffered that incontestable conclusion of an amicable divorce. Ti was most generous in providing for me so that I could live out a worry-free life in a place that I had grown to love. We stayed in touch through the years, but I only saw him again maybe five or six times. I wanted to tell you two things: one was about his and my skeet shooting, and the other was what a wonderful provider he was. He never questioned anything I asked for, and he never denied me or his children any experience or time with him. The real happiness in life that I remember today was spent with whom we all know as Titanic Thompson."

****

"Looks as if we are having a parade of women up here, one following another. But we ex's are truly here to sing the praises of our former husband, Titanic Thompson. My name used to be Jeanette Bennett before I married Titanic. I knew I was his fifth wife. I knew he had lost one wife in an automobile accident, and he was divorced from the other three. But that didn't matter to me. I didn't marry him for money or for his bodybuilding looks, because he never told me how much money he had, and he didn't have a bodybuilding look – although he was quite handsome, even at age 62. You know how old I was when I married Ti?" Several sounds of "No, no – tell us" came from the audience.

"I was almost 19 – I was really 18 years old! But my father made me tell everyone that I was 19! My dad had known Titanic for years in the oil business in and around Tulsa, Oklahoma, and although we had a huge age discrepancy, dad gave his all-out approval.

"With my father as an adviser and sometimes partner with Titanic, we settled down in the oil fields of Oklahoma and lived a very respectable life. Then, in 1957, oil was discovered in supposedly large quantities in New Mexico, and we were about the first lease hounds in the area. While there, when Titanic was 65 years old, we had Ti's second child, and the apple of my eye – my son, Ty Wayne Thompson. We remained in New Mexico doing very well financially for another two years before Titanic yearned for more of his past action. He said that he figured he had about three or four more years of action-filled fun to live, and New Mexico just wasn't where that kind of fun was. So we moved to a quiet little neighborhood in San Antonio, Texas. I've never seen Titanic happier. I kept up my chores in raising Ty Wayne, and Titanic scurried around Texas playing golf and dabbling in a few poker games. He said he wasn't interested in the high stakes anymore, but he absolutely had to have the action to cure his habit. Like Maxine said before, Titanic was a principled man, a good provider, and a loving husband and father, but his women had to understand that he was much like a born-to-be traveling salesman – he had to satisfy his necessity for action in golf and poker. Thank God he was good at them, and, together with those still-existing oil leases, those two games provided all of us our livelihoods.

"I know there are some more people that want to share their experiences with you about their times with Titanic, and I, too, want to hear them, so I'll have a seat now and wait my turn a little later if I think something got left out!" Jeanette was ushered to her seat with thunderous applause.

Chapter 10

The gentleman rose from his chair at the insistence of his fellow funeral service attendees seated with him at one of the tables in the banquet room at the River Crest Country Club. He was dressed casually in an extra-large, light green golf shirt, typical golf slacks, also green, tan leather loafers, and a brown Arnold Palmer leather belt. As he slid his chair back under the table, he balanced himself well on his left foot with only the toe of his right foot touching the deep pile carpet. The middle-aged country club pro had been stricken with dreaded polio when he was a child. His body surrendered only a withered right leg to the disease, and his will and dedication to fitness saved the rest of his body. In fact, his strength and coordination surpassed most athletes in every part of his body except that withered right leg.

During his boyhood, he participated in every sport: in football (but only as an immobile lineman), in basketball (as a distant reserve), and in baseball (as a better-than-decent pitcher). But somewhere along the way, he tried out the sport of golf. It offered him the best chance to excel within the bounds of his partially crippled body. He worked at it with all his might. Soon, he was able to hit it long with the rest of the boys, and his natural touch in the short game became notorious. He confessed to himself right away that he had no chance to be a touring pro because of the necessity to walk, but more than anything he wanted to be a resident club pro. He had no delusions of grandeur; he was a realist from the start, but he knew he could make his dream a reality if he worked hard enough. Swinging from the right side, he had to develop a unique style of only partially shifting his weight back to his right side on the loaded-up backswing. He developed another unique move that initiated his downswing that put him in perfect hitting position in the hitting area. And he learned to repeat it all – all the time – regardless of being tired.

He thanked God every day for being born in a time when he could use an electric or motorized golf cart, otherwise he would have been relegated to short, par-three courses where and if they existed at all. He captained his high school golf team, and he played well at the college golf level, but soon his desire to be a club pro won out, and his dedication persevered until he won his PGA Club Professional card.

Walking is a series of controlled falls for all of us, but for this club pro, it was more pronounced and required total attention to balance. As he took one legitimate left-legged step forward, and then a thrown right leg forward, he made it easily to the steps leading up to the podium. Without use of a handrail, he slung that withered right leg up each of the three steps and perched himself behind the microphone just like all of his predecessors. The guests clapped in honor of his dedication, and they sat on the edge of their seats waiting to hear what toast he had to give.

"Many of you have heard about my experiences with Titanic Thompson, but just in case you haven't, my compadres at my table insist on me telling those who haven't heard. My name is Gene Shields. All my life, I wanted to be married to a woman who would tolerate the long hours of my profession, and I wanted to be a PGA Club Professional. Of course, I wanted children, and I wanted to be a good teacher to them and other youngsters. I've been blessed to have accomplished all of that, and hopefully I will have a lot more time left to give back some more of my blessings. I can't hide the imperfection in my body, and I want you all to know that I consider it a blessing, and not a bit of an inconvenience – except when I have to have all my pants altered after I pull them off the rack." The crowd erupted in laughter and applause, and for Gene, the ice was broken – he didn't relish the opportunity at being a public speaker.

"I know it's getting a bit late, so enough about me; I want to tell you about my brief experiences with the legend, Titanic Thompson.

"I was at the PGA qualifying school to take all my tests to become a club professional – as you'll remember, other than my family, my number-one goal in life. After sitting in one of those testing rooms all morning, my other applicants and I were all given the opportunity to hit some golf balls out on the practice tee after lunch. I remember it was hot, and not everybody wanted to get sweaty before going back to the classroom, but a few of us could never turn down the opportunity to hit golf balls. Anyway, the practice tee was less than half full with the fun-seekers while most of the guys napped in air-conditioned lounge chairs.

"I had hit maybe a half bucket when a stranger approached me. He was tall and lanky, he was dressed in golfing attire, and he had a manila folder under his arm. He introduced himself as Titanic Thompson. I got weak-kneed. I follow golf like no other person in the world. I can give you golfing statistics on every touring pro, and I know every golfer who has a chance to make it on the tour. I know college golfers, and I know who is who in Texas high school golf. At the time, I had read everything printable on Titanic Thompson – every story, and every bet he had made – he was already a legend. And that doesn't even count the untold number of stories I've heard about him in clubhouses and golf seminars. I'm telling you, I could hardly speak when he introduced himself. I finally got a little composure, and I reached out my hand to shake hands with him. I remember his grip: it was firm and almost everlasting. As someone said before me tonight, he had a very sincere handshake.

"After I told him my name, but couldn't get another word out if I had wanted to, he got straight to the point of his visit. I can remember every word – just as if he were speaking to me today."

"'Gene, I'm surprised that we haven't run into each other before, but I want to tell you what a pleasure it is to meet you. I've been watching you swing for about 15 minutes, and I've only seen you hit one ball less than perfect. I mean no offense, but you've got the best swing of any golfer, considering your handicap, that I have ever seen. You know you could make it on the tour?'

"I gasped, and said that he was too kind. I told him that I've heard about him all of my golfing life, and that I was flabbergasted that he knew who I was. Then I asked him why he was there, and if he had a game on that course that day.

"'It may be a little presumptuous on my part, but I'm here to offer you a proposition.'

"Wow," I said. "Do I get to be your partner or something?"

"'As a matter of fact, you do. I don't want to take up your time if I am interfering with your testing, and if there is a better time today to talk to you about my proposition, I'd be glad to come back.'

"No, no. Would you rather go into the pro shop or the locker room where it's cooler?

"'Why don't we do that? Come on, I'll buy you a Coke.'

"I followed Mr. Thompson through the pro shop and into the men's locker room. He picked out a pair of comfortable chairs that were facing the practice tee window, and we sat down.

"'Here's the deal. First of all, you indicated that you have heard of me. I hope all you've heard wasn't all bad.'

"I assure you, Mr. Thompson, that I envision you as a living legend. From what I've heard, and from people who have actually seen you play, I understand that you're still probably the best golfer in the world. Anyone who can break par right-handed and left-handed has to be the best in the world."

"'Well, thank you very much. I used to be a lot better than I can play today, but I would say I'd still play anybody that would light. I'm still crazy enough to think I can still beat anybody alive – particularly for a large amount of money in match play. Does that bother you?'

"No, sir. Every time I tee it up, there is a bet of some sort. I'm certainly not against gambling – unless it's excessive, of course."

"'Well, I guess I've been more than guilty of gambling excessively. But I'd be willing to bet that I've won more than 90 percent of the time. Let me tell you why I'm here, and what I want to propose to you.

"'Every year up in Chicago, at one of their famous courses, some of my gambling friends who run some of the rackets in Chicago and New York get together for a father-and-son golf tournament. I've been playing golf with these guys for over 20 years, and I've played golf and poker with most of the fathers' fathers. There isn't a more honest golf tournament in the world. I usually take one of my sons to play, but I heard about you, and I thought we'd pull a fast one on them. They will love it. They highly respect someone who out thinks them and gets the best of them. I've won more than a million or two from them, and they keep inviting me back. In fact, I'm always the first person asked to be there. I know that because they ask me what date is best for me for the tournament – they always adjust to the date I pick!

"'I don't really get excited about a set up anymore, but after seeing you swing the golf club, I see real possibilities in this plan. They are going to love it, and you and I are going to make a lot of money. Are you interested in money?'

"Mr. Thompson, I am certainly interested in money. I'm getting married next month if I am successful in getting my PGA card. I've already got a job lined up, and it's my dream to be a club professional and a family man. But you know I haven't got any money, at least your kind of money. I'd love to be your partner, but I'm afraid I couldn't come up with my share of the money to make a decent gamble in your style.

"'You don't have to worry about the money. I'll handle all the risks. I'll fly you up there, take care of your room – all your expenses, and whatever spending money, within reason, you'll need. You certainly want to bring back a nice gift for your new bride. I'll fund all the money for both of us, and if we win – whatever we win – I'll take 75 percent, and you can take home 25 percent. You don't have to repay me any of your expenses out of your winnings. The way I've got it figured, we're liable to win a half a million dollars – at least a couple of hundred thousand. They pay off in cash, and there ain't no taxes. I'm not going to guarantee you the winnings, but I will guarantee you a fun trip with nothing out of pocket for you. The tournament will be in two months on a Thursday, Friday, and Saturday. You need to get there on a

Wednesday, and come back on Sunday. You'll make your own travel arrangements, but I'll send you the necessary money before-hand.

"'Here's my plan: I've had my lawyer draw up some adoption papers to make this thing legal, and to quash all objections from the tournament field. There won't be any trouble. They'll love my ingenuity. The course will be closed to the public and to all other members – we'll have the best time you ever had on a golf course. I will adopt you for the week, then we'll get it annulled or something so your mommy and dad won't be upset with me. Are your parents still living?'

"Yes, sir."

"'After you sign these temporary adoption papers, I'll enter us in the tournament, and I'll start booking all of the bets. The bets are usually per day plus a grand total of the three days. We'll have bets with every two-man father-and-son team there. There'll be at least 50 teams, and we'll have a minimum of a thousand a day per team plus a grand on the overall total per team. To be honest, I can't see us losing a single bet. There are a couple of decent play-ers, and they all try to bring in a ringer, but all we have to do is beat half of the field to break even, and that'll be like falling off a log. We'll catch a little ribbing, but everybody will treat us like family, and the whole thing will be fun for everybody. None of them care how much money they lose. They just point to their bodyguard, and tell him how much to give us. These are old friends, and there is nothing to worry about.

"'When you get there, I don't want you to get near a golf ball. I don't want you to practice a putt, a drive, or a pitch. I want your first shot to be the biggest surprise in the whole world. They're going to see your limp, and they're going to load the wagon with bets. They're going to figure they're going to get all of their money back from what they've lost over the years. I can't wait to see their faces when they see you hit that first ball. I'll probably have to give them some shots off my ball, but they'll never ask for a thing on your ball. Considering it'll be a best net ball for each hole for each round, I figure we've got a lead-pipe cinch. What do you think?'

"Gosh, Mr. Thompson. I am so honored that you'd think of

me as a partner, but I'm scared to death just thinking about it. I know I wouldn't let you down on the golf course, but unless my heart is in something, I don't think I could enjoy it or the money. All my life – at least since I've taken up golf – all I've really ever wanted is to be a PGA professional and get married. I'd have to tell my wife to be about it, and I don't think she'd let me go – not that I'm henpecked or nothing, but to be honest, it's her life, too, that I'd be putting on the line."

"'I understand son. Just remember, you'll probably make more money in that tournament than the next 20 years of your life as a PGA course pro. All tax-free, and all in cash at one time. There are no strings attached to further playing, and you can go to your new job in complete anonymity after we're through. Why don't you give it some thought? I'm staying at the Hilton downtown, and I've written down the hotel number and my room number on this piece of paper. Talk it over with your wife-to-be and get back with me tonight. If I'm not in when you call, try paging me around the lobby, otherwise just leave me a message as to your decision. You have no obligation to do anything, and you owe me nothing for hearing me out. I really hope you'll give it some hard thought – it could really make your life easier over your first few years of marriage, particularly if you're going to start a family.'"

"The tall, aging man then stood up, offered his hand again for a handshake, and said he looked forward to my message. I went back to my classroom for further tests and instructions. How I made it through the rest of that day with passing marks, I'll never know. I couldn't think of anything other than Mr. Thompson's proposition. My concentration was absolutely nil. Nevertheless, I got through the afternoon session, and I went back to my cheap hotel to call my fiancée.

"She was against the whole thing right from the beginning, and she said that I'd be risking my whole future and our marriage. She said that I should step back, count all of our blessings, and turn the offer down. If I wanted to, she said that I should invite Mr. Thompson over to our house for dinner the next time he was through our town, and for sure, we needed to invite him to our wedding, but it was out of the question to go through with this type of deal. She said Mr. Thompson was very generous, but the offer just didn't fit our kind of life at this time, and in all probability it wouldn't in the future either. I had already reached the same conclusion, but I wasn't completely sold on turning down all of that money. I knew there wasn't two non-pros in the world that could beat Titanic Thompson and me! But, I had to turn it down – for our already dedicated future.

"That phone call to Mr. Thompson's room was the hardest call I'd ever made. I happened to catch him in his room around nine o'clock, and I thanked him so much for the opportunity and for thinking about me, but I just couldn't do it. I just couldn't take the chance of throwing away all of my hard work. Mr. Thompson didn't say much, and I know he was greatly disappointed in me and the fact that his plan had gone awry. But he was a real gentleman, and he said that he understood. He wished me well with my new job. He said there was no doubt that I would get my PGA card, and that I'd make a great club pro and teacher. He declined the wedding invitation, but he wanted me to tell my wife that he wished us a very happy honeymoon and marriage. He also said that he thought we'd run into each other again someday, and that he looked forward to that time. He wished me good luck, and he said goodbye.

"May I have a glass of water? I don't have much farther to go, but I don't usually address crowds, and my mouth is a little dry. Thanks

"It was maybe five years after that father-and-son invitation-from Mr. Thompson that I ran into him again. As thrilling as it was for me to meet him the first time, and to be invited to be his playing partner – regardless of the ulterior motive – that day, it may be the second time that I had the pleasure of meeting Titanic Thompson that I'll remember the best the rest of my life. For a reason maybe only I can feel, my next encounter with him was a dream come true.

"My wife and I had a few days off in early July from my job, and we decided to spend the few days in San Antonio. When I had had all the shopping and River Walking I could stand, I decided to visit one of my fellow club pros out at Pecan Valley. I got there around 11:00 so that I could have lunch somewhere with him. His name was Bill, and we went back a long time – we even went to Q-School together. He is a great guy, and I was really looking forward to hearing how he was doing, and to find out all about his family.

"When I got there, he was so busy that he could barely get out from behind the main counter to greet me. We talked for a few minutes, and then I let him get back to business as I decided to scope out the merchandise in the pro shop – trying to see if there were any lines of clothing or accessories that I needed to have at my shop. They had a lot more people coming through their shop than mine, so they had more margin for error when they made their reselling selections. I had to be certain that what I picked to sell really would sell. I knew my clientele very well, so I could visualize what I thought might interest them, and on most occasions I could pinpoint the exact person who would be the buyer of choice before I got the merchandise home. My touring of the shop and hall displays went on for almost an hour until Bill was able to break free.

"Bill apologized profusely that he wasn't going to be able to go anywhere other than the club for lunch, and I was invited to the men's grill instead. We both had their big hamburgers, fries, and Cokes. The problem with eating where you work, particularly in the golf business, you are a continuing sounding board for every member's best shots, best scores, and all the tragedies that get mixed in. Time and time again, we were interrupted by stories and a need for a quick tip from Bill to cure someone's ill-tuned swing. When you depend on teaching lessons for a living, you have to make the most out of these little conversation tips so that you build a rapport that will carry you on to more lessons and other opportunities. I made it clear to Bill that he was to tend to business first, and we'd share our time together when time permitted.

"We finished lunch – concluding it with a celebratory Pecan Ball made of rich vanilla ice cream and topped with chocolate syrup and sprinkled with fresh pecans. Then I decided to stick around a few more minutes to finish our conversation while Bill held down the counter in the pro shop. When Bill got a rush from several golfers checking in, I went over to the window and looked out at the practice tee.

"Way at the far end of the tee that we call the anthill was a long, lanky gentleman who was hitting a bucket of balls left-hand-ed. There could be no doubt, it was an older Titanic Thompson. I watched him hit the rest of that bucket, and hoped he would finish and come by the pro shop; there I would encounter him for a re-introduction. His bag was lying flat on the ground, and when he moved it to get another club, it hid another couple of buckets of balls, so my original plan had to be abandoned. He was going to be out there awhile. I decided to formulate another plan to meet the maestro of golf – at least in my opinion he was the maestro.

"When Bill got a break from the maddening stream of golfers, I asked him if he knew the man on the far end of the prac-tice tee. He came over to the window to have a look.

"Of course, it's Titanic Thompson. I know you've heard of him in all of your golf circles. He comes out here quite often, but as of late, he's been here every day. He hits four or five buckets, and it's true that he hits from both sides. His name should be the Mirror Man because his swing from right to left or from left to right is the exact mirror of each. I never saw him play in his prime, but he must have been something. I certainly would bet on him. For my money, in match play, I don't think any man alive could have beaten him in his day – and that includes everybody on the tour. The amateurs were big in his day, and many of them were at least equal with the pros, and I know for a certainty that he beat all of them, and he gave most of them at least the equivalent of a shot a side in doing so. Something's up with him, 'cause I've never seen him work so hard. Look out there, it's at least 98 degrees out there, and he's dressed in a long-sleeve shirt, long pants, and that crazy lookin' sombrero on. He doesn't say much to anybody, and he keeps pretty much to himself, unless there's an impromptu poker game that springs up. He rarely plays 18 holes with anybody, but he does play nine holes about twice a week. Despite his quietness, he is revered around here. People don't confront him, but they all know of his past exploits. He treats everyone around here with the utmost of respect, and he is always courteous when he needs some-thing from one of the employees. That tells me a lot about a person. Give me a friend who can be kind to those who he doesn't have to be kind to – like a waiter or waitress – you know what I mean. In our profession, we kinda take the same abuses that a waiter or waitress does. It is a pleasure when we run into people who don't take advantage of us.

"I've never told anybody except my wife about my earlier offer from Mr. Thompson, so Bill was in the dark as to whether I had ever met him or knew much about him. So I asked Bill if he thought it would be all right if I walked out there to say hello to him. I told him that I had met him once, and that we actually had a bite to eat together. Bill replied that I was indeed a lucky fella. He said that in all the years he'd known Mr. Thompson, he'd never been invited to sit down with him for any reason. Then Bill suggested that if I thought that he'd remember me, I should go out there and say hello because he frequently just went straight to his car after his workout.

"I slowly finished my Coke, and tried to rehearse just what I was going to say. Finally, I got the confidence that I thought I needed, and I headed his way. There were maybe two or three other golfers on the practice tee that I passed by, but I hardly notice them. It's a wonder that I didn't walk right through their swings on the way to Mr. Thompson because I was so focused.

"As I got to within 30 feet or so, Mr. Thompson glanced up at me from his address at the practice ball he was about to hit. He stopped, put that iron club back in his bag, and pulled out a right-handed stick. He then turned his back to me and addressed the same ball right-handed. He struck it as if he had been hitting that particular iron all day. I stood there and watched from about 20 feet as he hit another two or three balls, then I felt that Mr. Thompson really didn't want to be bothered – judging from him switching sides – and I turned to reluctantly walk away.

"The slight wind was coming from Mr. Thompson direct to me. It was hot as blazes, and there wasn't a sound in the air but a few clicks of practicing golfers making contact with their practice balls. Then I heard some of the sweetest words I've ever heard.

"'Hello Gene. How've ya been? He kept hitting his practice shots.

"I stopped in my tracks – I wasn't going very fast." The crowd was so glued to Gene's story that it took several seconds for it to reply with laughter and light applause.

"I didn't intend to bother you, Mr. Thompson, but I happened to be in the pro shop looking out the window, and I recognized you. I couldn't take the chance on not being able to say hello, and to ask how you're doing."

"Ordinarily, I'm a pretty tough individual, but I had to stop talking, I was choking up fast, and I had boocooles of tears forming in my eyes. How could he remember me? I thought. And how in the hell could he remember my name – after nearly five years? I was strung out in emotion.

"'I've been okay, Gene. You know you missed one hell of a tournament. I don't want to rub it in on you, but I won a quarter of a million with one of my real sons, and he couldn't hit it a lick – doubt if he broke 95 all week. You and I could have tripled that at the least. But, there could be another day, and maybe under different circumstances, you might concede to be my partner. How about that?'

"God, I could hardly talk; tears were coming down my cheeks, and all I could do was turn into the wind and hope the wind would dry my face.

"Mr. Thompson, I'd rather be your partner than anyone alive. You have always been my hero, and after that invitation you gave me to play several years ago, I constantly think about what I missed, and what a good time we would have had together.

"Titanic kept right on hitting balls while he was talking. 'What brings you out here to Pecan Valley?'

"I have an old friend that works here, Bill – in the pro shop. I've never told anyone about your past offer to me, so he doesn't know that I know you from Adam, and he was kinda hesitant in letting me come out here to say hello. I told him that I got to sit down with you one day in another life and have a bite with you. Only then did he agree to let me disturb you.

"'There's no disturbing me, son. You've really made my day. Let me finish this bucket, and let's get Bill in there and go have a bite of lunch or a drink. Why don't you go set us up a table, and I'll be right there.'

"You've made my day, Mr. Thompson, and I'll go and do just that. See you when you're finished.

"Bill wasn't busy when I walked into the pro shop, and in fact, he had watched my conversation with Titanic through the same window I had seen Mr. Thompson. He asked how it went, and I told him that it went fine. I asked him who I was to see about setting up a private table for the three of us in the grill so that Mr. Thompson could get a bite to eat, and that we'd join him with a drink – all at his invitation. I told him that this was his chance to become a real friend to one of his members, and he better get a sub in here quick to take advantage of the lunch opportunity. He did just that, and I was directed to the head server to make the table arrangements.

"Bill and I were seated when Mr. Thompson came through the doorway into the grill. It wasn't manners, but respect that caused us simultaneously to rise and greet the legend when he approached. He shook our hands and asked to be excused to wash up in the men's locker room. He sat his big sombrero down in the vacant chair and went his way. Bill was as excited as I was, and it was hard for each of us to know what to say to each other. In five minutes or less, Mr. Thompson got back to our table and pulled up a chair.

"I opened the conversation with a serious question about Mr. Thompson's health. I asked him if anything was wrong that caused him to be hitting practice balls in the middle of the day, in near a 100 degree weather, with a long-sleeve shirt on, with two golf gloves on, and with that big sombrero covering his head.

"About that time, the waiter appeared and asked us if he could take our order. Mr. Thompson ordered a hamburger without a bun, and Bill and I ordered more Coke. Then Mr. Thompson addressed my earlier question.

"'First of all, my health is fine. I feel great. I'd like to hit it a bit farther, but I guess that's too much to ask, but thank you, I feel fine.'

" Then he kinda chuckled and looked both Bill and me in the eyes.

'To tell you the truth, I've got almost the same kind of tournament up in New York with my racketeering friends that I told you about years ago, Gene. For about the last 40 years or so, we've enjoyed an invitational tournament together for strictly family camaraderie. We've all been friends so long that we're really just like one big happy family. Well, last year I had to miss the tournament because I had hurt my back. It's well now, but they don't know it. About a month ago, I got a conference call from almost all of them saying that the tournament was going to be called off if I couldn't attend anymore. I told them that I was better, but I wasn't sure I could swing a club – and at the time of the conversation I hadn't tried to swing since hurting my back. I promised them that I would be there – next week – but I wasn't going to give any of them a shot on any bet. They indicated that the tournament would never be held again if I wasn't a participant, and the standard thousand dollar bets would continue, but without me giving strokes. I got to feeling a little sorry for the boys, so I agreed to all the matches, but I would alternate consecutive shots from left-handed to right. Now, you asked about my golfing attire today. I can't let those guys know I've been practicing – can't let them see a suntan!'

"I thought Bill was going to laugh right out of his chair. The laughing was contagious, and the three of us were causing an absolute scene in the restaurant. Mr. Thompson answered a few more questions from Bill and me while he finished his lunch, and then Mr. Thompson asked me about my new wife, who wasn't new anymore, and if we had any kids. I told him that life couldn't be any better for the two of us, and that we indeed did have a couple of kids, and they were fine as well. When the waiter came to clean up our table, Mr. Thompson had a question for both of us.

"'Does anyone around here know Gene? And do they know how well he can play?'

"Bill replied that he knew me, and that he was a pretty fair player, but he said he always seemed to come up short when we played – and in the past we'd had some pretty good matches around here. But he said that he doubted that any of the folks around now would remember those matches, and was quite sure that most would not recognize Gene.

Mr. Thompson finished his burger patty amongst Bill and my small talk. All the while, you could see the wheels turning in Titanic's calculating mind.

"'I've got a friend up in the hill country who plays a lot of golf, and he calls every once in a while asking me to get myself a partner and to play him and his partner up at his club. How about me showing up there with my ol' limp-along friend here and challenge him and his partner for some pretty good money? Same deal as I talked to you about years ago, Gene. You've got no risk, and you'd share a third of the winnings this time because I won't have to foot any traveling expenses for you. How about tomorrow – if I can arrange it. Call me tonight.'

"He wrote his home number on one of the cocktail napkins and gave it to me. Bill and I stood up to shake his hand again and say goodbye. Then Bill came out of the blue with a question.

"'Mr. Thompson, I've got a couple of days off. Do you think it would be possible if I took one of those days off and caddied for you?'

"Titanic stood back, paused a little, and looked at Bill.

"'If you'll come dressed as a caddy and not a golf pro, I would agree, but you got to show up dressed in scrubs – no shined shoes, a pulled-down hat so no one will recognize you, and a closed mouth – can't speak to anyone – you gotta act like I just picked you up off the road. If you can do all of that, I'd love to have ya. You two get together and call me tonight,' he said as he walked to the door.

"I left right away to get back to my hotel to tell my wife. For some reason, she wasn't as excited as I was." Again the laughter and the applause was slow because everyone was so enthralled with Gene's story.

"A lady answered when I called Mr. Thompson that night, and I immediately thought that somehow I had the wrong number. I asked for Mr. Thompson, and she said I must be Gene, and he was waiting for my call. I'm telling you, I was about to pee in my pants,

I was so excited. Mr. Thompson said the match was on at 10:30, and he would meet us there. He told me to stop on the way if I wanted to hit some practice balls somewhere, because he didn't want me to show off my swing until the first tee." The laughter and applause were anticipated and the crowd's eruption was well-timed.

"Bill and I showed up in my car ten minutes before tee time – only because we'd been circling the place for an hour before to make sure we didn't miss our destination. Mr. Thompson introduced me to our competitors, and pretended that he didn't know I was going to bring a caddy along. I told him that I wasn't sure that they'd have carts, and with my leg and all, I'd sure need a caddy on these hills. He smiled at me, then at his friends, and asked them if they wanted to share a fore-caddy? He also said that at his age, the game required everyone to ride in a golf cart. Everyone agreed, and incognito Bill had a caddying job.

"The bets were a $1,000 Nassau per man. That means that each player was betting a grand on each nine plus a grand on the total 18. I probably shot 38 on the front, but I had two birdies that helped. Mr. Thompson only had one birdie, but he shot 35 – no holes over par. We won the first nine by two holes, and we were two up on the 18 bet going into the backside. We had them two down on the backside when we turned the 15th, so they were out of the 18 bet, and they were two down with three to play on the last nine-hole bet. They elected to press both the back nine bet and the 18 bet. Titanic birdied the last hole – a par five – to win everything. We had won $5,000, and my share was $1,666. – more money than I have ever dreamed of in winnings on a golf course. But the money really didn't matter. I had redeemed myself with Titanic Thompson, and I can always say that I had the privilege of being a successful partner of his. What a thrill! I insisted that Bill split my winnings with me because if it weren't for him, none of that would have ever happened. What a vacation – playing a round of golf with one of my best pro friends as my fore-caddy, winning enough money to buy my wife a special dress, and being a partner with Titanic Thompson in a real-live golf match. Thank you so much, Mr. Thompson – you made that day the happiest day of my life."

Gene Shields exited the platform rubbing his crying eyes with the sleeves of his short-sleeved golf shirt, but around him was a thunderous standing ovation of appreciation for two very fine people.

"Have any of you been to the Redman Club on Ervay Street in Dallas?" Half of the crowd began to hoot and holler in the affirmative.

Chapter 11

"My name is Ace Darnell, and that, I'm proud to say, was my establishment. One of my favorite customers who visited my establishment with some regularity was none other than Titanic Thompson. I can confess, now that much time has passed since the things I'm going to tell you about really happened, that we did have some exciting gambling activity around there. The biggest draw and the best of my patrons from far and wide who was involved in some of the biggest poker games that this state has ever seen was none other than Titanic Thompson.

"High-stakes golf games and other revenue-producing events were organized and created there. Everyone who participated there was on the up-and-up with every other participant. There was never any alleged cheating or rigging, and there were never any collection problems. There were never any fights or threats, and there were never any underworld ties that threatened the integrity of a game or an event. Now I can't say that everyone there left as a happy camper." The crowd broke out in spontaneous laughter and light hand-clapping. "After all, no one likes to go home a loser, and in the world of gambling somebody's goin' to win and somebody's goin' to lose.

"Before I get to one of the greatest one-on-one golf matches that was organized there, and before I tell you who the participants were, I want to tell you some Titanic stories that happened within the confines of my club, and just what a fantastic nose for wagering our friend Titanic Thompson had. Let me get my little cue card out here so that I don't miss anything." Ace seemed to apply art at having trouble finding which pocket his treasured cue card was in, but he found it, and the stories began to roll.

"Titanic would usually give me a call a few days before his Dallas arrival. He would suggest that the two of us play a little golf, and then he'd ask who was around that might be interested in a good-sized poker game. At that point, we'd both silently agree that the golf would in time take care of itself, and I'd begin to think who was in town and who was available to sit in on Titanic's type of poker game. Now, let me describe Titanic's typical poker game. It was never an open, no-limit game – it was almost always a pot-limit game. There were always rules such as three bumps, $1,000 ante, and a list of about three or four approved games. There were very few games that allowed a joker to be included in the deck. The house would always furnish the cards, and it went without saying that the house stood by the fact that the cards didn't favor anyone – the deck was not marked. There was never any prohibition on no checks and raises or you had to have jacks or better to open or anything like that. This was real poker that accented the drawing of cards, and the ability to bluff. All of that was rolled into one word that the winner usually did better than anyone else at the table, the ability to analyze. A-N-A-L-Y-Z-E. If the game lasted long enough, the cards would supposedly even out, and that is why no good poker player wanted a short game. A good player wanted a minimum of a 24 hour game. That always played right into the hands of a really good poker player. The problem with everyone who felt that way was that the losing player for the moment had to have the bankroll to weather the storm and hold out long enough for the cards to turn if they weren't falling for him early. If the cards were running early for a particular player, he'd rat-hole a percentage of his winnings and play the rest of the game as a staunch conservative. Titanic knew all of these tendencies. He knew the odds on everything. In fact, in his early gambling days in New York, Titanic sought out a practicing mathematician to teach him all the odds, and to ensure him that the two of them had thought of all possibilities. I think his name was Pat McAlley, a college professor who had a reputation of being one of this country's best mathematicians. I can still remember Titanic teaching me some of the odds that he learned and verified with Professor McAlley.

"Call heads or tails on one coin toss – it's an even 50-50. Calling two coins that are tossed at the same time either both heads or both tails is four to one. When you add another coin and toss all three at the same time, the odds are six to one that you can call at least two that match either heads or tails. In rolling the dice, it's eight to three you can roll a particular number on one roll of a pair of dice. In poker, on a five-card hand, it's 51.5 to 50 that you'll be in possession of at least a pair. If you're in a game to try and draw the first Ace, on the average, you're going to have to wait for eight and one-half cards. That's about all I can remember, but Titanic Thompson could quote you the exact odds on almost any draw or combination. When you added his remarkable memory to the equation, he knew what everybody had by the third or fourth draw around the table. He was conniving, no doubt about it, but he was brilliant at everything he touched.

"I saw him win more that $700.000 – paid off in cash – in a three-night poker game, and I was his partner on the golf course when he was 76 years old and bet a gallery full of people that he could shoot his age on a new – reconditioned – public golf course that he had never played before. He intentionally bogeyed the last hole to squeak in a 75. When he finished counting over 100 one $100 bills, I lost count and went to the car.

"Oddly enough, we had football pools, individual college and pro team sports bets at the Redman, but I never saw Titanic place a bet on any team or individual sport that he wasn't a part of. If he couldn't have some odds in his favor because of his analytical mind, his personal skill, or his memory, he wasn't about to make a bet.

"In his younger years, after he got into town, he'd always play golf by day and poker by night. I don't know who his banker was, but Titanic must have been a better account than Brinks!" The crowd roared with approval. "When he was in town, I was a part-ner with Titanic every other day – just about, and the other days I was a spectator. To see that man maneuver a golf ball was some-thing special. I saw him play every good golfer in town at one time or the other, and I can honestly say I never saw him lose a match in head-to-head competition that wasn't a setup. And I guarantee you

– except for his old - 'I'm playing right-handed, and now I'll switch to left-handed if the money's right – on almost all of his other setup bets, the victim knew what was going on, but he couldn't help himself from trying to be the one that broke the tide – who won when he wasn't supposed to win. Also, I guarantee you that many of Titanic's victims knew they were going to lose, but they wanted the honor of losing to the master – Titanic Thompson.

"I gotta tell you about the time that Titanic and I had a lead-pipe-cinch match between us and a couple of real scatter-drive players. I hadn't played with them before, but I had heard plenty about them. They had to cheat to break 80, and they bet more money than water behind a dam. With us, we knew they wouldn't cheat – no one would dare be caught trying to cheat Titanic Thompson. Titanic won all of his bets on skill, intuition, careful planning, and coolness under pressure. There has never been even an accusation that Titanic ever played less than a totally honest game – now he carefully fixed a few….." The crowd clapped for two hard minutes on that line, because they knew the comment was exactly true! In the world of humor, nothing is funnier than the truth when told in a joking manner.

"The day started late because Titanic got to the course late – a first for Titanic. When I asked Titanic if anything was wrong, he replied that he was under a new prescription for sleeping pills, and he just woke up too late. After six holes, I began to feel a little ashamed at having asked Titanic about his lateness – we were up four holes after six. Then, you'd have thought someone had hit Titanic on the head with a ball-peen hammer. He could hardly swing. He always made contact, but he had no clue where the ball was going. That was the only time I can remember losing money as a partnership. We lost $400, and neither one of us was very happy. For the first time ever, we got in an argument about who was responsible for making the losing bet. When I finally confessed to being the one that suggested the bet, Ti said that from now on, he was not partnering with me again, and that he was going to make his own bet – then he took a taxi to the hotel and went to sleep. The cab driver said he had to carry Ti to his room. After sleeping for 12 straight hours, Titanic reappeared at the same golf course. I was on the practice tee when he arrived.

"Titanic asked for forgiveness if he had said anything out of character the day before. He said that he now knew he had been drugged – not intentionally by anyone else but himself – he had taken the wrong medicine. And then he began telling me about this bet he had made at the hotel over breakfast. Seems he had breakfast across the aisle from a twosome that was talking about playing this very course later in the day. Titanic made friends with the two and told them that he was planning to play the same course. He told me that he could have finagled a partnership wager for the two of us, but he knew he had to make the bet right there, and he wasn't sure that I'd play anymore with him, and he said that he wouldn't blame me. Then he told me that he was betting the little rich one of the two – and he was blind in one eye! The match was not to begin until mid-afternoon for one reason or the other.

"When I finished my modest gambling round, Titanic was on the 16th hole. I cornered him for a few words out of the hearing reach of the others and then grabbed a cart and went out to follow Titanic's match. As he approached the 17th tee, I asked him how much he had won. He smiled and said he was down several grand, but he was fixing to put it in first gear and bring home the bacon. He reckoned that it was going to get pretty dark pretty fast, and he would have the decided advantage with two eyes over one. I told him that he was wrong, that the other fella had been playing all his life when it was half dark, and he had the advantage!" The crowd loved that punch line, and let Ace have a well-deserved hand.

"Titanic shrugged off my comment and pressed every bet he could. Poor Ti was still suffering from his day-before mix-up with his new sleeping pills. He just couldn't get it into gear at all. He lost a bunch. He congratulated his opponent, paid off with cash, and took another taxi to the hotel. I came over to that hotel that night to buy his supper. Now don't get me wrong – Titanic still had plenty of money, but it was a shock to both of us to see him lose. I didn't want him to bask alone in his sorrow. He soon got over that loss, changed his prescription for sleeping pills, and went on to win at least 100 straight more times on the links. That's an estimate, but I'd bet it was at least that.

"He was a great man in more ways than what we've heard here tonight. One of his great attributes was to recognize talent – particularly talent on the golf course. At the time of the incident that I've been dying to all of you about, Titanic was pushing his late 70s – he was getting old, like me, and he knew it. However, he was always up to a bet when he thought he had the advantage. If he couldn't play like he used to, then he'd convert to betting on somebody who played and thought like he used to.

"That brings me to one of the best one-on-one challenge matches that was ever organized. Of course, I was the primary mover in getting the players to agree to participate, and I was the primary moving force to get the dates, the location, and all of the other elements in order. One of the participants in making this match happen was Titanic Thompson, but I'm going to fool you on this one – Titanic was a participant, but he wasn't a player, just a sponsor and a bettor. I just mentioned that in Titanic's older years, he couldn't guarantee the sub-par rounds of his earlier years, so if the opportunity presented itself with the kind of player he liked, he wouldn't hesitate to back him or bet on him – within certain guidelines and parameters.

"In 1968 or there-abouts – give or take a year or two – I talked to Titanic about being a part of a match that I was in the process of promoting between two of the younger up-and-coming pros of that generation. One of the players that I suggested he back and bet on was a new tour player named Raymond Floyd." Everyone in the house knew that Raymond was in the audience, and all turned at once – just like the crowd following a tennis ball at a tennis match – to locate the already-famous PGA golfer.

"My earlier arrangements for Raymond had him coming to Dallas on a layover before traveling to the match site in El Paso, Texas. I suggested to Titanic that I change Raymond's reservations and have the three of us fly from Dallas a day or so prior to the match date so that Ray could play the course a couple of times before the big action took place. Titanic was agreeable on all fronts. Titanic had heard great things about Mr. Floyd – a good driver, a great iron player, and as good a short game and putter that had surfaced on the tour in a long time. Besides that, he had been successful at every level he had played – he would be the favorite against almost every player anyone could think of.

"Titanic was suspicious of whom he would be playing, however. Before Ti finally committed, he wanted to know which tour player was going to be the opposition. When I told him that the opposition was not a tour player – not even a foreseeable qualifier, although he was in town to try out at the Horizon Country Club – he was a Mexican kid from El Paso who was establishing himself quite well in the game. Titanic's quote was 'How could we be so fortunate; there must be a hitch somewhere.'

"I told him that I wouldn't bet against Raymond Floyd against anyone, but that I am sure not underestimating this Mexican character. I've heard that he can do it all, but his forte is his gritty nature that controls his game. People say he just never loses. He is a great putter – particularly under pressure, but he is just average in length. However, there was one quote of a rather famous golfer who had seen him play a few rounds, and that famous golfer had even helped him refine some of his practice techniques. All he said was, 'This kid may be the finest striker of the golf ball I have ever seen.' I told Titanic that such a quote was routine from a lot of players just trying to get someone started, or just being kind after beating his brains out in a bet or two. But that wasn't the case here – the quote was attributed to none other than Bantam Ben Hogan! Titanic looked like someone had dropped an anvil on his foot. His face wrinkled in consternation.

"'Tell me more about this Mexican kid.'

"Well, one of the funniest things that I have ever heard of on a golf course, this kid did: he played a complete nine-hole round of golf on a regulation golf course averaging a bogey a hole – PLAYING THE ENTIRE ROUND WITH NOTHING BUT A COKE BOTTLE!

"'God Almighty Ace. What are you getting us into? That sounds like me in my younger years. I'm ashamed that I didn't think of that one way back when. I'll tell you something right now. When you get a guy thinking about betting on the unusual, that means he's mastered the usual. He isn't going to be called a fool with some off-the-wall bet when he can't back up a standard golf bet. I'm scared of this guy already. Floyd is a great player, and he has the experience factor over the Mexican kid in a match that should draw a pretty big gallery, but the kid sounds like he has grit, and he ain't going to back down from anybody.'

"I told Titanic that I agreed with his assessment, but how could anyone hesitate to bet on the best – or certainly one of the best – a guy on tour against someone who hasn't yet even made it to the tour? I knew immediately I shouldn't have said that! Titanic looked at me like I was crazy, and then sarcastically told me off in one little sentence.

"'Dumb-ass, did you ever bet on me? Remember, I couldn't even spell the word t-o-u-r!'" The crowd got a kick out of that retort, and appreciated Ace being honest about his short, thought-out comment to Titanic.

"I wanted to tell Titanic that in the world of today's golfing folks, the tour was everything. In his day, the tour was wonderful, and did possess the best group of golfers in the world, but there were other great golfers – amateurs and professional bettors that were the tour player's equal. But I had taken my medicine, and I didn't want to get in a comparison situation that quite frankly, I didn't believe in myself. Present company excepted, of course, I do believe that Titanic could beat any man alive in match play when he was in his prime.

"In Floyd versus Trevino, each participating player was to automatically receive 20 percent of any action that flowed through the organizers for any and all bets that were on them, and the original backers of the match had guaranteed side bets of $20,000 each to the two participants without any down side risk. So, from a moneymaking standpoint, compared to the lifestyles that each participant was living in, the edge was overwhelming on the side of whom we were later to know as the Merry Mexican. Nevertheless, who in the world would expect a young Mexican kid from El Paso, Texas, to readily compete with a world-renowned tour veteran?

"Mr. Floyd showed up in Big 'D' right on schedule, and the threesome of Mr. Floyd, Titanic, and myself took a noon flight out of Love Field directly to El Paso the following day. Raymond slept the whole flight, so Titanic and I figured that the best time to tell him our plan of scouting out the course could wait until he finished his rest – we didn't want to take a chance that he was dogged tired for one reason or another. After we checked into our hotel in downtown El Paso, we set up a meeting time in the lobby bar before having dinner. At the bar, Titanic suggested to Raymond that he pay a visit to the course a couple of times to familiarize himself to probable pin placements, where to position his drives, where it would be prudent to use a lesser-length club off the tee of some holes, etc. Titanic also told Raymond that he had secured a caddy for Raymond who knew the course like the palm of his hand. The caddy was a suggestion from a real good friend of Ti's from earlier gambling days, and his loyalty was vouched for and that loyalty could never be a question. Besides that, he was of Mexican origin, and he could interpret anything that Mr. Trevino would say in Spanish that might affect the match. It just might prove useful.

"Well, a slight disagreement ensued between Titanic and Mr. Floyd. Raymond was so confident that he saw no need of checking out the course against an unknown, and furthermore, he languished that his rest was far more important than any review of the course to be played. After a few words were exchanged – you all know that Titanic could be rather convincing; Titanic convinc ed Raymond that over the years he had a few notches on his gun barrel.

Raymond agreed to ride the course, plus play a practice round prior to the match. During a hasty ride over the course two days before the match, Raymond and I were riding together and watching a foursome finish its play on 18 when I noticed our opposition walking up to the green. I remember asking Raymond if he had ever met the Mexican kid who was named Lee Trevino. He said that he had not, but not to worry, he was a safe bet. That's when I told him to pay special attention to the next player to hit – it was Lee. He fired a short iron to the long par five. The ball hit hole high and jetted past the hole by 15 feet, then it bit, and pulled back to within three inches of the cup. I had to ask him if he thought a practice round was in order. He replied that he had promised Mr. Thompson he'd play one, and now, he really thought it was a good idea. He also asked if we could find out what Mr. Trevino shot today. I told him that wouldn't be a problem. I suggested we watch them putt out, and then I'd introduce Raymond to his opponent, and he could ask him for himself. He agreed.

"It turned out to be a rather social occasion as Raymond and Lee both gulped down at least four beers apiece getting acquainted. When Raymond later rejoined me, he said Lee had told him that he played the course purposely trying to leave the ball in precarious positions all day except number 18 where he decided that he wanted to end the day on a high note. He said Lee wasn't concerned with his score because he had nothing riding on the round – yet he still shot a 69 on the par 72 course. I think Mr. Floyd had a reawakening, and he was eager to make his practice round a necessary learning experience.

"The first day's weather for the match was hot as blazes. I don't know whether it was the cloudless sky, the blistering sun, or what, but Raymond's 69 was no match for the Mexican kid's 67. As I recall, Lee birdied the fourth hole and never looked back. The closest Raymond got to Lee was during the handshake after the match. Titanic and I lost $9,000 each, while my recommended backers of Mr. Floyd lost a total of ten grand apiece. My side of the fence was not too happy.

"The second day's betting schedule was to be for the same amount. Lee shot another 67 and Raymond improved to a 68, but the score was not indicative of the match, and I think Raymond would tell you the same thing. Lee was on a roll, and Raymond hadn't felt his best game kick in as of yet.

"To Raymond's credit, he was about as mad as any golfer I've ever seen. He was embarrassed at losing two days in a row, but he thought he had been robbed with some of his putts not falling. He even commented that maybe gravity doesn't exist at this altitude and this close to Mexico – he truly couldn't understand his losing posture. Titanic and I had then lost $18,000 apiece, and our comfortable backers of Mr. Floyd were down even more. So, following Titanic's lead, we sought out the opposition bettors at the hotel that night and told them we wanted to double up and catch up.

Unfortunately, the opposing gamblers had different ideas –

like they had already spent our money! They wouldn't budge off our original bet, although we only had one more day to go – one more match. They stuck to the same amount of money that was already on the line.

"The third day helped us out, but Titanic and I were still net losers of $9,000 apiece. But that third day of watching Raymond Floyd hit the golf ball was classic. The wind was up, and the greens were like lightning. But none of that affected Mr. Floyd; he shot a cool-running 66 to Lee's struggling even par. Our side was the losing side for the combined three days, but we had introduced two super golfers to one another, and I personally got a lot of satisfaction out of that plus watching some of the best golf – close-up – I have ever seen. Now I don't know whether I enjoyed it nine grand worth ….." The crowd's laughter drowned out Ace's self-induced laughter.

"Ladies and gentlemen, if you'll all look back to that back table next to the main banquet room door, you'll see the fantastic golfers I've been talking about. Please thank each of them for being here, and I know they are feeling the same reciprocation toward you."

Each of the players stood up and acknowledged the welcome and the illustrious story. The applause lasted a full two minutes with inter-sprinkled shouts of "more – more." Finally the crowd quieted, and Ace Darnell was back in control.

"Before I sit down, I want to share one more story with you about the unbelievable Titanic Thompson. Granted, it cannot match the one I've just previously tried to impart to you, and certainly the characters are not going to be as well-known as a Raymond Floyd or a Lee Trevino, but the story is just about as interesting, and it forever displays the confidence of a man who absolutely knew his own talents and how they would hold up under the toughest of pressure.

"The story began again at my place – The Redman Club on Ervay Street in Dallas, Texas. Titanic was in town again to play poker and golf. As I recall the year, it was sometime around 1950 somthing. For the fear of revealing some names and places that might cost someone a pension, or a job, or a college some sort of sanctions, I will keep the names and places in this story a secret. I will say that the event happened near here, somewhere in the Texas/Oklahoma territory that was then college golf's most hallowed ground. But before I get to the actual event, I've got to set the stage.

"Titanic had been in town for three or four days playing golf by day and poker by night. On the night of the fourth day of his current visit, the poker game stretched into the next day. It was a contagious game that captured all the original participants and a slew of want-a-be alternates. The game was pure high-stakes poker – no frills, pot limit, and a three-bump regulation. When the game took a lull because of a prolonged bathroom break by a couple of participants, the conversation turned from cards to college golf. There had been a recent article in the Dallas Morning News praising the current NCAA collegiate golf team of this renowned university as the best assemblage of golf talent in the history of collegiate golf. At the end of the article, the author summarized his assessment of the team as never again to be matched. I didn't notice it then, but when I think back, I'm sure I should have noticed the wheels turning in Titanic's head as to how he could capitalize on the article and such an interest being shown by his fellow gamblers.

"On purpose, Titanic never joined in the discussion, and he purposely let the interest peak before he made a comment."

"'Hey, Ace. How much in advance do you have to book one of those big party buses that you regularly lease for football games in the fall? Can you lease a big one on a week's notice?'

"I nonchalantly replied that I could get one of those damn buses right then and there if he wanted it bad enough. Then I turned toward Titanic expecting an immediate comeback. Instead, he just sat there, kinda set his jaw, and then cleared his throat to get everyone's attention.

"I really don't know much about college golf, but I know not many of them make it to the tour. That doesn't mean they aren't talented, but I suspect their popularity and the assessment of their game is hinged more on their college alumni support than actual abilities. I'm about to either make a fool out of myself or I'm about

to make my point. Tell ya what my proposition is: if all of ya'll will
rent the bus, and if Ace will set up the match – the time, the home
course of the team, and with, of course, the coach's permission. I'd
like to play their three best players – heads up; my ball against their
best ball of the threesome for 18 holes on their course – sight
unseen to me before the day of the match. Now, here's the kicker.
I'll entertain a maximum of 50 bets for $1,000 each, but for every
$1,000 bet on the four-ball bet – my ball against the other three –
every bettor has also got to bet another thousand on two out of the
three of my opponents against me – you can choose any of the two,
but you have to designate the two before the match begins. I'll
have a total of 100,000 bucks riding on my own ball. We'll play it
from the tips – the very back tees for all you non-conforming golf
addicts – and we'll play the ball flat – just like they play their little
tournaments, but, we're going to be playing match play – by the
hole – what the final scores are for each player doesn't matter a tin-
ker's damn. Do I have any takers, or are you all of the same mindset as me as to how college golf can stand up to an old hustler like
me?

"The poker game was a secondary subject now; everyone
started talking with everyone else about what kind of odds Titanic
was proposing. The consensus was that Titanic had finally made a
proposition that he couldn't live with. On a neutral course, maybe
Titanic would have a reasonable bet, but there was no way he could
beat the current NCAA champions on their own course with his ball
going up against the best of three! That bet seemed a cinch for all
the inquisitive. The mandatory second bet was less attractive – of
course. But if everyone was going to win the four-ball bet, then
everyone would be playing on Titanic's money on the second bet.
Titanic had successfully conveyed his proposition where the bettors
had fallen in love with their position. Titanic asked for a piece of
paper and a pencil to list the accepting bettors on his proposition if
Ace could arrange the encounter. The list reached a total of 21 individuals with promises of the remaining 29 before sunset on the following day. I was officially put in charge of the event, and I virtually guaranteed everybody that I could follow through on all of the
plans.

"Sure enough, when I got in touch with the coach of the collegiate champs, he was tickled pink at giving his top three players a chance to show their wares against the legendary Titanic Thompson. He indicated that he couldn't speak for each one of them, but that out of his top five players, he was certain that he'd have no trouble coming up with three of them who would be dying to accept the challenge. Coach and I had known each other for several years. We had played in fund-raisers together, and I had done some investigative work for him in the past on a couple of questionable scholarship cases that he needed to know some inside facts about. He also knew that I would never allow any of his players in my joint, and he knew I was good for any report on when any of his players had a tendency to visit other establishments that might jeopardize their scholarships. So he wasn't hesitant at all to call on my trustworthiness to guarantee silence prior to the event. The match was going to be a fun one for his boys, and although a certain amount of bad publicity was sure to get out afterwards, coach indicated that he could handle it. He did set certain requirements, however. The match would have to be played before school started, and none of his players could bet a dime. He said that he couldn't control spectators as to how they bet, and on whom. So the time and place were agreed upon, and the two party buses were rented to hold 50+ riders and a few wives and girlfriends.

"Because all of the action was previously booked, Titanic chose to drive himself to the site of the match. He figured that he had plenty of time after the match to socialize. As usual, he calculated and planned his preparations well. He got in touch and hired one of last year's team members as his caddy, and he showed up at the course four hours before the match. He got permission to substitute his practice ball session on the practice tee with the actual playing of all four par threes and the two ending par fours or par fives on each nine. After his practice was completed, Titanic took a cold shower and laid down for an hour to rest his weary legs. The caddy woke him 30 minutes before tee time. Titanic didn't hit another practice ball, but he did fine tune his putting stroke before the bell rang.

"The call to the tee was accomplished by the official starter stationed at his umbrella stand next to number one's longest tee box. When the participants arrived with drivers in hand, the starter unerringly introduced the players to the then-growing gallery. The game was announced as a friendly match between Titanic Thompson, from parts unknown, versus the individual players of the school and from their particular hometowns and high schools. At every introduction, the gallery murmured in anticipation of the big-money match. Cordial handshakes among the players followed the intros, and a coin toss between Titanic and one of the collegians determined the order of play. The collegians won the honors, and all three teed off before Titanic took the tee. Those young guns hit the ball out of sight, and the thought of Titanic not being able to keep up was paramount to Titanic backers. However, when Titanic's ten-degree driver smacked the three hundred plus dimpled, one plus inch, tightly wound ball, the game was officially on, and all of the fears from the young guns' drives were put to rest. Titanic's ball came to rest right in the middle of the fairway – a good ten yards further than any of his younger predecessors. The second shots were now the order of anticipation. The college player furthermost away hit a solid four iron toward the small, hourglass-shaped first green, but his sphere landed well left of the well-manicured green. The next two collegians hit the green, but the closest was 30 feet away from the pin. Titanic flushed his second shot, a seven iron, and it flew 20 feet beyond the pin placement. All of the collegians got up and down to halve Titanic. Except for Titanic out-driving his younger opponents, the first hole proved uneventful.

"The second hole was a medium iron over water to an elevated green surrounded on either side by deep sand bunkers. Two of the three college phenoms came to rest on the frog-hair while Titanic's ball came to rest right in the middle of the green. Unfortunately for Titanic, the pin was cut just over the water's edge at the very front of the green. Titanic's "greenie" was the third-closest to the hole. Again, everyone got up and down for team and individual halves.

"The third hole was a medium-length par five whose fairway was narrow and whose surface slanted heavily from left to right. All of the home course participants landed in the fairway but rolled into the heavy rough on the right. Titanic, known for his ability to work the ball, started the drive down the right side of the fairway, but drew it slightly toward the middle. Despite an unfavorable kick from left to right, Ti's ball held the fairway, and gave him a clear shot to the hole from a good fairway lie. All of the youngsters' shots went awry and missed the green. Titanic's ball rolled up to within five feet of the toughly placed back pin. The chip shots of Titanic's competitors were all short, and the closest one to the pin was six feet with a horrendous side-hill breaking putt from left to right. Titanic missed his eagle putt, but unbelievably, all three of the junior players failed to get up and down for their birdies, and he won the hole with a gimmie bird.

"Holes four, five, six, and seven were miraculously tied by Titanic. The boys couldn't buy a birdie putt, and everyone settled for pars.

"Going into the eighth hole, all of the competitors to Titanic were still one down. The eighth was a downhill par five that was long and narrow. Titanic was first to drive, and his tee shot barely rolled off the fairway into the first cut of the rough. Although Titanic was again the longest hitter, he was the one away from the green because he was on the long side of the fairway. Titanic hit his second shot first, and he laid it almost exactly 100 yards from the pin – right in a perfect opening to the green. The young guns couldn't help themselves in trying to reach the green when they saw Titanic lay up. All found trouble, and Titanic was clearly in the driver's seat to win the hole. Win it he did. His third shot almost found the bottom of the cup, but was knocked away by a stubborn pin that was slanted directly toward his approach. Titanic's gimmie birdie caused the other players to try too hard to get it close, and all the others settled for pars.

"As the ninth was parred by all players, the front nine tallied a two-hole lead for the old man versus the young guns.

"Titanic lost both the tenth and the 11th holes to birdies, and the four-ball bet was now even. However, the three-ball bets were all in Titanic's favor at one up. The 12th and 13th holes were halved, and the match moved toward the long and difficult 236 yard par three 14th. Titanic was now last to play, and he took advantage of the learning experience. The wind had picked up, and none of his opponents made the green. Titanic was a quick learner of the others' perils and selected to cut a three wood into the left-to-right banked green with his finest left-handed shot of the match. Titanic rolled in his long 20 foot putt for the win while the other players could only watch and cry.

"The number 15th hole was a par five that was far from a birdie hole, but everyone in the foursome managed one. The 16th was a tough par four against the now-growing wind. The odds of anyone coming away with an under-par score against that wind was at least 20-to-one in the odds market. True to the bookmaker's odds, all participants walked away with struggling pars. Titanic had to make a five-footer for the half, and he was later to say that putt was the key to the entire confrontation.

"More times than not, the 17th hole on a championship course is a par three. The rule held up in this case. Two of the collegians burned the hole for birdies, but gravity would not cooperate. The hole ended in a tie for all, and all bets went into the final hole dormy to Titanic's one-up lead on the four-ball bet while the combination three-ball bets had been closed out by Ti.

"The 18th hole was a par five dogleg left that held strategically placed traps interwoven all over the traditional landing area for the initial drive. Not a single player executed an acceptable shot for the caliber players that were involved on their respective drives. The second shots were just as miserably misplaced, and the match looked destined to a settlement for par at best for all participants. A couple of the young guns made good runs at hitting their third shots close, but all failed. Going into the 18th hole, the match was predicted by all of the spectators to end as if the 18th hole were never to be played due to the difficulty of the fairway bunkers. Certainly, Titanic was going to par the hole, and because of the difficulty factor under the present conditions, none of the others stood a reasonable chance of hitting their third shots close to the pin. However, something happened to the handicappers, and the match truly came down to the last putt. All of the youngsters drilled their third just past the pin. Titanic again elected to lay up to his traditional 100 yard range and stuck his third five feet under the pin. By the time everyone had assembled their third shots to the green, there wasn't a single golfer more than ten feet from a potential win. Time was clearly running out for the collegians, and everyone was aware that Titanic was about to run away with the wagon unless one of the youngsters made his difficult putt. Prior to Titanic's noble effort, all of the boys put forth their finest efforts, but it was not to be. Titanic then slopped in his five-footer without pressure for a convincing win on all fronts.

"Magnanimous Titanic walked over to the other players and personally congratulated each for a game well played. Drinks were served all over the clubhouse and out on the veranda. Ace – that's me – collected all of the monies due one to another and counted it out bank-style to the victor, Titanic Thompson. As the bus loaded up its passengers, Titanic offered to outfit the two buses with new liquor from the up-the-street liquor store, and the party started and departed.

"Later on, I had a chance to ask Titanic how he came up with such a bet, and if he were ever the slightest bit scared at the potential outcome. He told me that he had all of the betting angles covered in his favor. Pressure was his greatest ally. The boys were playing for their coach. At critical times, they were playing not to lose instead of playing to win. They loved the gallery, and they were not going to hit less than an aggressive shot if anyone was watching. 'To tell the truth, Ace, I figured it would be a cakewalk. If I had been in their shoes, I would have folded like a cheap skirt. I thought it was remarkable that all of them played so well. It was one of the most enjoyable experiences of my golfing career. In fact, I am a little ashamed at putting those young fellas down, when we were first organizing this thing – I'm telling you now – no doubt these kids can flat-out play!'

"Titanic played one more night of poker until he decided to get out of Dodge. The cockleburs were at work on Titanic's back side and he was ready to succumb. Although Titanic didn't have anything officially planned for his next hustle or his next destination, anyone who knew him knew he was already beginning a thought process designed to expect the inevitable – a wager that had a significant advantage for one Titanic Thompson.

"Titanic Thompson was one of America's most intriguing characters. He was a friend of all of us. He was a loyal husband – be it five times - and he was an honest gambler. I can say without hesitation that Titanic Thompson would never collect a dime on a bet if he thought there was a misunderstanding of the terms and conditions of the bet. That's why he always wrote down the specific terms. Like the casinos in Las Vegas, he always stacked the odds in his favor, yet there was always a gamble to it. Everyone involved in any wager with Titanic had a chance to win; he just made the proposition sound more in the favor of his opposition than the later facts would reveal. His secret to his own success: he handled pressure like no other individual player of any game that ever lived!

"I thank you all for being here. I thank you for your time in listening to me proudly tell of some of my experiences with the great one – Titanic Thompson, and I pray that all of us will treasure our time with the most entertaining human being who ever lived on American soil. Good night, my friends!"

Ace Darnell departed the speaker's stand amidst thundering applause and a standing ovation. Everyone who knew of Titanic Thompson also knew one of his best friends, Ace Darnell, and they all appreciated his reflections.

Chapter 12

With only modest prodding from his distinguished table in the back of the ballroom came one of Titanic's favorite local partners, direct from the now-named Ridglea Country Club, another of Ft. Worth's finest golfers, T. A. Avarello.

From his voice or his stature, no one would believe T. A. was 52 years old – here was a man that in 1947 was Titanic's partner in a couple of major partnership matches – at a ripe old age of 25. T. A. himself was next to legendary on the various courses in and around Ft. Worth, and his clutch performances that helped Titanic win a couple of famous partnership matches out at Ridglea are in themselves a local legend. Not everyone in the crowd recognized T. A. on his way to the podium, but enough catcalls from his present friends scattered around the gathering made everyone aware that T. A. was going to be something special for the audience. Dressed in his respectful blue pinstriped suit with a matching tie and front-pocket handkerchief, T. A. gently took hold of the microphone.

"My name is T. A. Avarello. I am a native Texan, and Ft. Worth has been my home of choice for more years than I care to remember, but I have enjoyed every one of those years. Because of this occasion, I am reminded of one particular year when I had the distinct honor of partnering with Titanic Thompson on a golf course. The year was 1947. The place where the action happened was a semi-private course at that time – Ridglea Golf Club. The professional at the time there was Raymond Gifford, and he is here tonight. Please give the other Raymond in this house tonight a hand. Stand up, Raymond, and take what you are due - he was also a wonderful friend of Titanic's."

When the crowd's applause died down, T. A. resumed his narrative.

"For most of my golfing years, I had been a fan of Titanic Thompson, and every chance I had, I was always a spectator when I had advance notice that he was going to be involved in a local match. It was my dream to play with Titanic Thompson. Some of my athletic friends wanted to be on the same ball field as Mickey Mantle, but I wanted to be playing in the same foursome with Titanic Thompson. How my dream became a reality is a short story that I would like to use as a prelude to Titanic's most famous challenge match of all time – between His Noble Honor, Sir Byron Nelson and our friend Titanic Thompson.

"My story begins this way. I was putting around the putting green with some regular players out at Ridglea Golf Club in the summer of 1947. We always assembled there about thirty minutes before noon every weekday except Mondays. Occasionally, there would be a challenge match of some sort that would come out of our gathering, and occasionally one of the regulars would bring in a ringer from out of town or another course in Ft. Worth, and then we would try to pair up with as even a match as we could muster using our established handicaps and reputations. By 1:00 or 1:30, all the games were set, and we would take consecutive tee times off number one till about two o'clock.

"On this particular day, for some untold reason, we were all slow in formulating our games. Then, almost right next to the putting green, the longest black Cadillac that any one of us had ever seen rolled up. What looked like a chauffeur got out of the driver's side door. He had a chauffeur's-type hat on – one of those short-billed hats that one only associates with a chauffeur. I was the first to notice that the tall, lanky gentleman who seemed to be posing as a chauffeur was none other than my golfing idol, Titanic Thompson. All of our attention was then momentarily disrupted when what all of us agreed was the most beautiful blonde woman any of us had ever seen exited the passenger side of the stretched Cadillac. Her hair was shoulder length and golden. None of us doubted that it had to be Veronica Lake. The truth is, however, none of us ever really found out who she was.

"Titanic strolled over to the pro's shack, as we called it. It was like a portable building – with a tin roof. Another gentleman got out of the backseat, opened up the trunk, and got out Titanic's golf clubs and shoes. After bringing the bag and shoes to the door of the pro-shack, the younger gentleman returned to the Cadillac, got into the driver's seat, motioned for Veronica to get back into the car, then turned that big bus around and left.

"Raymond Gafford, our pro, and the guy you all so generously welcomed a while ago, gave Mr. Thompson a welcoming handshake. The two of them had a private conversation for about ten minutes in closed quarters, and then Raymond summoned me over to the shack.

"'T. A., I want to introduce you to Titanic Thompson.'

"I'm telling you that I could hardly speak. How I did it, I don't know, but I stuck my hand out for a handshake and said that I was glad to meet ya.

"'Titanic is an old friend of mine, as you know, and he has dropped by to ask me for a favor. He wanted me to join him in a friendly little betting game this afternoon right here on my home course, but because my good friend didn't get to me in time, I have already committed to driving my wife to the dentist this afternoon. So he needs a replacement for me. He asked me if any of you hustlers out there had the gumption to stomach a real game of betting golf. I didn't have to look twice when I saw you out there, T. A., so I told him I would recommend you being his partner. What do you say?'

"I was dumbfounded. But I also saw an opportunity to live my dream, and I said that it would be my honor to play along-side Mr. Thompson. I also indicated that I had heard big-time stories about how much money Titanic had to bet in order to make it interesting, and I certainly couldn't carry my load on that front. No sooner than I got that statement out of my mouth than Mr. Thompson chimed in.

"'Young man, you don't need to worry about money. In fact, I rather like it that way – there'll be absolutely no pressure on you at all. You are in a no-lose situation. I'll finance the whole match, and if we win I'll cut you in for 25 percent of the action. Now, if I happen to place a few side bets along the way, they'll be mine alone – you'll only have action on the main bet and any presses that come after the original. Now it's important that all of this money talk stays with the three of us. I can get by speaking for the two of us, but I'm sure our worthy opponents will be thinking that you are on your own as far as the partnership bets are concerned. Also, I don't want you to be suckered into any side bets on your own – not from a bystander, and no individual bets at all. This is serious business for me, and I want my partner to have no other interest than in making our partnership come out on top. Got it?'

'Yes, sir,' I said. This was truly a dream come true for me, and I didn't stand to lose a thing – not that I would have ever expected Titanic Thompson to ever lose. So I agreed to all of the conditions, and I asked when it was tee time.'

"'The game is set for two o'clock. I told my two friends who aren't here yet that I would prefer to play at Ridglea, but I'm supposed to call them if I can get us the two o'clock tee time. Raymond says the course is ours at two, so, if you'll join me, I'm fixin' to give them a call if I have your word that you're going to be my winning partner.'

"As Mr. Thompson finished that remark, he smiled and looked right into my eyes. I told him that I never planned on losing at anything, and by all means, I wasn't goin' to let that happen today.

"When I went back out to that putting green after thanking Raymond for the setup, I didn't have to worry at all about any spike marks – I was high as a kite. I didn't let all the details be known to the guys, and I wasn't sure whether Mr. Thompson wanted a gallery or not, so I emphasized that this was a strictly private match that I'd tell them all about the next day. I then gathered up a couple of large buckets of balls – one for me and one for Mr. Thompson – and headed for the driving range.

"Side by side on the range, it was evident that Titanic Thompson was not a serious practicer on that day. He was joking around on every shot. He asked me to fade a shot, hook a shot, knock one down, and pop one up – then he'd do the same. I knew he was sizing up my game. But at the same time, he relished the opportunity for me to see him hit all the shots that he asked me to strike. He never missed a shot; he was mister automatic. I guess there was a method in that ceremony as well – he was building my confidence to the fact that he could really play! Finally, at about half until two, another new Cadillac pulled up, and two obvious-looking golf hustlers got out and fetched their bags. In those days, and now too, I could spot a hustler a mile away, and these two fit every qualification of a hustler.

"Back then, there was only one course at Ridglea – the North Course. It was semi-private, but anyone who had enough money for green fees could play it. There were several caddies who hung out there to be picked up in some of the big betting games, so the place really was a wagering golfer's paradise. The course played just over 6,100 hundred yards, and it was as tough a par 71 course as there was in the area. It was tight, and there were enough hazards to keep anyone honest on going for spectacular shots. The greens were splendid for those days even though they were all Bermuda.

"At just before two o'clock, all of the participants opted for a Coke, and then we walked together toward the number-one tee. The game was solidified along the walk. We agreed on a thousand dollar Nassau per man – as a reminder to you golfing novices, that's a grand per side, the front and the back, plus another grand for the overall 18 holes. It was always a match-play bet – only by the hole. One's gross score never mattered. In those days, that was a ton of money, and the original bet was sure to be doubled or tripled with presses. A press is a separate bet that originates out on the course when the losing side gets mad enough to want another bet. If it happens that the losing side gets down on the second bet, they can press again, then if they get mad enough again, if they are down on all preceding bets, they can press again. I'm telling you, I've been in on matches where there've been 50 presses in a single 18-hole match – that's 50 extra bets that are all at the same denomination of the first bet, it can really get out of hand. Now, at a grand a nine, and a grand for the 18, I didn't expect very many presses – even if I was with Titanic Thompson.

"As usual, one of our opponents flipped a tee in the air to determine who went first off number one. As I recall, our opponents won the toss. They were a couple of touring Texas hustlers from around the Dallas area, and I had never seen either of them play before that day – I hadn't even heard of their names before. But after they both hit it good right down the middle on their first tee shots, they got my attention.

"The front nine was a struggle. Of course we were playing by the hole – match play, but if it had been medal play, I know I would have taken home the booby prize – I'm not sure I broke 40. Mr. Thompson held us in there, though, and I can't explain it, but I really got it going on the backside. I had clear winners on three holes with uncontested birdies. We ended up winning the 18 hole bet by three holes with two to play. We won the backside by the same margin, and because we carried the tied front nine bet over to the backside, we won it by the same score as well. There were a couple of presses of a grand each on the last three holes, but we won only one hole out of the three – they won only one as well, and we broke even on the other, and the presses had no effect.

"Complications between all the contestants kept us from playing again the next day, but several days after the first match we hooked up again. This time, Mr. Thompson gave them two different kinds of bets on the front side: he gave them a one-up start on one bet, and a shot for one of our opponents on the fifth hole – a par five. Then Mr. Thompson agreed to give them another shot on the first par five on the back if we were net winners on the front side – net dollar winners. The 18 hole bet was without strokes – just a plain one grand bet by the hole.

"I've forgotten which bets we won and lost on that front side, but I remember we were down one of the bets, and we broke even on all the others – we were even on the 18 hole bet as well. On the backside, a I got hot again – I had two birdie winners, and Mr. Thompson had one. We ended up winning a net of five or six bets counting our one-bet loss on the front side. Without a doubt, those two days of being a first-time partner of Titanic Thompson were the highlight of my golfing experiences. I've been fortunate to win some local tournaments, and I've played in a bunch of pro-ams with some pretty famous people, but nothing was as thrilling as my times with Titanic Thompson. I had the privilege of playing a few more times in groups and occasionally in the same foursome with Mr. Thompson later in life, but I wasn't his major partner, and there wasn't any pressure on me to succeed for him. Those last experiences probably ranked second in my golfing career as my most exciting times on a golf course.

"Now I want to re-hear, and I want all of you who haven't already heard about the match of the 30s between Titanic Thompson and our immortal Dallas resident, Byron Nelson. May I introduce to you someone who I'm proud to share my table with back there, one of our most respected elders, Warren Williams."

Warren Williams and T. A. Avarello met in the aisle on the way to their new destinations – T. A. back to his dining table and Warren up to the front at the speaker's stand. A warm handshake slowed the progress of each, but the crowd was appreciative of both gentlemen and certainly didn't mind the wait.

"I was nearly 50 years old in 1934 when I was privileged to watch one of the finest golfing contests anyone has ever seen. As T. A. has eluded, it was between our favorite tour champion, Byron Nelson, and the man we are here tonight to honor, Titanic Thompson. The match was organized by three rich Texans from the area, and I won't bother to mention their names or identity for their privacy protection. They had a fancy for organizing the unbelievable, and this match was true to their form. Each offered a modest sum of $1,000 to the winner. For tour standards in that day, that was a big sum, but in the gambling circles that Titanic Thompson visited, that sum was paltry. The three businessmen were smart, though. They knew that if they could schedule the match at the convenience of both players, it wouldn't be the money that carried off the contest, it'd be the challenge! They were right! Both players signed on with freedom to each to handle their own side bets. For Titanic, that was music to his ears, and for Byron, his only motivation was his immense following from his loyal Texas followers who wanted to see him carry the tour torch to victory over a common hustler.

"The match was to be held at either Tennison Park in East Dallas or at Ridglea Golf Club in Ft. Worth. As it turned out, Ridglea was the easy choice, and arrangements were quickly accomplished. In the golfing community around both Dallas and Ft. Worth, word of the match spread like wildfire. Parking along the streets next to Ridglea was a policeman's nightmare. If parking tickets were issued in those days, they would have been as popular as napkins at a barbecue house. In spite of the terrible logistics in getting to the course, and in spite of the parking fiasco, boy, did the people come to the show. P. T. Barnum couldn't have planned it any better.

"I have no idea about how many or how much Titanic booked in side bets, but I know it didn't compare to all of the bets that were being wagered one to another throughout the crowd. Before I knew it, I had at least 20 bets going with people I had never seen before. The moment was magic, and I got so caught up in the circus that when I finally figured out all of my bets, I had to break even – I ended up booking the same amount of money on each guy, Titanic and Byron. It didn't matter, though, I saw one hell of a match!

"As I mentioned earlier, back then Ridglea was not a private course, and they only had one 18 – the North Course as we know it today. The yardage was about the same then as today, about 6,100 yards, par 71. The greens were well-shaven Bermuda, and the fairways were plenty narrow. As I remember, the course record at the time was 65, but back then there were no sanctioned records that were witnessed by very many people. The anticipation by everyone who knew golf was that everybody there was bound to witness a true new course record. But regardless, everybody was going to witness golf like no one had ever seen before. If it had been like today, the ticket sales would have topped any tour event but back then it was free entertainment.

"I can't remember which player won the honors on the first tee, and I might be a little fuzzy on the exact details of the rest of the match, considering it took place 30 years ago - and I wasn't exactly a 20 year-old at the time, but I'll do my best. There are certain memories that I can retain in my golden years – those things that have a special place in my heart as well as in my mind. Needless to say, this was one of those events. Please forgive me if I make a few mistakes on the exact numbers because it was the overall match that counted. The match has meant so much to my life that recollecting the experience is one of my greatest treasures, but every day that goes by, my memory of the details gets fuzzier and fuzzier. Well, enough for the disclaimers, let me share with you one of the most memorable days in my life and in the lives of all who went to the extra effort to see the match of the decade in person.

"The first hole was halved – both players hit short irons into the almost 500 yard par five for birdies. On the second hole, both escaped with rather lucky scrambling pars. On the third short par four, Byron birdied it and went one up. Byron knocked it close and converted for a birdie on the second par three on number seven. Byron had one more birdie on the front side at the ninth to finish with a two-stroke lead, and up by two holes for the match-play bettors. As they related to par, Byron was three under with no bogeys while Titanic had no bogeys either, but he only had one birdie – at number one.

"Both players got a drink and a candy bar at the turn. The lines at the restrooms were so long that both players had to take a detour to get to the tenth tee. Byron Nelson was the clear winner in every respect on the front side, and most of the gallery believed that that trend would continue. Titanic hadn't really hit anything close since that first hole, and everyone had virtually forgotten that piece of work because it was so long ago. Nevertheless, no one went home, and the backside was held in great anticipation by every golfer and non-golfer in the crowd.

"Titanic birdied one of the first two holes on the backside, and Byron birdied the other one. Both parred the third hole, and then Titanic got in the groove – he strung together three birdies in a row while Byron couldn't buy a putt. Byron rolled in a snake on the 15th to Titanic's struggling par. Both guys parred the 16th, and then Titanic caught fire again. Titanic banged in a birdie on the 17th and Byron settled for a par. For all practical circumstances, most of the bets were based on match play, and the match was over after the 17th, and Titanic was the winner. Both golfers were real gentlemen as they congratulated each other after 17 with Titanic the match-play victor. Then the two headed to the final tee. For the medal-play enthusiasts, the two had to play the 18th to determine the best in total stroke scoring. The par-five 18 was another 500 yarder. Titanic almost made the green in two. It was evident that some of the enthusiasm in Byron's camp was lost, and he decided to lay up the traditional 100 yards from the pin. Then both hit it close and each made his respective putt to close out a superlative day of unbelievable golf.

"Byron didn't lose anything to Titanic, he made his living with consistency on the tour – regularly beating the very best pros in a 72 hole format. When he won a tournament, he didn't have to win every round – it was the total of four rounds that paid. Byron beat Titanic handily on the front, and tall, lanky Titanic took it to Byron on the back. Incidentally, Titanic's 29 on the back gave him two records at Ridglea – the back-nine lowest score ever, and the overall 18 hole best score ever – a 64.

"As evidenced by the finest gentleman in the game being with us here tonight, Byron Nelson is a gracious competitor who will go down in history as one of the greatest tour players ever, and certainly its greatest gentleman among hordes of golfing gentlemen.

"As for Titanic Thompson after that heralded match, he took a pay cut for just being a winning participant! We all know that he went on with his regular lifestyle – whipping everybody who thought he had a chance against him – right-handed or left-handed.

"Golf is a funny game. The differences between a real match player and a real medal player are as different as a swimmer and a diver. Both use the same pool – the swimmer and the diver, just like the medal player and the match player use the same golf course, but it is really a completely different game. In match play, which all of us do every time we tee it up for a little wager or two on our home courses, it's match play. For the occasional barbecue tournaments that we all try to play in, it is a deviation to medal play, and if the truth be known, we don't fare so well under that format.

In the game of golf using the match-play format, there will never be, and there never has been, a greater golfer from either side as the wonderful Titanic Thompson."

The crowd began to stand in anticipation of Warren Williams's last remarks, and the loud cheers and clapping was thunderous to everyone on the River Crest property. Even the guard at the guardhouse gate had to hear it. It took Warren Williams a good ten minutes to get back to his seat. Of course he was slow due to his age and arthritic joints, but the real reason it took so long for him to get back to his table was that all of the well-wishers stopped his every step to shake his hand and wish him well. All the occupants of the great dining hall came to pay their respects to him regardless of where their own tables and seats had been. This fine gentleman was a local hero of sorts just because he was a witness to such an event, but he was also a respected man in the community who never refused an opportunity to talk about his favorite pastime – golf – and his favorite player of all time, Titanic Thompson.

Chapter 13

As Warren Williams took his seat among friends, Dwayne Douglas was already on his way to the podium.

"Ladies and gentlemen, tonight has been one of those rare experiences that each of us will treasure for a lifetime. We have been treated to extraordinary tales of meaningful experiences from very special people. For those of us who were listeners, such as I, it was just a plain, over-the-top experience. When I woke up this morning, I expected another day at the office; instead I have had the privilege to meet and hear from some of my all-time favorite people in history. In all my dreams, I could never have imagined being dealt this hand – I will remember you all for the rest of my life.

"I have been informed that the crew here at the club is out past their bedtime." Dwayne looked at his watched and gasped. "My God! It is half past one o'clock in the morning.

"What I have been sent up here to say is that we're all out of food, and the only drinks that will be left after this announcement are the beverages in the big black buckets over on the iced drink table. The entire club crew that so graciously volunteered for this lengthy duty is going home. We have been left the keys to continue on with our remembrances, but most of the refreshments are hereby declared gone. Please, let's all of us give a big round of applause for these fine people who came out of nowhere to accommodate us."

Dwayne led the applause, and then everyone rose from his seat to clap and hoot as loudly as he could in appreciation for the way everyone had been treated and accommodated. Then Dwayne brought the microphone back up to say a few more words.

"The funeral is scheduled to begin at one o'clock tomorrow – that's less than 12 hours from now. I have no intention to cut this appreciation reception short – by no means – but I have heard some hints that some of you are rather tired from the unexpected day's travels, and those folks want to get to bed before the sun rises." That brought a mixture of a few boos and some hardy laughter.

"So, having said that, I would like to suggest to those who wish to depart back to their hotels and motels, drivers are standing by out in front of the club to be of assistance to you. Because of previous commitments, I would like to remind everyone that each of us will be responsible for our own transportation to and from the services tomorrow at one o'clock. For those departing souls that just cannot take any more fun, we all wish you a safe journey, and we will see you tomorrow."

The crowd had naturally been thinned by a 100 or so, and was down in numbers to somewhere around 300 people when Dwayne finished his remarks. Then another 100 or so decided that sleep was the better part of valor, and they joined the already departed for places unknown.

Dwayne then addressed the remainder of the guests. "Just as a suggestion, let's all kinda regroup and consolidate around fewer tables. All the guests in the back, please pick a table a little closer to the stage up here and take up a new residence with some fresh new acquaintances. There's simply no telling how long we are going to be here, and new entertainment at some of the closer, half-empty tables will surely be a good thing. Now who wants to take a crack at our new-situated audience with some more famous Titanic Thompson stories?"

Several hands went in the air, and Dwayne pointed to the one furthermost to the rear of the banquet room. As the gentleman who was next to vociferate made his way to the podium, Dwayne reminded the audience, "Further appearances would continue on a spontaneous basis – whoever wants to be next, just come on up here and have at it – you don't have to be selected to join this party, and whenever the spirit moves ya, just come on up here and tell us what you've got on your mind. I assure you, we'll want to hear it."

Except for the immediate family that was still in attendance, almost everyone who had not taken the speaker's rostrum did so. Most just wanted to say that they wanted to at least be counted in this parade of well-wishers for Titanic's family, and they wanted to be on the record for paying their respects to their departed friend.

All of the living immediate family members of Titanic Thompson were present and still accounted for, but most declined their respective table companions' suggestions of saying a few more words. All were still awestruck by the magnificent attendance from so many of their's and Titanic's friends, and they still found it hard to believe that all of these friends had chosen to be there, and for many at great expense and some with great hardship. They were very grateful, and none of them wanted to be guilty of leaving early before everyone who had made such an effort to be there could be heard.

Nora Trushel, Titanic's first wife, who then married the noted bank robber Pretty Boy Floyd was seated at a separate table with friends who she thought she'd never see again. Titanic's second wife, Alice Kane, was a topic of conversation for all who knew Titanic back in his younger days, and all were so regretful that Alice never got to live out her life because of that terrible automobile accident in Pittsburgh. Joanne Raney of Topeka, Kansas, was Titanic's third wife and the father of Titanic's first-born, Tommy, and they sat comfortably together at the same table with friends who had meant so much to them when Tommy was a growing young man. From Norfolk, Virginia, was Titanic's fourth wife, the indescribably beautiful Maxine Thomas. Her sisters, Betty and Bonnie, joined her among other mutual friends from the past. Maxine was Titanic's junior by 40 years when they were married, and the years since their marriage had been very kind to her beautiful appearance. Jeanette saw the wonders of Titanic Thompson when she was only 18 years old, while Titanic was already 63. By the time Jeanette was 20, she had given birth to Titanic's second son, Ty Wayne, born in 1959 – only 15 years ago. Ty Wayne was proudly dressed and was proudly sitting next to his beautiful mother that had yet to reach her 36th birthday. The sprinkling of these family members amongst the gathered throng of Titanic's many friends was an unscheduled plus for the festive remembrances that had been so eloquently delivered. The occasion was so intimately close for everyone that the world outside did not seem to even exist.

After another almost two hours of one after the other participants in this unscheduled wake in which every single person made it to the podium to announce his or her name and a short rendition of his or her favorite occasion with the illustrious Titanic, the immediate family members sensed it was their time to make their appearance with a spoken word.

The group gathered on the narrow stage, hand in hand – arm in arm, at the invitation of host, Dwayne. Flashbulb after flashbulb made their sudden burst of light; it was almost like the Fourth of July. After all of the snapshots were taken, Jeanette took to the speaker's platform and caressed the mike.

"Because I was the last person here to see and hold our man, Titanic Thompson, I thought it appropriate that I should be the master of ceremony here concerning Titanic's immediate family. This is an unrehearsed gathering, and none of us up here expected anything like the tribute that each of you has made, first in being here, and second, in offering up such kind remembrances about our favorite fella.

"I want to personally thank each and every one of you for being here. I want to say that Titanic thought about each and every one of you on so many occasions that it is impossible to remember the times. Titanic died in his sleep undoubtedly unconsciously remembering several of his many experiences with some of you. His only suffering came from his lack of physical ability to continue a lifestyle that brought him such great pleasure in associating with each of you. Before I monopolize this opportunity, I just want to again say that I thank you all so much – again – for being here, and for being by Titanic's side whenever he needed you.

"Now, may I introduce to you Nora Thompson – the first Mrs. Titanic Thompson."

The remaining crowd stood and clapped in respect.

"Thank you all for your kindness to me, for your undying loyalty to Titanic, and for the special effort that each of you have made to be here. God bless each and every one of you."

After the applause died down, Jeanette introduced Joanne.

"Unfortunately, we are skipping another of Titanic's wives, and although I never had the pleasure of meeting her, I understand that she was a wonderful person. Please remember the late Alice Thompson as we will all remember each other at this gathering. I can't begin to tell all of you of one millionth of the happy times I had with my former husband, Titanic Thompson. He was generous, he was fun-loving, he was considerate, and he loved our son more than anyone knew. I am so grateful to God for my life with him, and I am so blessed by our son, Tommy. Thank you all for being here. You all have made this day more than a special remembrance for Titanic. You've made it a most special day for his family."

Again, the applause was almost deafening as Joanne resumed her place in the family line.

Jeanette then introduced someone more her age – only a little bit older – Maxine Thomas.

"Thank you, Jeanette. I first want to thank each of Titanic's family members for being here. I don't know that any of you have ever seen a gathering of four ex-wives of one man before - without a few shotguns." That really drew a chorus of laughs and clapping. "But it is a tribute to Titanic and to all of us that we can all still be grateful for the limited time each of us had individually with Titanic, and that despite all of us sharing his last name, we do not let that be a handicap to us being nice and loving each other. There isn't a one of you that is unfamiliar to me – I know I have heard Titanic talk about each of you. Thank you all for being here. I love you all!"

Jeanette gave Maxine a big hug, and then regained control of the microphone.

"I don't want to necessarily close out the opportunities for anyone else in the audience to come back and say a few more words, but for us on the stage right now, we have saved the best for last: Titanic's two boys. I don't know which one of you should be first to say hello to most of your daddy's best friends, but I know you'll both be appreciated equally as well regardless of the order in which you speak. Ty Wayne, why don't you lead the siblings off?

Ladies and gentlemen, I give you the last vestige from the life of the immortal Titanic Thompson, Ty Wayne Thompson."

The standing ovation was loud, spontaneous, and sincere. It lasted for a full three minutes. Then the almost 16 year-old took the mike.

"I'm really not the speaker type, but my mother said that I needed to say a few words, and now that I've been up here for a few minutes it doesn't seem so scary." The light applause obviously relaxed the youngster.

"My mom and I are honored to be here. Not even I know all of the stories associated with my dad, and I have been thoroughly excited listening to all of you. No doubt, my dad wasn't a perfect person, but I'm told that if you die with a bunch of friends that would go to the trouble to come to your funeral, you must have lived a worthwhile life. I call all of you a bunch of friends, and that makes my dad a special person. All of us up here feel that way, and it is comforting to me that you all feel the same way. I guess that's all I can say, except I thank all of you for being here as well."

Another standing ovation followed Ty Wayne's every step back in line. Then the applause grew into a crescendo to welcome Ti's first son, Tommy.

"My dad never told me that I would have to shake so many hands in such a short period of time. My right hand is about to fall off but I'm not complaining. Like Maxine said, I've heard about every one of you, and I am absolutely thrilled at being able to finally put a face to the names I've heard about so much. I've had the privilege of meeting a good number of you before, but now the book is complete – I've met the rest. I guess convenience is a terrible thing because I know all of us up here at the podium and all of you out there in the audience are having a wonderful time, and we all wish we had done this sooner if not more often, but it was always just too inconvenient. That's a shame. If I could carry one wish forward out of my dad's going- to-rest experience, it would be that each one of us never forget each other again. That would make my dad happy, and it would make all of us up here happy. All of you, make it a point to look me up when you come to my town, and I'll try to do the same when I come to yours. Thank you all for going out of your way to be here. I know my dad is so proud, not necessarily because you're here, but because you are his friends – always have been and always will be. Thank you very much for honoring him and all of us up here."

Everyone on the crowded podium gathered in one great big monstrous hug. Tears running down everyone's cheeks were common, there wasn't a dry eye in the place. For half of the audience, Tommy's last words signaled the end of the evening, and they gathered up their cameras and other belongings and headed either for their own transportation or the furnished limousines and cabs.

For those who remained, including Titanic's oldest son, Tommy, someone had discovered an open liquor cabinet. After little food for the last couple of hours, and still consuming large quantities of hooch, only the rowdies remained. The stragglers weren't thinking about free booze, or a chance to get drunk with their friends, they were just having the time of their lives being with and enjoying friends of the past.

It took about 30 minutes for the departing guests to say their final goodbyes, give the appropriate hugs, shake hands, and load up. Then the house remainders huddled up at five adjoining tables to continue the night. One of the previous servers was a real golf enthusiast, and actually asked his supervisor for permission to stay and look after the guests. No one associated with the club was afraid of not accounting for all charges because the local paper was good for anything and everything. The late-staying server saw no need to alert anyone because someone found an open liquor cabinet – he'd just note the consumption and add it to the bill.

Cigars were broken out with the assumption that anyone who didn't like their smell would have long been gone. The lighters were flaming all over the place, and the server decided that he needed a better answer than to suggest that there be no cigar smoking. He quickly ran to the men's lounge to see if continuing the party there was an option for the reduced-sized crowd. To his surprise, the cleaning crew had completed its job of cleaning the lounge, so he hurried back to spread the news. He told the group that since there were no more women present, it would be more convenient for everyone left to continue their evening in the men's lounge plus it was certainly more comfortable. Someone suggested that the idea was sound simply because the men's restroom was closer and more convenient.

The club employee offered to gather up everyone's drinks on a big serving tray and meet them in the lounge, and everyone expressed his appreciation but opted to carry his own drinks and cigars to the new party location.

The tables in the men's lounge were all four-place, square tables. The seats were all arm-rested leather mid-backed chairs. Cigar ashtrays were everywhere, complete with matches and coasters for the sweating drinks. Someone bunched up two groups of tables until there were two long rows of four tables each, packed full of Titanic friends and one son as the only relative. Then there were some threesomes and foursomes who occupied the remaining ten tables or so.

The conversations and drinks continued for another hour until someone decided that he had a better tribute to Titanic Thompson than the standard funeral that was supposed to take place in another nine hours. That someone was one of the grandsons of one of the alleged Mafia family leaders of days gone by, Tony III. He talked his plan over with his two other present family members, and they then called the head of the family corporation back home to run the idea by the boss of all bosses. Then he called for quiet and addressed his new-found buddies in the smoke-filled lounge.

"I need to get everyone's attention for a moment." A few of the guys hurriedly sought a stopping place to their stories and then turned to listen to their new-found friend.

"My family members who made this trip with me have joined me with a proposition that I think you all might like. We have taken the liberty of calling our senior family members for permission to make an offer to Mr. Thompson's family and to you – the stay-with-it-group – that's still here. There is a great deal of probable expense to our offer, and my family is prepared to cover all costs and to indemnify everyone who might object to our actions. I know your curiosity is about to kill you right now, so let me tell you what we've got in mind. Again I say we will cover all responsibility if you all agree with our proposition.

"Before I get into the meat of the plan, I need everyone present here to make a kinda pledge to me and my family." The entire listening audience – all in unison – squirmed from one side of their chairs to the other.

"Now I think you all know that my family and I take these pledges most seriously. We don't want to talk anyone into supporting our plan, but if we have a solid majority of support, we hope the ones that might not be sold on our plan at first would give way to the majority and lend their unqualified support. This is an expensive proposition, and I remind you all that all expenses, foreseen and unforeseen, will be totally my and my family's responsibility.

"Here's our plan: Titanic Thompson has been known for his golfing prowess more than anything else. He loved the game, he loved its players, and he made his living dealing with both. All of the people who put aside their business and personal responsibilities to be here to honor Mr. Thompson until now were going to leave with two things: a grateful feeling that they had the privilege of being among all of Mr. Thompson's friends, and an empty feeling that each one of us couldn't do more to say a proper goodbye to our beloved friend. Does Mr. Thompson – our friend and the source of ours and my family's greatest memories – deserve to be buried in a public cemetery? After careful thought, my entire family thinks not and they hope you agree. Mr. Thompson deserves to be buried within the confines of what he loved most – a golf course – and a golf course that he loved to play – like right where we are tonight – at River Crest Country Club in Ft. Worth, Texas, near where he loved to live, and near where he ultimately died.

"My family and friends who are here have already talked to several of you who have some expertise in golf-course maintenance, and we have an employee of the club with us who can tell us where everything is that we need to use. Now it comes as a pretty easy chore for any of my family members to do or assist in doing a quiet burial." That comment really got everyone squirming, but squirming in laughter and hand-slapping.

"We propose that we go back to town, reverently gather up Mr. Thompson in his casket, and drive him back to the club where we are right now. While a group of us attends to the task of bringing Mr. Thompson back here, another group of us will summarily start to destroy a part of the 18th green. Now you know I don't really mean destroy it, but we are going to damage it a bit. We'll pick the highest point on the green to disturb, and we will dig a six-foot-deep hole just big enough for Mr. Thompson's casket to occupy. I'm telling you, we've had plenty of experience in doing a job like this, and aside from a few lines that signify the installation of some newly sodden putting green grass, no one will be able to tell what we've done – only the group here right now will know what happened. We'll clean up all of the spare dirt, we won't leave tracks, and everyone except the greens' attendant will just figure the maintenance crew replaced a patch of grass. Someone will have to clue in the greens' superintendent, but I never sweat the small stuff – I assure you all that he will be a happy camper with this idea. The key to this event being successful and independent of local knowledge is for us all to take an oath of silence.

"I want to take a vote right now. Mickey, will you tear up some of those gin rummy score pads and pass out some of those pencils? This is going to be a secret ballot vote. No one is twisting your arm – you're either in or you're out with this plan. Vote by writing a yes or a no. Now, Mickey, get these votes in quick and put them in that big punch bowl over there." Tony III pointed in the direction of the enormous bowl on the buffet next to the door.

In five minutes, the bowl was half filled with penciled-in votes and it was handed by Mickey to the obvious senior member of his family, Tony III. Tony then addressed Mickey one more time.

"Mickey, grab yourself another gin rummy pad over there and keep track of the votes as I count them out loud."

Tony III then began to pick out the folded paper contents of the punch bowl.

"The first vote is a yes – in favor of the project. The second vote is also a yes."

The tally went on as fast as Tony III could open the folded votes. Not one single nay. When there was only one vote remaining, and all of the previous votes were in favor of the plan, Tony III stopped and, almost crying, re-addressed the suspended audience.

"I'm not going to open this last vote because the plan clearly passed, and I want this damn thing to be unanimous. If there is any one of you that wants a negative last vote counted in the negative, then speak now or forever hold your peace!"

The whole room exploded in yells and back-slapping.

"Now, we've only got about four hours left before daylight, so we're going to have to get to work fast. Mickey, you're in charge of taking five or six guys back to the funeral home and pick up Titanic. My other family member that's here – scar head – he got that name from bumping his head pretty bad when he raised up too quick in one of our family pickups , probably going out to bury someone just like we're goin' to do – ha! ha! Anyway, scar-head, you get the club server over there and take Jim and Bob over at table number one, and head to the maintenance barn to get the tools we're going to need. Jim and Bob know all about golf course maintenance, so they'll be able to recognize what we're going to need to leave this place like we found it – except with our beloved Mr. Thompson buried where he ought to be – underneath the putting surface of his favorite 18th green. Jim and Bob, you're our two architects, so get your thinking caps on – we're all counting on you two to get this plan workable. There'll be plenty of time to celebrate our completed task later, but until it is completed, please – no horseplay, no jokes, just plain work. Let's go get it done!"

Chapter 14

Tony III remained outside the main clubhouse next to the 18th green awaiting his two subordinates' actions that would bring him Mr. Thompson's body and casket and the necessary maintenance tools to accomplish the task at hand. He was the supreme coordinator. He kept a bevy of other volunteers who were on call to do anything that might arise to get the final job done. They were to relieve any future bottlenecks. One thing that Tony thought the requisitioners would not think of was a broom. Without thinking to use a courteous tone of voice or a pleasant choice of words, he grabbed the first funeral attendee who was closest to him and barked out orders to go and find him a broom. Tony III was thinking that the whole surface of the green would be needed to be swept clean after burial was complete.

Mickey had requisitioned the only remaining funeral home limousine that remained at the club when the plan was approved. He introduced himself to the limo driver, Steven Clinton, and tried to foster a quick rapport – he knew he was going to have to trust him explicitly as the night would wear on. He then commandeered a taxi to carry the other two members of his team in the kidnap party that was going to retrieve Titanic Thompson's casket and body. On the way to the funeral home, Mickey was able to concoct a plan that would accomplish his assigned task and still protect the limo driver who would surely be fired for cause if anyone found out about him being an accomplice in the ordeal. Mickey first slipped the limo driver a cool $500 in hundreds to begin his plan. Then Mickey made the driver swear that his silence had just been bought, and that he understood the consequences in opening his mouth thereafter. For emphasis, Mickey made sure the limousine driver knew from where he came and he asked repeated family questions. Mickey also agreed to pay him another 500 the next day if the plan went off without a hitch tonight.

The limo and the taxi pulled up to the front of the funeral home at about the same time. Mickey went over to the taxi driver and paid him off with a handsome tip to not remember his last fare – then sent him on his way.

Mickey and the limo driver then instructed the rest of his crew to hide out of sight until he whistled the all clear from the rear of the building. Then they were to come running, but they were to stay in the shadows, and certainly stay out of sight.

When Mickey tried the rear door, it was locked – predictably. But, thank goodness, the key to open that door was on the key chain belonging to the limo. Steven was only a few steps behind Mickey, but he had anticipated the locked door, and he carried the key ring that held the door-opening key.

Steven slipped the key into the rear door lock and turned it easily to open the door. Because of a couple of late-night pickups of cadavers in recent weeks, he remembered the security code to the security system that was located on the wall just inside the main back door, and he moved quickly to the code box and inserted the proper numbers in the proper sequence. Both Mickey and the limo man waited intensely for the three minutes of waiting time until a bad code insertion would trigger the alarm. When three and a half minutes went by, they sighed a sigh of relief and Mickey opened the back door to whistle for his companions. They came running, and Mickey hurriedly rushed them through the door and into the hall that led to the various viewing rooms.

The limo driver then motioned Mickey and two of their helpers to follow him to the casket storage room. They entered without a problem and turned on the light. There were no windows in the storage room so they were safe to operate in lighted circumstances. Steven remembered the type and style of Titanic's casket and removed one just like it from one of the storage shelves. The two helpers then carried the new casket down the hall and into Titanic Thompson's viewing room. The ever-thinking Steven secured a collapsible rolling casket dolly, and rolled it into place, then with the help of his tag-along helpers, Steven instructed the crew on just how to transfer Titanic Thompson's casket and remains to the sturdy dolly. The empty casket that was the exact model and color of the one being removed was carefully placed in its place. It was not unusual for the caskets to be closed during closed viewing times, so the limo driver closed the bodyless casket and straightened up all of the flowers and drapes that surrounded the former casket – everything was put back in place just as it was found. Unless someone opened the casket, the switch would never be noticed, and it was customary for no employee to ever open a casket unless he was in the presence of a family member or one of the funeral directors. The limo driver then directed the loading of Titanic's casket still strapped to the folding dolly into one of the hearses in total darkness – the outside parking lot lights had been extinguished by Steven.

Steven was now a common name for everyone in the group who knew the limo driver as if he were an old brother. Steven then took over the driver's seat and loaded the rest of his crew into the back of the hearse lying down and out of sight. Mickey took the commanding right front seat, the shotgun seat as he and his friends referred to it. As the limo was put in forward gear, Steven suddenly stopped the vehicle and asked that everyone stay where he was, and to be patient – he had to go one more time through the building to make sure that nothing was out of place – turn back on all of the parking lights, and then reset the security alarm.

In another five long minutes, Steven returned with a smile on his face, and reentered the long-black hearse. Steven chose all of the freeways for his route back to River Crest because they would be the least conspicuous for a hearse to travel at that time of night.

During the same time that Mickey was fetching his body and casket on his individual assignment, scar- head began working with his crew under several red-lens-coated flashlights. They gained entrance to the maintenance barn through a lucky window that had been left open. They were also lucky that there was no security system on the barn, and there was no roving security person to worry about other than the night watchman at the faraway entry gate.

Thank goodness, the entry gate was over a mile away, and completely hidden from view from the maintenance barn. Because the maintenance barn was in a secured area that no one on the outskirts of the club could see, scar-head's crew could peruse the contents of the barn in light furnished from a typical light switch. They found the following as necessary tools that all agreed were absolutely essential. They commandeered two maintenance golf carts that had been altered to be electric golf cart pickup trucks. One even had a power-tilting dump-truck assembly. Into these, the crew loaded numerous shovels, a couple of mattocks and picks, a grass removing machine, two five-gallon cans of gasoline, four 50 foot extension cords, a green roller that had to be filled with water to make it heavy enough to press down newly planted or laid grass, and a 50 foot water hose to fill the canister in the grass roller. Additionally, the crew loaded up a tamping tool, two foot-powered edgers, a hoe, and a power blower.

The six-man crew of scar-head then drove its stash to the burial site at the back of the 18th green. Tony III saw them coming in the moonlight, and was waiting for them at his choice of digging sites. Scar-head was smart enough to stay on the cement cart-paths throughout his journey – even to within a few feet from the back of number eighteen. Before they unloaded anything, Tony, III wanted an explanation of all the tools brought to him and their purported use. When Jim and Bob had explained their acquisitions and their intended use, Tony asked if they had noticed a large tarpaulin or two. Scar-head looked to the others for their answers, then he replied that they had not noticed one. Tony III then dispatched Jim back in one of the golf carts to go back to the maintenance barn to to look for one.

Scar-head was back in five minutes with a 20 foot by 20 foot square tarp. It was perfect to load the shoveled dirt onto, and it would prove a superb cleaning mechanism later on for the residue dirt that could not be removed from the site by just a shovel. Tony was an advanced thinker.

While Jim was running his newly assigned errand, the others began to take direct orders from Tony III in starting their undertaking. Bob was assigned the task to draw out the parameters of the intended hole. One of the crew was sent into the clubhouse to switch on the porch lights that would give them enough illumination to accomplish their job, and another was given the task to pay a visit to the entry guard house and the enclosed night watchman. The best dressed of the bunch was the chosen one for the night watchman duty, and he was to assess the situation to determine what course to take for the expected entrance of the hearse, and for all of the activity occurring around the 18th green should the night watchman have a hankering to take a little walk. One of the instructions that Tony III gave was to find out when and why the guard might leave his station – like a restroom visit, or to just run the grounds.

While interrogating the guard after a careful entry into his shack, the hearse with Tianic's body rolled up to the gate. The nattily dressed businessman who was sent to the guard house by Tony III started to laugh as the hearse stopped for clearance to pass. The guard got up and asked what was so funny?

The businessman replied, "What a funny sight this is. The funeral home sent word that they had an abundance of canned drinks and some beer in their fridge since the club had shut down the kitchen. They just want to help, and their choice of a delivery vehicle is certainly comical."

The guard began to laugh, and motioned for the big black hearse to proceed. The businessman then began to interrogate his new-found friend. The resulting answers gave the businessman a lot of comfort. The guard was listening to an all-night radio station, and he said that he rarely ever left his post for any reason. Once or twice a night, he would go outside to take a leak, but he never ventured up to the clubhouse for any reason. The businessman then offered to bring him a drink, but he thought he had been gone long enough from the continued party. After earlier explaining the funeral wake, the assigned businessman left the guard house confident that all was well, and that the guard posed no problem to their plan – especially now, after the awaited hearse had just gained clearance.

By the time the businessman and the hearse arrived at the clubhouse entrance, they could see the remarkable progress being made by Jim and Bob under the direction of Tony III on the burial site. All of the grass had been stripped away with the grass stripping machine, and it was all rolled up in one-foot widths in ten-foot lengths, ready to be re-sodden at a moment's notice. The hole was surprisingly deep already, and the sides were as straight and measured as possible. Jim and Bob's crew took turns with two diggers at a time employed to do the digging. Tony III had suggested only a three-minute tag team because time was of the essence, and fatigue was a time-limiting factor that they simply could not afford. The once-well-dressed shovelers were now absolutely filthy. A forethought to undress down to the bare essentials was certainly a good idea. They could always take a shower when the job was completed. Their shoes were the problem. Tony, III recognized that as a problem almost immediately after the grass stripping had begun. He sent Jim back to the maintenance barn to search for rubber boots, but only three pairs were found, and they didn't fit all of the digging volunteers. Nevertheless, they managed.

Two and a half hours after the deceptive burial plan was approved, the grave was pronounced deep enough, secure enough, and ready for a dropped casket. Steven had had the forethought to bring spare ropes for the sole purpose of letting down the casket into the grave. Very carefully, using all of the ropes that Steven had brought, the entire group of the masquerading funeral directors lowered their best buddy into their hand-dug gravesite. When the casket hit the bottom of the hole, the ropes were pulled clear, and one of the associates climbed down to make sure the casket was level and secure. When the associate was pulled by hand out of the grave, Tony III wasted no time in ordering the shovels back into motion to refill the grave from the dirt on the tarp. Again, the tag team approach was used. It took almost 30 more minutes to hurriedly refill the hole, level it with the rest of the green, and reinstall the once-removed sod. The leftover dirt was shoveled onto the dump bed golf cart and driven off to the nearest creek bed for a quick drop. The tarp was carried off in the other cart to be shaken clean at the same location with the other removed dirt. Two men had already filled the roller drum canister of the green roller and began to roll the re-sodden turf to make it level – on the same plane

– with the four bordering sides of the green. Almost at the same time, another two-man crew began the sweeping exercise to rid the area of recognizable dirt. When all was done, the 50-foot water hose was brought over to give the sod a thorough wetting. All the tools, the hoses, the stripping machine, and all of the other paraphernalia were loaded back into the two now-emptied electric golf cart pickups and were put back in the exact places within the maintenance barn from which they had come.

Tony III gave one further order. "Everyone return every conceivable thing to its rightful place where it was prior to this exercise – then everyone clean up in the men's locker-room – I'll meet everyone back here at this spot in exactly 30 minutes. That'll give us a good hour to vacate this place before sunup. Now get going – you all did one hell of a job! But remember, one out-of-place tool or anything carelessly left exposed could cause us tremendous problems – be thoughtful to leave everything just as you had found it."

In less than 30 minutes, everyone had cleaned up, and all were meeting without a sound at just the prescribed spot that Tony III had designated. Then again, Tony took charge and addressed his proud troops.

"Gentlemen, you have done our friend Titanic proud, you have done me proud, and most importantly, you have done you and your friends proud. We accomplished what we set out to do, and we did it well within the time-limit parameters that were available to us. I'm telling you just like it is – I've never been prouder to be associated with as fine a bunch of guys. I don't know if any one of you has pastoral experience, but I'd be glad to defer to anyone that would be kind enough to offer a prayer for our fallen hero. Silence gripped the morning night air, and everyone was rooting for a volunteer. Finally, finally a familiar voice broke the silence with the Lord's Prayer. After his revered rendition, he addressed the Lord himself in the name of the Thompson family, and then on behalf of all the standing volunteers to this most unusual event.

He ended his prayer with, "and God bless my Daddy."

Everyone was emotionally moved, and without exception everyone knelt on the grass next to the now fabled 18th green and offered his own private prayers for future guidance of his own life, and to please remember Titanic Thompson's family. Tony III broke the silent prayers with a loud and sturdy Amen. Then he said that there were a couple of more problems to take care of before and during the regularly scheduled funeral.

He said, "Somehow, first thing before the funeral home opened its doors, he would get the family members to agree to a closed casket visitation and funeral. The funeral in all respects should go on just as if this night had never existed. Someone at River Crest was going to have to inform the head greens-keeper, and explain what actually happened, or make some excuse for the relayed sod. Either way, there should be no afterthoughts about what happened. Quite honestly, if anyone had told you what you have just helped do, you would have called them crazy. So a made-up story would be better believed, and the greens keeper would be more likely to believe what made us replace his turf. I will take on the two tasks involving the greens keeper and the closed casket within family. I'll want your help on the closed casket issue, Tommy, if you can see fit to do so.

"The other thing that must be adhered to, come hell or high water, is to remember our code of sworn silence; this event must not leave the lips of all of us who have been involved. We all swore to secrecy, and secrecy it will be. We should all take those oaths very seriously – I know that I do.

"Enough said already – let's go get some shut-eye, and let's look for one another at the funeral parlor tomorrow just before one o'clock. Be careful when talking around strangers – we're not really hiding anything, we just have a secret. Goodnight all.

Chapter 15

The morning wakeups for all of the burial crew from the night before were especially hard. For everyone who wanted to get to the scheduled funeral on time, they would have to leave their night's lodging by noon. That meant everyone had to get up by ten or so to allow enough time for a quick breakfast or snack and enough time to get dressed in proper attire. Everything considered, that meant that the hours available for sleeping would be only three or four. After all of the night before's activities and all of the consumption of inebriating substances, sleep was going to be one ingredient of the day that all would wish they had more of.

Somehow, all the friends of Titanic Thompson who came to Ft. Worth, Texas, with the intent of paying their respects at Titanic's funeral made it to the church on time. The best dressed were Tony III, Mickey, and scar-head. The funeral was to begin at one, and Dwayne Douglas and his boss, Ben Winkleman, were satisfied that everyone who Dwayne had told him about was present and accounted for. The parking lot was overflowing to the tune of serious street blocking from all of the cars parked and double parked along the curbs. The funeral parlor, the foyer, and all of the hallways inside the medium-sized funeral home were packed shoulder to shoulder and heel to toe.

The organ musician began his playing shortly before one o'clock, and all of the funeral-home-supplied vehicles were in their places by the same time. As if the funeral directors had a premonition concerning the overflow crowd, they were ready in all respects.

Last night's limousine driver, Steven, was Tony III's key to everything going as planned for his wrap-up chores. He was to be the second person to arrive at the funeral home when it traditionally opened its doors around nine o'clock. He was to be well-groomed and showing no wear from the night before. After he was inside in the presence of one or more of the employees, he was to call Tony III, leave a short message, and then hang up the telephone and wait for a return call.

Tony III called back as scheduled, and pretended to be Tommy Thompson, Titanic's first son. By proxy, Tommy left instructions that the family had decided that they would prefer to remember Mr. Thompson as they had left him last night – in the company of all his friends. He emphasized that each of the family members had said his or her private goodbyes, and they would prefer that those remembrances be their last. They requested that the casket be closed first thing this morning, and that it remained closed throughout the services and burial, and he was the one whom they had elected to call the funeral home to deliver the request. Steven tried to write down Tommy Thompson's instructions as fast as he could, then he delivered them to the now-present director who had just walked in the back door. Steven then took it on himself to go into the viewing room, check the casket, seal it, and rearrange the flower blanket to cover the top of the now-sealed casket.

Steven's next stop was to the early arriving director's office for a personal request.

"Mr. Jamison, I've got a special request concerning the Thompson funeral. I know that I'm your number-one limo driver, but for this funeral, I'd like to go back to my old job, and drive the hearse. I've gotten rather attached to the deceased and all of his friends and family. I admit that this is a strange request, but I have my reasons and I hope you'll consider the change."

"Al (the scheduled hearse driver) isn't in yet. When he comes in, you work it out with him; it's OK with me. You know you're probably forfeiting a pretty good tip. If I were you, I'd try to get Al to split it. He wouldn't be getting any of it anyway if he were the hearse driver."

"You're right. I'll see Al when he gets here, and I'll proceed just like you suggested. Thank you – we'll both do a bang-up job. By the way, how many other limos have been scheduled?"

"Five, other than our regular three. They are coming with their own drivers, so you and Al will have to organize them. For God's sake, make sure they know they should drive with their lights on!"

With the duties of being the limousine driver automatically comes the responsibility of loading the casket, unloading the casket, and lowering the casket into the grave. Mickey and Tony III had done an excellent job of recruiting, paying, and building a faithful relationship with Steven, and it was handsomely paying off.

Not wanting to wake Tony III up, Steven called Tony III's motel and left a written message for him with the morning attendant. He relayed the message that everything was well in control, and that he would meet him in the funeral home parking lot around 12:30.

Tommy Thompson called all of the family members at their overnight locations and suggested a family meeting at a quarter after noon at the funeral home. He also offered to pick up anyone of the family who needed transportation, or if they preferred the funeral home limousine would ferry them to and from the services.

At shortly after 12:30, the family members entered a closed-door family meeting held in one of the other vacant viewing rooms. Tommy had decided on coming clean with all of the family members after he had talked separately with each one of them when they arrived. He sized up the situation perfectly, and he was convinced that there would be no dissenters. Then, with all present, he informed the group of the previous night's activities.

"I have something very important to share with all of you. Some of you might not know me as well as the others, but there is not a family member or another person on earth that could ever say that I didn't love my father more than anyone else in the world – except my mother." Tommy looked Joanne's way with a wink and a nod.

"I want three things to come from this funeral – I want my dad to get the kind of funeral he deserved. I want all of his family members to remember the funeral as a wonderful goodbye to my Dad, but more importantly, to remember being with all the rest of this now close-knit family unit. And lastly, I want all of those special friends of my Dad's to leave here with a glad heart, a heart full of love and remembrances of my Dad and his thoughtful friends that came to honor him.

"That leads me to what I want to share with you. Last night, after all of you left that wonderful tribute to my Dad, about a quarter of the original crowd remained. They were not the crazies or the drunks; they were the real appreciative friends of mine and Ty Wayne's dad, and all the rest of yours husband. When the stories continued among that group that remained, each one would have brought tears to your eyes because of the sincerity that was attached. Finally, one of the guys who was here representing a couple of the families from up north – you know who I mean – the mobster-looking guys, but I'm sure that doesn't really exist today. Anyway, he called me aside and said he had just checked in with his family, and he wanted to run a proposition by me. I was all ears.

"He said that all of the family had loved my Dad so much that they wanted him to be buried in someplace special, and whatever the costs were, it didn't matter. Of course, I was taken by complete surprise, and my first thoughts were of all the planning, and etc. that has gone into all of this by Jeanette. I immediately thought that they wanted to ship my Dad somewhere else or something. But they didn't. They just thought that my Dad would appreciate someone thinking about his life enough to want to have him buried in someplace where he truly would want to be. He said that when all of the family and the godfathers got together, they couldn't get away from one primary thought. If Titanic Thompson could pick his own burial site, it would have to be on a golf course, and it would have to be on one that meant a great deal to him.

"They proposed to me that we bury my Dad on the 18th green at River Crest Country Club here in Ft. Worth. I nearly fell out of my chair. The guy, Tony III, was the one telling me all this. He grabbed me, looked at me with tears in his eyes, and said that we could do it. I didn't know what to say. I thought about each one of you, but according to Tony, we couldn't do it as a regular funeral – there might be too many objections. We had to do it under the cover of darkness right then and right there. He said that he was overpowered with the thought, and he didn't want to meddle in the family affairs, but the offer was too good to pass up without a vote of some sort, from everybody available. He even asked me to call all of you, but I told him that I didn't have all of your numbers at the time. Then he had another suggestion. He said that all of the people that were still there represented the salt of the earth to my Dad, and that absent the first consideration – the family, they should be given the right to vote as to whether it was a good idea or not. I'm not copping out on you, but I just didn't know what to say, so I told him to get everyone's attention, explain the plan, and then see if they were for it.

"Tony did just that. He was marvelous with his praise for my Dad, and he kept stressing that his family would be totally responsible for any and all costs, for any negative publicity – which he said there wouldn't be if all went right – and for any costs down the road if something unforeseen came up. He conducted a secret ballot among every single person present after his thorough explanation of how the plan should be carried out. After he passed the hat to collect all of the folded-up votes, he read them each one at a time. It was unanimous – every single soul voted to have his friend buried under the 18th green at River Crest. He even set the unfolded votes on the table for anyone wishing to examine them; they could do so.

"Now, again, I couldn't think of anything else but all of you. I tried to put myself into each one of your shoes. I tried to think of all of the negatives, but I kept coming back to a bunch of dedicated friends who were willing to risk their lives if they got caught, and a bunch of sincere friends who wanted to pay for the whole thing. How wrong could that be? I kept asking myself. Finally, I gave my go-ahead, and I spoke for all of you. I realize that I had no right to do that, but I did it, and I thought then as I do now that each one of you would approve my actions. Now, if you want to shoot me, then go ahead. I'd rather be dead than to disappoint any of you. I haven't told my mother this because I thought that we were all in this together, and no family member should be told before another."

Nora was the first to speak with an interrupting shriek. "My son, and you are my son to me – you and Ty Wayne – I'm so proud of you. You did the right thing; you did exactly what my husband, Titanic Thompson, would have done for his father, and he would have been proud of it – I for one am in full support of you. But you'll have to tell me one thing: What are we going to tell all of those folks waiting out there to go to a funeral that they've been expecting for two days?"

"Nora, Tony has thought of everything. We – everybody who was left in that ballroom after you all left – buried dad early this morning. The burial site is so cleaned up that nobody could possibly tell what had happened. Tony, Mickey, and their family brother, scar-head saw to it that another casket replaced the one that Dad was in – same kind and same color. The casket sitting in that chapel right over there doesn't have a body in it. It is totally empty!

"What we're goin' to do, if everyone agrees, we're goin' to have the funeral that was planned all along. Only there won't be a body in the casket. There will be all the tributes, the prayers, the eulogy – everything – but Dad will be there only in spirit. He will enjoy it just the same as if his body had been there."

Now it was Maxine's time to interrupt. "Tommy Thompson, I cannot believe what I'm hearing. I can't believe someone would think of such a thing, but God bless them for it. I cannot think of anything more than our family getting together that would make Titanic happier. Let's face it. Our man wasn't cut from a cookie-cutter. He was a true individual, and he loved to deviate from the norm. You just made that possible. My only question is, how do we thank these people? How do we know who they are among all of the others? And, can we tell them that we know all about it? And how and when do we express our gratitude to them?"

"I can think of nothing more pleasant than for every one of them to hear your exact words. Thank you so much, Maxine. My heart is pounding. I wanted so much for you all to be pleased with my sudden decision."

"Jeanette, I can't stand it any longer. What do you think?"

"Well, I don't know how you're ever going to make a nearly 16 year-old young man keep this kind of secret, but I think it is the best tribute to a loved one I've ever heard of. Ty Wayne, I want you to let us know your thoughts, because you are burdened with having to keep this secret longer than any of us – you've got the longest to live!

"Mom, I'm kinda in shock, but if you think it is right, and if Tommy thought it was right last night, I'm sure not going to be the one who says it isn't. My Dad loved golf. It was his job, his hobby, and his life. To know that he is buried where he would love to be seems very fitting to me. I really think it was a neat thing to do. I just wish I had been there to take part in it."

"Ty Wayne, when all of this is over, you and I will go by that gravesite late one night, and I'll show you every step we took – just how it all happened. Believe me, you were there. I thought about you every minute.

"Mom, you're the last one who hasn't said a word. For some reason, I think you're going to be right with me and us, but I want you to voice your free will."

After a pause that guaranteed absolute silence, Joanne stood up and spoke up. "You all know that I wouldn't vote against the majority no matter what, but I think it is important for my son and all of you to know that I am 100 percent with each and every one of you, and I think what was done was done in the right spirit, for the right reasons, and by people without a thing to gain from it. How could anyone not be for something so noble?"

"Mom, you are exactly right. It is a shame that we must keep this our little secret, but we need to protect those who made it happen. We can't dodge the fact that we trespassed on someone else's property to bury my Dad. We don't really know if there are state laws here in Texas that prevent such a burial. All we know, and quite frankly, all we care about, is we've made the spirit of my Dad very happy, and we've made his friends and family members even more happy that they could give Titanic Thompson something very special, something that no other man has ever had – a burial on a golf course right where he loved so much to be."

Just at that time came a knock on the door. It was one of the funeral directors with one of the out-of-town travelers who had come to pay his respects for his absent family – it was Tony III. Tony thanked the director for the knock, and entered the isolated room and closed the door.

"I just wanted to come in here and either take my whipping or let you know that whatever is needed in money or support, you can count on my family."

Tommy was nearest to the intruder, but he stepped back to allow the other family members to give the big brute an individual hug of appreciation.

"They know all about it, Tony. You have made them very happy, and they are very grateful. Time is short. We've got to get in there, but I know they would like to hear a few words from you."

"Tommy, you know I ain't much of a speaker, but I ain't really scared of nothin'. But I'm pretty scared right now – I wish I had some of the boys here with me to back me up! All I can say is that my family and the other associated families wanted to do something special for the man we all called The Man. He meant so much to all of my elders, and he loved on all of us kids every time we saw him. You all know that we have nothing to gain by all of this – we just wanted to do something special. Despite our good intentions, none of this could have happened without a lot of those guys out there. I'm at a loss as to how we can tell them how we feel, and I know they're not going to come begging for patronage, but I want you all to know what a loyal bunch of guys they are."

Nora then burst in again. "Tony, I think we ought to make them the pallbearers – you know we haven't named any. I think you and your brothers, Tommy and Ty Wayne, and then all of those friends who helped should be our pallbearers.

Tony then turned to the other family members. "What do you think?"

Everyone began to smile, then laugh. The consensus was; WHAT A GREAT IDEA!

Joanne suggested that they all – Tony included – hold hands and say a silent prayer. After one minute, just like it was scheduled, another knock on the door was heard. The director said it was time.

The family was seated in front of the overflowing chapel. The pastor who was earlier chosen by Jeanette and her and Titanic's attorney stepped up to the pulpit. Before he could say a word, Jeanette rose and asked him if she might address the mourners. The pastor nodded his approval, and Jeanette turned to speak to the quieted multitude.

"Ladies and gentlemen: The family has a special request for some of you who are in attendance within the chapel and for some of those who are listening to the service in the halls and in other rooms within the building. We would like all of those gentlemen who remained at the River Crest Country Club last night after we early birds had gone to be the family's choice as the official pallbearers for our beloved Titanic Thompson."

If anyone could have looked backwards, he would have noticed the giveaway smiles of all of the participants of last night's deeds.

The service was short by that day's standards, and then the pastor asked for all of the pallbearers to step forward and prepare the casket for the ride to the cemetery. About a quarter of those in the chapel stepped forward, and others who had given up their seats came in from other parts of the building. As people passed each other coming and going, soon only the official pallbearers occupied the first ten pews of the chapel. The family then asked the pastor if they could address just the pallbearers.

Tommy took the microphone first and thanked each and everyone of last night's loyal posse. Then he introduced each of the other family members who were delighted to say their thank you in person and with special sincerity. Tommy then turned over the proceeding back to the pastor, who then summoned the funeral home person responsible for coordinating the loading of the casket. No one in the first ten pews was surprised when Steven Clinton stepped forward and called Tim, Bob, Tony, Mickey, and scar-head by name to lend him a hand. Then he motioned for every other pallbearer to assist.

The first limousine following the hearse included the four ex-wives of Titanic: Nora, Maxine, Jeanette, and Joanne.

The second limousine contained the two sons of Titanic, Tommy and Ty Wayne, plus two special friends, Mickey and scar-head. Conspicuously absent was Tony III. He was riding shotgun in the hearse with a make-believe Titanic, and his new friend, Steven.

The procession was over a mile in length. Every attendee at the funeral home was in the line of lighted cars. As the hearse pulled onto the grass in front of the designated gravesite, the other cars scrambled for parking on every side street available. Steven and a group of the pallbearers positioned the casket for lowering as the crowd gathered. One of the pallbearers whispered to another, "practice makes perfect." The immediate family was seated in the only chairs that were available under the small green tent. Titanic's attorney, Dick Clark, said a few kind words to the family, and then he turned over the last rites to the attending pastor. The pastor was again short and sweet with his remarks. He was particularly moved by all of Titanic's friends who came from far and wide to be with their beloved friend.

After all of the immediate family grasped hands circling the casket, the casket was carefully lowered to its resting place by Steven, Mickey, Tony, and scar-head. Tommy then addressed the crowd and asked each to come forward and let the family have the opportunity to personally thank each present guest. Tommy asked that all of the pallbearers be last in line.

For two hours, the family didn't endure. They enjoyed seeing all those friends one more time and when it came time for the pallbearers to pay their respects to the family, they were individually hugged and kissed by every family member.

One month later, Ben Winkleman and the Ft. Worth Star Telegram got a bill from his club, River Crest Country Club. He held it two more days until the funeral home bill arrived, and then he took them both down to the accounts payable department. He instructed the clerk to pay the bills immediately – as he walked away – the clerk heard him mumble, that'll be the best payment for services that this paper will ever make.